CLOCKWORK

Twist

~ BOOK ONE ~

Waking

Emily Thompson

ISBN: 1482766507
ISBN-13: 978-1482766509

Acknowledgments

On this most auspicious day, of Twist's first publication, I would like to thank just about everyone I know, because I have received such abundant support. My family in particular has been a great encouragement in so many ways that I would run out of words if I tried to thank them properly. I must also thank my editors, Janice and Stanley, Michelle, and Richard for their unwavering diligence and patience. Most of all, I have to thank Twist for taking me along on such a fantastic journey.

Upon his bench the pieces lay
As if an artwork on display
Of gears and hands
Of wire thin bands
That glisten in dim candle play
—*Janice T*

Twist always had steady hands. No matter how intricate the device, or how tiny the springs and cogs, his aim never wavered. After minutes of silent work on the small brass pocket watch, he finally allowed himself a smile of satisfaction. He placed the last cog and then closed the back of the watch, admiring the glinting metal in the dim glow that seeped in through the window over his desk. He held the brushed brass up to his ear and closed his large, steel-blue eyes as he listened to the faint pulse of clockwork life.

A silver bell set beside the window rang out like a thunderclap. Twist's slight frame shuddered at the sudden sound, his eyes flew open to stare at the bell in fright, and his grip on the watch slipped. He clutched at the chain as it fell through his fingers, catching the watch a moment before it crashed onto the desk. The unexpected success stole a breath from him as the bell rang again. Twist placed the watch in the pocket of his thin waistcoat and hastened to his feet, turning to the stairs at the back of the room.

The blackness of the room, out of the candlelight, stalled his steps. He snatched up the candle in its tin holder and set his jaw in annoyance, which only gave his

angular features an even sharper and more delicate
appearance. The bell rang out a third time as his feet
flew quickly down the stairs. On the ground floor, Twist
blew out the candle and hastily turned the key on the gas
light at the front door, filling the small room with amber
light.

Thick-paned windows flanked the heavy, dark,
wooden door and spilled the ghost of damp light on the
bare floor. There were no clocks on the walls of the
shop, only framed mirrors of different sizes. There was
nothing on the open floor save for a pair of red velvet
couches that faced each other over a table made of
disused gears from a tower clock. The silver mirrors
multiplied the gaslight to a strange brightness that most
people found unsettling. Twist didn't even look at it as he
quickly took his short black coat from the rack by the
door and threw it on over his white shirt, black trousers,
and still-unbuttoned silver waistcoat. He only had time to
straighten the collar and run a hand over his constant
mess of wild and curly black hair before the bell rang out
impatiently again.

Twist threw open the locks and pulled the door back
just enough to peer out through the crack. A young
woman stood on his step, her hand still on the bell pull.
She was no older than him—older than twenty, but not
yet thirty. She wore high boots over trousers; under a
short, lace-rimmed skirt, and a velvet bodice. She held
no umbrella, and wore only a thin jacket to shield her
from the rain. Her blond hair looked dark from all the
water in it, hanging in a loose braid at her neck. Her sea
green eyes locked onto Twist's with a strength and
determination that startled him.

"Oh thank heaven!" she breathed out in relief. "I
thought no one was here."

"Can I help you?" Twist asked, his voice as loud and

clear as it would ever get.

"What?" the girl asked. "I didn't hear you."

"Come in," Twist said, his small voice colored darkly with disdain. He pulled the door open for her and turned away, taking a seat on the center of the couch that faced the door.

The young woman let herself inside and closed the door behind her. She looked around the room in the reflected gaslight until her eyes fell on Twist again. He saw the same pause in her gaze that he usually did when others got a clear look at him. Feeling reassured, he remained perfectly still, leaning forward on his knees and staring at her steadily: expressionless. The girl seemed to shiver slightly, either from the chill of the rain or from the effect of Twist's efforts, but she stepped forward all the same and took a seat facing him.

"You are ... Twist, aren't you?" she asked. She pulled the small shoulder bag that had hung behind her into her lap as she sat. Twist saw the rain water drip onto his couch and did his best not to grimace.

"I am," Twist replied, his voice stronger in the silence of the small, mirrored room.

"I'm Arabel Davis," the girl said pleasantly. "I need your help."

"Have you brought it with you?" he asked.

"Brought what?"

"Whatever you need fixed," Twist toned, as if to a child.

"Oh," she said, smiling to break the tension. Twist focused on keeping his breath shallow so that his small form would seem even more still. Her smile frayed slightly. "Well, I can't bring it here. I don't actually have it yet, you see."

"Bring it here and I'll see what I can do."

"I don't think you understand," she said, almost

pleading in her eagerness. "I don't need you to repair a watch for me, or anything like that. I need your help. I need you to come with me."

Despite himself, Twist blinked into a confused frown. "Where?"

"Well, Nepal, but—" she began.

"Isn't that in Asia?" Twist asked, hanging onto his placid expression for dear life.

"Yes, I have an airship," Arabel said, obviously meaning to continue.

"No," Twist said instantly.

"It wouldn't take more than a few days to get there," she tried, leaning closer over the table. Twist straightened up and leaned away.

"I'm not going halfway across the world, and I'm certainly not taking an airship to get there," he said as firmly as his soft voice would allow. "I'm sorry, but I can't help you."

"I can pay you, of course."

"No amount of worldly wealth will get me off of solid ground," Twist said, fighting to keep his anger hidden behind his chilly blue eyes. "I've never left London, and I have no desire to do so now."

Arabel's sea-green eyes flashed with such a sudden and keen annoyance—remarkably like the glow of a smoldering canon wick, Twist noticed—that for a moment, he worried that she might like to hit him. He felt his heart beat faster, despite his efforts to keep it slow and steady.

"I'm sorry," he said again, flatly. "If there is nothing else, then good day to you."

"Are you really just nothing but an ordinary little clock maker?" Her voice was suddenly sharp.

"Excuse me?" Twist asked, letting himself appear confused again by mistake.

"Do you only repair broken clockwork? Are the rumors about you all silly lies?"

"I'm sure you can find your way out," Twist said, getting to his feet as smoothly as he could, and turning for the back stairs.

"I've found the clockwork princess."

Twist froze in his steps. After a moment of silent bewilderment, he turned slowly to look back at his guest over his shoulder. "That's a myth."

"It's not," she said, a satisfied smirk now on her face. "I know where it is."

"You can't know where it is because it doesn't exist."

"It's in Nepal, right now," Arabel said. She reached into the bag on her lap, and pulled out a small clump of silver and copper gears, which she placed gently on the tabletop. "I've seen it with my own eyes. It's as real as I am."

Twist turned back as she spoke, and took the item off the table gingerly. The moment Twist's fingers touched the gears, his mind burned with images that he had never seen. He closed his eyes to see the vision more clearly in his mind: metal hands, elegant as a Vermeer maiden's now lying broken on the floor of a dark room—years of dust and neglect, like slime on the once-gleaming surface —those hands running lightly through tall grass in sunlight, long before—the sound of a girl's laughter, brighter than any sunlight Twist had ever seen.

A sharp intake of breath at the intensity of the images brought Twist's attention back to himself. His eyes flew open to see the gears in his palm, the clutching mechanism of a clockwork hand. He could just hear the echo of her laughter in the gentle shine. A shiver ran through his skin like an electric shock, making him shudder. She wasn't just a beautiful fairy tale.

"Are you all right?" Arabel asked, now standing just

beside him.

Twist looked to her quickly, surprised to see her so close. He nodded and took a small step away.

"It's in pieces now," she said. "But if anyone can fix it, I'm sure that you could. Only, it can't be moved until it's repaired. It was risky enough just taking that."

Twist hardly heard her. His thoughts were still wound tightly around the images he'd seen. She'd been left all alone for so long, broken and forgotten. Overwhelming sadness tightened in his chest until he feared that he wouldn't be able to breathe. He felt terrible guilt at holding a piece of her so far away from the rest of her body. He knew the old stories well enough to easily guess at her constant misery. How could she have been treated so badly? Who could have left her alone? How could he stand by and let her continue to be abused by idiots and time?

"Did you take anything else?" he asked, surprised by how strained and rough his own voice sounded.

"Well, no," Arabel said, drifting closer to him again. "I didn't think it would be safe." She lifted a hand to touch his arm as she bent her head to see his face.

Twist jerked away from her before she could touch him, and turned to face her. "When do you want to leave?" he asked, his features—under control again—held impossibly still and empty.

"That depends on whether or not you would be coming," she said, hesitantly hopeful.

Twist's fingers tightened on the gears in his hand, and for just an instant he heard the gentle ring of that childlike laugh again. "I'm coming."

"Wonderful," Arabel said, smiling broadly. "Then we can leave tomorrow."

Try as he might, Twist simply couldn't fall asleep that night. He tossed and turned until the sky outside his dark rooms grew bright enough to count as daylight. The drizzle hadn't stopped from the previous day, leaving the world in a gray half-light long into the morning. As he stood at the window in his attic workshop, looking out through thick glass at the soot-blackened city of London, Twist struggled to imagine a world beyond it. Nepal: the highest mountains on Earth, on the other side of the world. The idea of it was simply too big to fit in his head.

Packing only made Twist more nervous. In the end, he found himself with a bag full of clothes, his best clock-mending tools, and a pair of candles, just in case. He looked over his bookshelf next—adventures, histories, and a fair amount of chivalry—and selected a book of poems to pass the journey. The chunk of clockwork that Arabel had brought to him last night was wrapped safely in soft cotton and buried deep in his bag. Looking about his workshop, he was suddenly struck by the thought that he might not stand here again for a very long time.

His own personal clock collection covered the bare wooden walls, filling the room with their constant, stable harmony. He looked over them in their gleaming perfection, recalling quiet, comforting moments with each one. The sound of their regular, mechanical rhythm was as familiar to him as his own breath.

His newly mended watch was still in his waistcoat pocket, ticking gently like a second heart. Twist drew it out, opened the face, and then placed it gently on the desk in the dim light that seeped down through the rain. He held perfectly still and quiet for a long moment, letting the soft sounds of the rain and his clocks soak deep into the tension on the spring, into the brass gears, into every part of the little watch. Then he closed it and placed it back into his pocket.

With nothing left to pack and the meeting time a mere half hour away, he set out for the airship docks. Twist didn't believe in umbrellas, and so put on a pair of silver trimmed, blue-lensed goggles to shield his eyes from the fine drizzle and wrapped a thick wool scarf around his neck. Water collected on the heavy black cotton of his loose, hip-length coat and fell into rivers down his back, but he was so accustomed to the chill of the air that he hardly noticed it. His boots, black as his jacket, hit the cobblestones with purpose as he forced himself to banish all second thoughts.

He hurried through the dark, narrow, winding streets, rushing past the unnamed masses of London without a moment's glance. By the time he got to the airship docks, perched high in the air on exposed wrought-iron platforms, his wild, curly black hair was heavy with the rain, and his hands were shaking. He told himself that it was because of the cold. His heart beat so strongly that he feared others could hear it as he hurried up the stairs along with the other travelers. He followed the signs to the seventh jetty, but his steps slowed as he drew near.

The airship was massive, large enough to carry a full crew and a significant amount of cargo, though it flew no flags of nationality. The body of the ship appeared to have three decks, with the topmost deck hanging out over the back of the ship like a platform, while the front end of the second deck reached out forward into a point. All the open areas were rimmed with metal railings of varying shades of patina and rust, but the rest of the ship appeared to be made of gray wood, the same color as the storm clouds overhead. Above, an enormous white balloon was stretched from bow to stern, and was flanked with wing-like sails on either side. Huge brass propellers were set at the stern of the ship. In the dim of the drizzle, the vessel appeared nothing but menacing and impressive to Twist.

"Twist, you're right on time," said a girl's voice from farther along the jetty. This time Arabel had an umbrella, but she still looked a bit damp as she hurried closer to Twist. She was dressed much the same as the day before, except that her bodice was shimmering a deep green that matched her happy eyes, and there was a silver pistol strapped to her right hip. Behind her, Twist could see the crew turning to look at him. Each one differed in race, size, and shape. A few of them appeared to be armed as well.

"Are you ready for your adventure?" Arabel asked, a wide smile on her face.

"Are you pirates?" Twist asked, looking at her through the blue lenses of his goggles.

She seemed to give the question some thought. "No, not really."

"Explain that, in detail, please," Twist said as calmly as he could.

"I assure you," Arabel said, "that we are fine, upstanding gentlemen and ladies who don't seek out unlawful activity. Now, are you ready to leave?"

Twist's jaw tightened despite his efforts to stop it. "I'm not skilled with ... *violence*, you know," he said softly, even for him, causing her to tilt her ear to hear him.

She moved back, a laugh on her breath. "My word, you are cute!" she said, the words forcing their way out through the tightly clenched teeth of her wide smile.

Twist bristled at the accusation, and he opened his

mouth to tell her that he was going home and that she could very well leave him alone for the rest of his life.

"Oh, I'm sorry," she said, taking a breath to calm her apparent glee. "I see we might look a bit odd to you, but I can promise that you will be perfectly safe for the entire time that you are in our company. We need you, after all. So please, don't forget why it is that you're here."

A flash of memory followed her words, calming Twist's temper. He wasn't going on this trip for his health. He was doing it for the princess, because no one else ever had. He could almost feel her still, cold, clockwork, so far away, depending on him alone to bring her back to life. No one else would be able to do her justice.

"I'm ready," Twist said, looking to Arabel.

"Splendid," she said, guiding him towards the airship. "We're just about ready to cast off."

Twist had barely set foot on the open second deck before the crew began to throw off the mooring ropes. He heard the sound of the steam engine in the stern of the ship rumble to life below decks, and his blood ran cold at the sound. Arabel left him and climbed into the rigging at the side of the ship without a moment's hesitation. Rain fell from the balloon above in a curtain of drizzle around the outer edge. Twist found himself constantly in the way of the crew as they hurried about on the dry center of the deck.

He stepped to the damp railing reluctantly, and his gaze slipped into the distance below. Still hanging beside the docks, the ship was nearly a hundred feet off the ground. Twist's vision swam and he clutched hard to the railing, forcing his eyes to close. After a moment of standing still, head bent under the light rain, he began to feel his legs steady under him.

A curious sensation of rising crept over him gently. Against his better judgment, Twist opened his eyes to see London's blackened rooftops fall away beneath him as the clouds tumbled down. Terror gave way to a wild thrill as the airship rose to meet the wind. The air chilled, and the rain grew heavier and began to fly in strange arcs and angles, while the clouds fell faster and faster from the sky.

In moments, thick fog splashed down on the deck, blinding Twist to all but the space just around him. His breath caught, as if frightened to leave him now, and he clung to the railing as his only sure reality in this strange experience. But in another moment of that smooth rising feeling, the fog broke and fell away as the airship burst out of the clouds into brilliant, blazing sunlight and a pure-blue sky.

Twist blinked against the intense light of day, even though the tinted glass of his goggles. As the crew shouted in the sudden calm of open air, the ship stilled its rising pace to sail quickly through the puffy, twirling, impossible landscape on the tops of the pure-white clouds. Looking down, Twist saw the bottom of the ship barely submerged in the smooth valleys of the cloud tops. He looked up again to see an enormous mountain of twisting white pass by like an island in a calm sea. After a moment, the ship sped up to such a pace that a white, billowing spray began to fly off the bow, breaking like waves as the ship ran through inconsistencies in the surface.

Twist pulled the goggles off his eyes to hang around his neck and loosened his scarf to flap behind him in the rush of wind, while his hair flew free around his face and neck. The air was crisp as ever and stung at his skin, but the sunlight competed with it to warm him, stronger now than he'd ever felt it before. It took a few moments for his eyes to adjust to the extreme white and brilliant blue all around him, but he couldn't fight the desire to see it clearly, to experience this wonder fully.

"Welcome to the sky, Twist," Arabel said from above him. He looked up to see her hanging in the rigging, casual as could be, tying off a rope that was attached to the wing-like sails. "How do you like it up here?"

"It's..." he tried to respond, but no other words came to him at first. "It's so bright," he said finally.

"Compared to London, anything would be," Arabel said with a smile in her voice. "You should see Greece. Those islands are at least as bright as this, down at sea level."

Twist couldn't imagine anywhere on the surface of the Earth looking anything like the otherworldly vista before him, but he nodded anyway. As he watched, other airships appeared behind them. Each one broke up out of the clouds with an arabesque of white mist before falling to skim the surface the same way that this ship had done. Some of them seemed to follow the same direction, but most turned off for other destinations. Twist tried to wonder at where they might be headed, but he quickly realized that he had a very limited concept of geography. He couldn't even reasonably guess at which countries he might see between England and Nepal.

"Hey, landlubber," said a voice behind Twist. He spun quickly to see a young man with thin, black eyes and emerald-green hair, cut short and falling like feathers over his black-smudged face, grinning at him. "You're the clock guy, right?"

"Twist," he replied with a nod.

"I'm Zayle." He offered a handshake. Twist saw soot and oil stains on the boy's rough fingers.

"Nice to meet you," Twist said, bowing slightly but keeping his hands to himself.

"Wow, you're stuffy, aren't you?" Zayle said, giving him an uncertain look. "Oh well, come on, I'll show you where you'll be sleeping," he said, turning and reaching out a hand. Twist assumed it to be only a gesture, but Zayle's hand fell onto his shoulder with a solid pat.

In an instant, Twist's mind flashed with the vision of Zayle as a very young boy, suddenly aware that he was lost in the center of a huge, noisy, colorful marketplace. Zayle's mother was gone. People were talking, shouting, and laughing around him in a language Twist had never heard. The air was hot and full of strange smells. What if he couldn't find her? What if he would never see his mother again? Twist tore himself free of the image and backed away from Zayle with a jerk that tripped him. He landed heavily on the deck, his arms shaking as they tried to hold him up, his legs curled up under him, and his head ringing with the same fear and confusion as the little boy in the vision.

The crisp air above the clouds rushed in to ease his unsteady breath, but his vision and hearing only returned in waves. He saw a hand fly for his shoulder again and let out a terrified yelp, pulling away from it. Zayle stared wide-eyed at Twist as other faces appeared behind him, his hand frozen in its reach. Twist realized slowly that his own eyes were open wide with fear, and he was curled up into himself, pulling away from Zayle like a frightened kitten. It had been so long since anyone had touched him that he'd almost forgotten what it was like.

"I'm fine," Twist said, forcing what strength he had into his voice and pushing himself into a more dignified position. The emotions from the vision were still running wildly through him, but he did all he could to distance himself from them.

"What just happened?" Zayle asked, as the others began to circle Twist with a mixture of confusion and concern on each of their faces. "Are you all right?"

"Just don't..." Twist paused, not wanting to offend Zayle. "Don't touch me, please."

"But I hardly touched him at all," Zayle said to the others.

"Wait, did you just get a vision?" Arabel asked, kneeling down very near to Twist. He jerked again at her quick motion and found her peering at him intently.

"I thought it only worked with clocks," said one of the others.

"Apparently not," said another.

"It's nothing," Twist said, pulling himself to his feet on still-shaky legs. "Just try not to touch me, if you can," he said, straightening his clothes and not looking at anyone. Arabel stood as well, but seemed to hover much too closely for Twist's taste.

"What did you see?" Zayle asked, something like excitement in his bright voice.

Twist looked at him quickly, slightly alarmed that Zayle was so easily entertained by all this. As he looked at him, though, Twist realized that Zayle looked exactly the same now, despite the years. Somewhere, deep in his heart, Twist knew he'd never found his mother again.

"Nothing," Twist said stiffly, looking away. "It wasn't clear enough."

"Oh, come on," Zayle said playfully. "What did you see?"

Twist stared at him, still as he could be on the gentle sway of the sea of clouds, his steel-blue eyes cold and empty in the stark brightness. "Nothing."

Zayle stared back at him for an instant before drifting close to Arabel. "Is he a vampire, too?"

"No, it's sunny and he's not sizzling," Arabel said, shaking her head. Twist heard another in the crowd give an annoyed tsk.

"You were going to show me something?" Twist said, with what little dignity he had left.

"Oh right." Zayle began to reach out to Twist again, but stopped, pulling back when Twist's eyes flashed with fear and his form tightened. "Right this way," Zayle said, gesturing instead.

Twist didn't look back as Zayle led him away and down onto the first deck of the ship. The brightness of the sky outside fought its way through the small porthole windows set into the sides of the ship, pouring into the hallways of dark wood. Zayle took Twist down the center hallway to a door, and then into a small room with a hanging hammock against one wall, a small chest against the other, and a desk under the two porthole windows in the side of the ship.

"It's not much, I know," Zayle said as Twist looked over his new space, "but it's nicer than the cargo hold."

"It'll be fine," Twist said, already missing his clocks in the silence of the sky. He put his bag down on the desk, expecting Zayle to leave him alone to unpack. Zayle didn't move from the doorway. He had a curious expression on his face when Twist turned to look at him.

"So, what did you see?" Zayle asked, watching him carefully. Twist's reflexes blanked his face and stilled his form. "I know you saw something," Zayle continued, narrowing his eyes.

The strong emotions of loss, confusion, and fear still shuddered in Twist's heart. He turned away from Zayle to keep him from getting a good look at his eyes. "I saw a little boy."

"How little?" Zayle asked, a smile on his face as he stepped closer. "Was I cute?"

"You were afraid," Twist said, watching him and backing away slightly. "Lost."

Zayle paused, his smile gone.

"I'm sorry," Twist said quickly. "I have no control over what I see with people. I didn't mean to," he continued, running a hand through his hair as an excuse to look away.

"It's okay," Zayle said lightly, though his eyes were different now, cold somehow. "I'm not mad. I was the one who touched you, right? It's just…"

Twist struggled to remember why he had decided to leave home. "It's just that you didn't expect me to see something like that. I know. I'm sorry."

"It's fine, really," Zayle said, smiling more warmly at him. "If you need anything else, just let me or Ara know."

"Ara?" Twist asked.

"Arabel," Zayle clarified quickly, to Twist's nod of understanding. "Well," he added, glancing around the room. "I'll leave you to settle in."

"Thank you," Twist managed.

Zayle shut the door behind him, finally leaving Twist alone in the near-complete silence of his cabin. Down here, he couldn't hear the wind except for a quiet murmur at the porthole seals. He couldn't hear the crew unless they walked over the boards above his head. There was no drizzle of rain, or hum of city life. There were no clocks and no machines except for the low rumble of the engines in the stern, so distant through the thick wood that he had to strain to hear it at all. After a moment of unbelievable stillness, the faint ticking of his own pocket watch drifted gently to Twist's ears.

He drew it out and pressed the back of it to his ear, leaning against the wall. Closing his eyes, the complex workings of all its tiny springs, gears, and cogs filled his mind like a beautiful thought. He felt his form ease and release tensions that he hadn't realized it had been holding, as the tiny, regular, heartbeat ticked softly against his ear.

The watch felt no fear. It didn't realize that it was already far away from home. All of its thoughts were as cold and mechanical as its form: complex, methodical, and constant. Twist felt his heart ease as well as he opened himself to the little clockwork life in his hand, letting go of fears, both his own and external.

There was a knock at the door to Twist's cabin. He slipped the watch back into his pocket and pushed his wild black hair mostly into place before he opened the door. A woman stood outside it, her skin as dark as mahogany and her eyes as bright as silver. Red-and-gold silk was wrapped around her shoulders in a hooded shawl, over a tight bodice, and her strong arms were wrapped in black cloth all the way to her fingertips. A long, black lace skirt fell almost to the floor, where it met black boots with talon-like high heels. Her long silver hair hung in thin braids from a single tail bound at the crown of her head. Twist stared at her silently, fighting to hide the awe in his own eyes.

"Are you hungry?" the woman asked, her voice rich, dark, and colored with an accent unlike any Twist had ever heard.

"I suppose," he said, unsure.

"We are having tea," the woman said coolly, crossing her arms over her chest. "You are welcome to join us."

"Yes, thank you," Twist said with a nod.

He closed the door behind him as he followed the woman along the hallway and back to the stairs. She put the hood of her red-and-gold shawl over her head before climbing the stairs, leaving the cloth to hang far over her face. She took Twist out into the brilliant sunlight of the open deck, and then into the room at the stern of the ship.

It was a large, open room, rimmed with windows and richly decorated with rugs on the wood floor, paintings on the papered walls, and ornate-looking items of brass, gold, and silver placed on every open surface. A large table sat in the center of the room, its legs bolted to the floor, with a number of chairs placed around it and also bolted down. There was an array of food and drink laid out on the table, and the rest of the crew was already seated to enjoy it.

While his guide took a seat with the others, Arabel turned to Twist with a smile and insisted that he sit beside her. She began to pour him a cup of tea before he had time to object.

"So, Twist," said a man with gray eyes, sitting across the table from Twist, "where have you traveled to before?"

"I've never traveled," Twist responded.

All of the others at the table stopped whatever they were doing to stare at him.

"Told you," Arabel said brightly. "Isn't it wonderful?" Twist looked at her uncertainly.

"You're serious?" Zayle asked, pausing in his reach for a biscuit. "You've never been anywhere?"

Twist gave a shrug. "I like London."

"Why?" Zayle asked, confusion rampant on his face.

"Zayle, be polite," said the man with gray eyes. "This trip must be quite the treat for you, Twist," he said, sipping at his tea.

"Yes, it must all be very exciting!" Zayle agreed, nibbling at his biscuit.

The woman with the silver eyes laughed lightly to herself, sipping at a glass of red wine, the bright silk hanging gently at the side of her face.

"You don't think so, *ma chérie*?" asked a man with a strong French accent, sitting beside her. He wore gold, wire-rimmed glasses, a very well-trimmed beard, and decidedly the best-looking and most stylish clothes of the lot.

"He's terrified," the woman said smoothly.

Something about the way she said it made Twist shiver.
She glanced at him with a wicked gleam in her silver
eyes.

"Aazzi, you be nice now, too," said the man with gray
eyes. "Don't let them bother you," he said to Twist.
"They both get bored too easily." Aazzi gave him a
dangerous glance.

"Crumpet?" Arabel asked, offering Twist one on a
small plate. Twist took it purely out of politeness,
keeping an eye on Aazzi all the while. Her fingers
looked like sharp claws on the delicate glass of wine.

"Well, shall we have some proper introductions?"
asked the man with gray eyes. He then introduced
himself as Howell Davis, the owner and captain of this
airship, the *Vimana*. Arabel, his niece, was the ship's
rigging expert. Zayle was the ship's engineer, while Dr.
Philippe Rodés, the smartly dressed man with the glasses,
was the ship's doctor. Aazzi was introduced as Dr.
Rodés's wife and the ship's defense and security expert.

"Don't be alarmed, but she is also a vampire," Captain
Davis said aside.

Twist almost choked on his tea and looked at Aazzi in
shock and fright. She only smiled back at him, holding
her glass of wine to her lips.

"It's nothing you need to worry about," Dr. Rodés
said evenly.

"Besides, you're too small to make much of a meal,"
Aazzi said with a wink and false sweetness to Twist.
Pure animal terror shot up Twist's spine, rooting him to
his chair. He forced himself to speak, just to keep from
screaming.

"Why does this ship need to employ a doctor or a ..."
Twist paused, staring at Aazzi, "A defense expert?
Arabel told me you that weren't pirates." Some of them
laughed lightly.

"What a townie," Dr. Rodés said, shaking his head.

"We're not, really," Arabel said, catching his eye and clearly trying to look as trustworthy as she could. "Besides, what's wrong with having a crew of useful people?"

"It's the use to which you employ them that concerns me," Twist said back quickly. While Arabel waved a dismissive hand, new questions and fears bloomed in Twist's mind. "Wait, why are any of you even undertaking his journey? What value does the clockwork princess have for you? And when you say you found her —" he continued, his small voice speeding up.

"Twist," Captain Davis said gently, "why are you here? You're obviously troubled by most of this journey. Yet, here you are, sipping tea in the sky with the rest of us."

Twist's gaze lowered to his tea, though he hardly saw it. He knew she was alone, broken and forgotten in the dark, waiting for someone to put her back together. She'd always been loved, but now... Twist's fear dimmed at the thought, and he could hardly contain the unwavering, ravenous need to help her.

"She needs me," he said, softly even for him. No one seemed to hear him. "I have my own reasons," he said more loudly.

"So do we," Captain Davis said. "And so, here we all are."

Twist stared back at him coldly, his frustration breaking free of his clamoring defenses. "That's as much an answer as this tea cup is an elephant."

"My goodness," said Dr. Rodés, looking to his wife. "He hides his teeth as well as you do, my dear."

"He's smarter than you think, Howell," Aazzi said, smiling at Twist approvingly.

Captain Davis let out a thoughtful breath, staring at

Twist carefully. "I can assure your safety on the journey to Nepal, whatever help you may need to repair the clockwork girl, and then a safe return to London. What else would you have from me?"

"Considering that, I suppose an explanation really is asking too much," Twist said, sipping at his tea bitterly. Talking with people had never worked out well for him. He'd almost forgotten this, in all the time he'd spent alone with his clocks.

"How is our progress?" Captain Davis asked Arabel.

"We'll be over the continent in less than an hour," she responded. "We should reach Venice by tomorrow."

"Good," Captain Davis said, looking to Zayle next. "And how is the boiler holding up?"

"Well, it's running," Zayle said with a light sigh. "It'll get us to Venice for sure, and maybe as far as Constantinople without restocking our oil." Twist frowned in thought, wondering which country Constantinople was in. Sure, he'd heard the name of the city … or was Constantinople a country?

"Well, at least that's a good place to pick up more oil," Captain Davis said. "Remind me again why you haven't been able to fix it?" he added.

"I've been all through it," Zayle said. "I can patch it up all day, but until I find the source of the leak, it's only a stopgap."

"Wait!" Arabel said suddenly. Twist jumped slightly and looked at her, wide-eyed, to find her smiling at him brightly. "Twist, can't your Sight help with the engine?"

"How's that?" Zayle asked.

"Well, I heard that that's exactly what he's good at," Arabel said quickly. "His Sight shows him the problems in things. That's why he can fix complicated things like watches so well, because he can clearly see the cause of the problem, just by touching them. Right, Twist?"

Twist shrugged awkwardly, unnerved to hear his Sight talked about so casually. "I suppose."

"Then what, he just touches the engine and he can find the leak?" Zayle asked, his face awash with amazement. "That's just plain cheating!" he snapped, staring at Twist accusingly.

"Would you mind giving it a look, Mr. Twist?" Captain Davis asked. "It could speed up our progress. We'd then be able to get you back to London all the sooner." By now, the rest of the people at the table were all watching him. The weight of their gazes fell heavily on Twist's slight shoulders.

"I suppose," he muttered, shifting in his seat.

Once tea was finished, Zayle led Twist down into the engine room, buried in the dim, windowless, gas-lit stern on the lowest deck. Twist walked carefully on the dark boards, acutely aware that they were the only thing between him and an unimaginably long fall to the rough, frigid waters of the English Channel. Arabel followed behind, out of pure curiosity.

The steam engine made up the bulk of the stern of the ship, spanning it from side to side, and filling the space below the second deck. Pipes, gauges, valves, and burning hot metal shuddered with a constant growl, struggling to contain the pressure of the superheated steam that fed the propellers outside. In the low light of the gas lamps and the blazing fire that was held back by a small door near the floor, the steam engine looked every bit a manic and raging beast to Twist.

"Well, go ahead and touch it, I guess," Zayle said to him.

Twist remained silent as he stared at the horror in front of him. He couldn't remember another moment when he'd been frightened to open his Sight to a machine.

"Go on," Arabel said excitedly.

"You're not scared of it, are you?" Zayle said, a smirk barely hidden in his voice.

"Oh, leave him alone," Arabel said, swatting at him with the back of her hand. "Don't listen to him, Twist," she added gently. "Now go on. Don't be frightened."

The visible tightness in Twist's jaw betrayed his pride, though he still remained silent as he stepped closer to the colossus of steam and fire. A valve wheel stuck out significantly from the front, promising to be cooler to the touch than the rest of the hot metal. Twist took a breath to brace himself, and then reached out his slender fingers to fall on the metal wheel.

Fire, pressure, rage, and steam rushed through Twist's mind like a wild beast with a feral power beyond anything he had ever felt from a machine. He saw—knew—felt every bolt, pipe, chamber, and gear as if it were his own. The raw energy of the engine, so precariously contained in weakened steel, burst into him as if sensing a chance for escape, and stole the breath from his chest. In the moment before Twist lost his grip on consciousness, he caught a glimpse of a small, stinging pain in the raging chaos. Too much pressure was crushing in on too small a point, overheating the oil and forcing it to break out where it didn't belong.

Twist's fingers slipped from the wheel as his form sank to the coal-blackened floor. Arabel reached for him instantly, but stopped herself just before touching him. Twist's breath returned the moment the connection was cut, and he gasped as he knelt, hunched into a small ball before the still-growling, raging engine. Arabel and Zayle both knelt close beside him, peering fearfully at his face, now hidden behind his unruly black curls.

"Does this happen every time he touches anything?" Zayle asked, staring down at him.

"Well, at least he's not shaking this time."

Twist's blood still thundered with the reckless might of the engine, filling his heart with fire that didn't belong to him. He rose to his feet so quickly that the others jumped back a step in shock. Twist's cold blue eyes locked onto Zayle's, steady and fierce as a hungry wolf. He smiled subtly, his form held relaxed, still, and ready to destroy. Zayle stared back at him blankly, though something not unlike fear began to show at the edges of his eyes.

"Are you really so small, that you can only bolster your own meager ego by belittling me?" Twist asked, his voice level, cool, and razor edged.

Zayle opened his mouth to respond, but nothing came out, as confusion and alarm bloomed awkwardly on his face.

"Um..." Arabel began gently. "Twist? Are you all right?"

Twist looked to her with mild distaste, but something in her eyes steadied his thoughts. She was confused as well, bewildered, frightened, and somewhat disappointed in him. Something was wrong. He struggled to separate his own emotions from those of the vision, shaking his head to clear out some of the chaos. He reached for the watch in his pocket and held it tightly in both hands. It's tiny, constant, gentle heartbeat cooled his anger and soothed his disdain. He took a deep breath. By the time he exhaled, the fire in him had all but gone out.

"I'm sorry," he said softly.

"What did he say?" Zayle asked.

"I'm sorry," Twist said again, pushing his small voice harder. "Please disregard what I said," he added to Zayle. "There is a lot of anger in the heart of that engine." Zayle looked to the engine uncertainly.

"It has feelings?"

Twist looked back at him silently for a moment before he answered again. "There's too much pressure on this side," he said, pointing. "There is a weakness in the metal near the back and the pressure is overheating the oil and forcing it out through the seals. Lower the pressure on this side and the leak will stop on its own."

"Of course!" Zayle exclaimed, slapping at his own forehead. "I've checked the seals three times and never found a fault. But if there is even a small point of weakened metal then the pressure..." he said, rushing to the controls.

"See?" Arabel said happily. "I told you he could figure it out."

After all the noise of the steam engine, which had
rushed through his mind, Twist couldn't bear the near-
total silence of his cabin. He instead returned to the open
second deck and leaned his back against the railing. The
breeze tossed his black curls about playfully and tugged
at his scarf, now looped loosely around his neck. The
brilliant sunlight poured down his back like warm water
and reflected off the sea of pure-white clouds that the
ship sailed so quickly over. The ship still made no sound
as its bow broke the crests of the clouds along its hull, but
the rigging creaked softly as the balloon pulled against
the whispering wind. Twist closed his eyes to the
overpowering light and quietly savored the curious
combination of chilly air and baking sunlight in the soft
murmurs of the sky.

Before long, however, the warmth of the sunlight
began to fade. Twist opened his eyes to see vibrant color
splashed over the sky. Orange and pink brushed each
tower of cloud, while lilac spilled into the valleys, and the
sun fell slowly through the pale-blue sky. Twist turned to
look out over the vista, just as the clouds opened below
the airship, falling away to reveal a land Twist had never
seen. Emerald fields, rimmed and dotted with gray,
stretched out to the edge of the world impossibly far
below him. Tiny castles cast strong shadows against the
green, and small villages and towns appeared in clusters
here and there, as the land grew darker by the moment.

Twist looked behind him, but found only Captain
Davis out on the deck with him. He was standing at a
wheel not unlike that of a sailing ship, which stood at the

front edge of the top deck. Twist hurried to him, climbing the stairs two at a time.

"What land is that below us?" he asked.

"France," Captain Davis answered instantly. "We'll be flying over Paris soon."

"Paris," Twist said, his small voice filled to the brim with wonder. He'd read stories about Paris, seen paintings, and once touched a clock that was built there, but never in his life considered actually seeing the city with his own eyes.

"You can't miss it," Captain Davis said. "Just watch over the starboard side. We should keep the light long enough to make out the gardens at Versailles as well."

Twist hurried to the edge and looked over quickly, straight down, to see a town grow into a gray city through the abyss of empty air below him. Then, his vision realized the height from which it was looking, and it began to swim. Twist pulled back quickly, holding his suddenly horribly dizzy head in his hands.

"Be careful," Captain Davis said with a laugh. "It might be easier if you don't look straight down."

"There is a city down there now," Twist said, keeping his eyes closed for the moment and leaning against the rail. "Is that Paris?"

"No, that's Rouen," Captain Davis said lightly. "It's a large city, but not as large as Paris."

"How do you know so easily, exactly where we are?" Twist asked, opening his eyes again to look to Captain Davis. "You can't even see over the side from there."

Captain Davis smiled at him. "How do you know so easily, exactly how to fix your clocks?" he asked back. "We each have our skills. I don't have a clue about mechanical things, but I always know where I am." Twist gave his mind a moment to consider this—that this man could know the whole globe in such detail—but it only made him feel dizzy again to try.

"How many places have you been to?" Twist asked.

"I couldn't say," Captain Davis said. "You'd have to study more than a few maps to find a country I haven't been at least over." Silence stretched out between them again, while Twist let the thought of it play in his mind.

"I've been over two," he said softly.

If Captain Davis heard him, he chose not to respond. Twist turned back to gaze at the land again, though he tried not to look too far down right away. Just as promised, the towns continued to grow, filling the land with more and more gray, until Twist spotted a river winding through the buildings. There were two teardrop-shaped islands in the middle of the river, and there was a large cathedral on one of them. Long-forgotten maps of faraway cities floated back to his thoughts. Twist suddenly realized that he was looking at the Seine, the river that wriggled through Paris like a snake.

A shiver ran down his spine as he watched the sun fall over the French capital, filling the Seine with the reflected lilac and gold of the remaining clouds that streamed along beside the airship. Not long after, just before twilight claimed the land in darkness, he saw huge gardens and well-contained forests below as well, with impossibly long and straight paths cut cleanly through the green. Soon, the only light on the ground came from tiny, star-like points of gas light or candles, and reflected light in rivers and lakes from the last few rays that reached up to gild the clouds. The sun boiled itself into the horizon in a wash of red and copper before slipping wholly below the edge of the world and dragging a dark blanket studded with silver stars over the sky.

Wrapped awkwardly in his hammock, Twist struggled long into the night to find comfort. The silence of his cabin pressed in on him like a heavy fog until the beating of his own heart began to sound loud in his ears. Finally giving up on sleep, he carefully untangled himself from the hammock and found his watch.

He wrapped a heavy wool blanket around his shoulders, sat on the floor in a beam of brilliant moonlight that streamed through the porthole window above him, and turned the brass watch over in his hands. While the back was cleanly brushed brass and soft to the touch, the front cover of it was embossed with a delicate design—a sun inside a square, surrounded by decorative curling marks—that Twist's fingertips knew intrinsically. Twist let his Sight open slowly into the familiar pulse of the watch, his attention wafting over its gears and springs like smoke. After a moment, he opened the face of the watch.

The constant ticking of all his clocks in his tiny attic workshop, the dull hum of London's rain, the cool light that seeped down through the thick, drenched atmosphere, the scent of the old, dark wood and lingering soot, and the light flicker of a single candle all washed over him in a warm, comforting wave. The only emotions and memories that came to him were his own. Twist let go of his body and let his mind run free through the vision, basking in the safe emptiness of his own echo.

At some point, fatigue took hold. Twist drifted seamlessly from vision to dream, curled up in the moonlight. Some time later, he stirred to waking in a warm pool of sunlight on the floor of his quiet cabin. For a moment, he wasn't sure where he was. The watch in his hands was still open, the shadows of the attic room still coloring the air. Twist snapped it closed. The silence of the sky pushed back in on him like a cold shock. As he stood, stiff and still half asleep, the view beyond the windows caught his attention.

Snow-speckled mountains rose to meet the thin wisps of cloud all around the airship. For a moment he thought that they might be the Himalayas, but it must be impossible to travel so far in one night. Twist might not have had a very detailed map of the world in his mind, but he was sure that there was more than one country between England and Nepal. He dressed and made himself presentable as quickly as he could, and then hurried out into the hallway and up the stairs. Out on the open deck, the mountains looked all the more impressive. The ship had slowed to navigate through the high, snow-filled valleys.

Once Captain Davis had steered the ship through the highest peaks, he and all of the others shared a breakfast in the lavishly decorated second-deck cabin. Twist joined them, but did his best to stay out of conversations. As soon as he could politely leave the table, he headed back to his cabin to retrieve the book of poems that he had packed. He brought it out to the open deck and took a seat against the railing near the bow of the ship. He spent a long while in the quiet and colorful words of Percy Shelley, happily left alone by the others as they busied themselves about the airship.

"Twist, sweetie." Arabel's voice came to him from her perch in the rigging, just below the curve of the balloon. "Now would be a good time to look up."

Twist wasn't sure how he felt about being called "sweetie," but he looked forward over the bow nevertheless. His eyes were met with a sight unlike any he'd ever imagined.

A city of pale marble hung in a pool of white clouds, hundreds of feet in the air over a harbor city far below. Archways of stone and pale wood reached over the abyss to connect wide, open plazas and clusters of ornate buildings and tall towers. Domed roofs topped many structures, and stone filigree and statues seemed to adorn every surface. Ivy crawled over the balustrades, fountains flowed glistening in the sunlight, and countless people in colorful costumes strolled pleasantly through the city, apparently untroubled by the impossibility of their situation.

There were no balloons to hold the city aloft, nor any connection to the ground that Twist could see. Small boat-like crafts with wood and canvas wings hurried under the archways and around the buildings like gondolas of the air, and many huge airships were already docked at the edges of the city.

"Pretty impressive, isn't it?" Arabel called to him happily as she climbed down from the rigging. "I just love Venice," she said, stepping up to the bow beside him.

"I thought Venice was built on water," Twist said, staring bewildered as the flying city drew closer.

"Well, that part is on water," Arabel said, pointing down to the harbor below. "But this is the new section of Venice. It's much easier for the airship traffic. And it's a splendid view!"

"But how does it..." Twist waved his hand vaguely at the flying city.

"How does it stay up, you mean?" Arabel asked. "I'm not really sure," she said with a shrug. "It has something to do with magnetic rocks and electrical currents. But whatever the mechanical details, it's perfectly stable. It doesn't move from that spot: up, down, or to any side. It sure would be a bother if it did," she added with a light laugh.

The *Vimana* came in close, slipping in between other airships that were already docked at the end of long, wooden piers. Twist watched as the populace of the city became clearer to him. Each person was dressed in ornate costumes of silk, feathers, and lace, in bright and vibrant colors. Their faces were all covered with masks of impossibly endless variation: long beak-like faces, expressionless faces—of pure white or intricately decorated—masks shaped like stars and half-moons painted with gold, and large fan shapes. Medieval jester caps topped many, while other masks only covered the eyes.

"We haven't missed Carnival!" Arabel cheered and clapped her hands. "I was afraid we would," she said to Twist.

"So, it's not a city of mad clowns, then," Twist said with a reassured nod.

Arabel laughed and shook her head. "Only during Carnival," she said, before hurrying off.

The ship docked, while Captain Davis gave his orders to collect the needed supplies and then be back on board by morning. Twist headed back to the bow to continue reading, but Zayle ran to him before he could sit down again.

"You're not staying on board," Zayle said sternly.

"Why not?" Twist asked back.

"Because you're in Venice, of course!" Zayle said. "Now come on, let's go play."

"No, thank you," Twist said, sitting down against the railing with his back to the city.

Zayle put his hands on his hips and stared down at Twist. "I'll drag you off this ship if I have to," he said.

Twist eyed him carefully, wondering if it was safe to test his threat.

"What's the hold up?" Arabel said, coming closer too.

"He wants to stay here," Zayle said, pointing an accusing finger.

"What?" Arabel gasped. "Why, do you feel sick?" she asked Twist.

"What's going on over here?" Aazzi asked, joining them.

"Something is wrong with Twist," Arabel said, sounding worried.

"He wants to stay on the ship," Zayle said.

"Oh Lord," Twist muttered, rubbing at his brow. "Please, go and enjoy yourselves," he said. "I don't like crowds, so I'll wait for you all here on the ship."

The three of them stared at him as if he'd just announced himself the king of France.

Without warning, Aazzi reached out, took hold of the collar of Twist's jacket, and pulled him to his feet, his face within an inch of hers. Twist froze as a cold thrill of shock shot up his spine. His hands held back, he pulled away as best he could to keep her from touching his skin directly. Aazzi stared into him with her silver eyes, holding him only a breath away.

"You are coming with us," she said softly. "And you're going to have a good time. Or, I'm going to bite you. Is that clear?"

"Why won't you leave me alone?" Twist asked in a fast, high gasp.

Aazzi smiled. "Life's too short, darling," she said gently. Twist saw a flash of pointed teeth in the last word. His heartbeat sped up so quickly that he felt dizzy for a moment. "Now," Aazzi said, releasing his collar, "come along."

Now too frightened to protest further, Twist went

with the others off the ship. People moved quickly along the docks and Twist did all he could to stay clear of everyone. The dock ended at a wide, open marble plaza, filled with festival-goers. Flashes of bright colors rushed by him on all sides, and people laughed, sang, and spoke loudly in languages he didn't know. There was constant motion, sound, and color, but Aazzi stayed close to Twist's back all the time.

"Here," Arabel said suddenly, handing Twist a small mask of black silk trimmed in silver, with turquoise beads sewn at the edge of one eye like tears. When Twist looked up to her, her face was already covered with a golden mask shaped like the sun, with long waving points of stiff fabric reaching out around her eyes, and crimson detail throughout. Twist saw a small stand behind her, showing loads of masks, hats, and other colorful things for sale.

"Go on, little one," Aazzi said behind him, putting on a silver mask that was shaped like a crescent moon. "You would only stand out without a mask, here."

Twist tamped down his pride at the pet name, took the mask, and put it on. The moment he did, his mind flashed with the image of a woman with long, curling black hair that fell around a white full-face mask. She lifted her mask to reveal a wicked smile before she leaned in quickly to kiss him. Twist shook his head sharply to clear the image, and the vision wafted from his mind like smoke, just before her lips met his.

"Here, Twist," Zayle's voice broke in from behind a jester mask with green, belled points hanging forward. Zayle handed Twist a glass of golden liquid, saying: "This will help."

"Help with what?" Twist asked, taking the glass.

"Drink it quick, and you'll be fine," Zayle said, taking a healthy drink from his own glass.

Twist took a sip to find it was a sweet-tasting wine. "Now you're trying to get me drunk!" Twist accused with as loud a voice as he could muster.

"No, I wouldn't," Zayle said back, his voice sounding hurt. "I'm just trying to get you a little tipsy, is all."

"I never should have left London," Twist muttered, his words lost in all the other noise. He took a mouthful of the wine just to get Zayle to stop pestering him.

Arabel took hold of the edge of his jacket sleeve and pulled him farther into the crowd. Small clusters formed here and there as people gathered to laugh and talk together. Couples danced in open spaces to impromptu bands of masked street musicians. Food and wine appeared out of nowhere, while every building seemed to spill more and more people out onto the plazas and walkways. The noise was constant, the chilly air was charged with energy, and color filled every part of the world under the brilliant midday light of the so-close sun in the high atmosphere.

Twist's senses dulled under the assault and the city turned into a swirling blur. When Arabel came to a huge fountain at the center of the plaza and stopped, he took another heavy drink from his glass. Zayle was probably right, and there was no fighting it now. Twist felt his head start to swim slightly and let himself relax into it. Arabel, still holding his sleeve, waved and yelled as two masked men approached from the crowd.

"Uncle, is that you?" she yelled to one of them.

"Is not," the man with a blue silk mask said back, coming closer. "This is Carnival. I can be whoever I want, today."

"What wrong with being you?" Arabel asked back.

"Nagging nieces, for a start," he snapped back tauntingly.

"Oh, you beast!" Arabel said, laughing and throwing

out a hand to slap at his arm as he laughed too.

"Lovely lady, could I have this dance?" the other masked man asked Aazzi with a bow. Twist heard a distinct French accent in his voice.

"I should tell you, I'm a married woman," Aazzi said to him playfully.

"Then your husband is a lucky man," the man said, holding out a hand. Aazzi laughed and took his hand, and they both disappeared into the crowd, hurrying closer to the nearest band and empty space to dance.

"I hate to say it," said the man with the blue mask, whose voice Twist now recognized as Captain Davis's, "but we are mainly here to resupply."

"Yeah, yeah," Zayle sighed. "I'll go see about the coal and oil," he said, slumping as he moved off into the crowd.

"I'll handle the food supplies," Captain Davis said. "Arabel, do we need anything for the rigging or sails?"

"It's all fine now," she said with a shrug. "I'll get some more rope, just in case, but we have enough canvas to keep the sails strong for a long while."

"Thank you," Captain Davis said, already heading away.

"Come along, Twist," Arabel said, slipping her finger through a button hole at the edge of his sleeve. "You're with me."

With a resigned sense of helplessness, Twist let Arabel lead him deeper into the crowds. After slipping past countless moving bodies, Arabel made a happy sound and hurried her pace, heading for one of the buildings. She almost ran up the steps, and then stopped at a landing under an arch of stone filigree, before a huge wooden door.

"We have to stop here," she said to Twist, who was out of breath from the run.

"Oh thank heaven," he muttered. "What is this place?"

Arabel let go of his sleeve to push the door open. The building was many-leveled, with railed walkways around a central open space that was filled with dust motes and streaming sunlight. Books filled every wall in tall cases that reached to the ceiling, and sat in neat rows on high shelves that took up most of the bottom floor. A dome of glass made up most of the ceiling, spilling warm sunlight into the air with the help of the few thin, tall windows that stole some space from the bookshelves.

"It's the library," Arabel said, her voice suddenly lower in the muffled quiet inside the building. Once the door closed, the chaos outside was dimmed considerably. "It's not very crowded today, is it?" she said with a smile in her voice. Looking around, Twist found no one else in sight but an elderly librarian behind a tall desk, who peered at them critically over the edge of her half-moon glasses.

Arabel took him up two floors, and into the back of the building. There, beside a window that looked out onto a vista over the edge of the flying city and down to the sea below, she stopped and ran her finger over the titles of the books on the shelf. She pulled her mask up to see better.

"Here it is," she said, pulling one of the books out. "This is where I first found out about the clockwork princess," she said, holding the open book out to Twist. He pulled his mask down to hang around his neck.

The pages looked ages old, gilded and painted brightly in a style that reminded Twist instantly of flying carpets and magical lamps. The image, however, was deeply familiar to him. Taking the book, Twist gazed down at the drawing of the clockwork princess, dancing in her palace atop the mountains of the world.

As his fingers touched the page, his mind washed over with the tale in one beautiful, bittersweet wave: the loving father who brought people from all over the world to entertain her, the jealousy of the suitors as she grew older and more lovely, the arrow that was meant for her protective father and instead struck her heart as she leaped to save him, the puppet maker from far away who built a metal puppet to contain her dying soul, the happily-ever-after in her new clockwork body as she danced forever in the sunlight on the highest mountains in the world.

"That book has such wonderful pictures," Arabel said, "and the story is written so well that I got a clear enough image to find her when I read it."

"How *did* you find her?" Twist asked, looking up to Arabel.

"Well," she said, smiling at him smugly, "you're not the only one with a gift, you know."

Twist's eyes opened wide.

"I can find things," Arabel said with a shrug. "If I can get a solid idea of what I need, and I concentrate on it, then I just … know where to find it. That's how I found you, too."

"I wondered why you came to me," Twist said, thinking back.

"Once we got to Nepal and saw the state of the clockwork puppet," Arabel explained, "I knew we would need someone with great skill to fix her properly. So, I focused on the problem, opened my Sight, and suddenly I just knew. I knew your name, where you were, and that if you touch something that's damaged, you can see the cause. That's what makes you so good at fixing things. I knew you would be able to fix her."

"You learned all that? Just through your Sight?"

"Well, that was all I got, actually," she said. "I usually get just enough information to find what I need, and nothing else."

"Your Sight seems very pleasant," Twist said softly.

Arabel watched him silently for a moment before she spoke again. "When did you first notice yours?" she asked. "Did it shock you the first time? Or was it always there?"

"I was always good at fixing things," Twist said. There was a small seat placed against the window, so he sat as he considered his answer. "I got better and better at it as I got older. After a while, I started to see clear visions with sounds and emotions. By the time I was old enough to read and write, I could hardly stand to touch people anymore."

"Is that because the visions were too strong?" Arabel asked, leaning back against the railing in front of him.

"The emotions are overwhelming," Twist said, shaking his head, his eyes focused on his thoughts. "The first thing I see when I touch something is what caused any problems in it. If it's a clock or a simple machine, then it's fine. But people…" He looked up at her.

"Everyone is broken, in one way or another. Whenever I touch people, I see exactly why. I feel it like it's happening to me."

"So, when Zayle touched you," Arabel began. Twist looked away from her quickly. "But, what if nothing's wrong?" she asked, bending her head to catch his gaze again. "What happens if you touch something that isn't broken?"

"Then it's random," Twist answered. "Sometimes I don't see anything at all. Otherwise, I see a random memory associated with the item, or I'm just completely aware of how it works."

"But, the boiler on the *Vimana*," Arabel said, thinking back.

"Was very angry," Twist said, finishing her thought. "Big, powerful machines have a lot of pride and anger in them."

"Machines have emotions?"

"Of course," he answered. "They have heartbeats, they breathe. Why wouldn't they?"

"I never thought about it like that. Sure, the clockwork princess is supposed to be alive, but a wall clock with feelings? It just sounds strange to me."

"But being able to find anything you need just by thinking about it is perfectly normal?"

"Absolutely," Arabel said brightly. "Nothing more natural in the world."

"They say that there are many of us," Twist said. "But I've never met anyone else, before."

"Oh, I've met loads," Arabel said with a flip of her hand. "You need to get out more, my dearie," she added with a playful wink. Twist's mouth twitched against the taste of the pet name. "Sights are becoming a normal quality these days. Still, it seems that each new Sight is unique. I've never met anyone with the same kind as mine." She frowned slightly, staring at Twist for a moment. "But yours does sound familiar."

"It does?" he asked. "You've met someone with my Sight?"

"Well, not exactly." She came closer and took a seat in the window beside him. Twist shifted away slightly. "My brother is much like you," Arabel said, holding his gaze with eager eyes. "His Sight is so strong that it's become a problem for him. He couldn't stand to look at anyone anymore by the time he left."

"He can't look at people?"

"When he looks at things," Arabel said, "I mean, when he concentrates on something, he can eventually understand them completely. If it's a machine, he can use it as easily as if he'd invented it himself. Oh, he loves watching the sky too. He used to tell me the name of any star I pointed out. But, like you, it worked with people too. When he looked into someone's eyes, he could see things about them. He told me that he started to get visions of them as well, in different places, and he thought that some of them might have been future events."

"Some of us can see the future?" Twist asked, wonder blooming on his face.

"They say that some can," Arabel said, smiling with a nod. "It's still very rare, and apparently very difficult. Like it is for Jonas," she added with a heavy sigh. "As he got older, and his Sight grew stronger, he started to fear it because it was so hard on him. He said that the visions were so clear that they hurt. People were the worst. Eventually he stopped looking at people at all."

"What happened to him?" Twist asked. "You said he left?"

"He joined another crew," Arabel said, her eyes full and distant. "A rival of ours. Thieves and cheats. We had a horrible fight, and he left the *Vimana*. A month later, we found him on their crew. Now I only see my brother on the other side of a fight," she added, as if trying to make it sound like a joke. Twist listened silently, wondering what it might be like to have a brother.

"Well, let's carry on, shall we?" Arabel said suddenly, standing up with a smile on her face. "It's Carnival and I want to have fun," she said, pulling her mask back into place.

After Twist and Arabel left the library, they continued on to finish their errand. They met Zayle again when the sun started to fall. Unbelievably to Twist, the city became even more crowded and the festivities even more energetic as the darkness grew. Parties poured out of houses and common buildings with their golden light and music. Dances sprang into existence wherever there was room on the streets and plazas. Wines of all types found their way into every glass, and the volume of all conversation grew to such a constant din that Twist gave up trying to speak at all.

Thanks to Zayle's diligence, Twist drank enough to give up complaining as well. Leaning over an empty spot of ivy-covered balustrade, Twist looked out over the world far below as the moon rose into a velvet sky. Though his vision swam when he looked straight down to the terrestrial section of Venice—glowing now with golden fires and lamps in its own version of the Carnival spirit—the height didn't bother him anymore.

"Are you having fun yet?" Aazzi's voice asked, stepping beside him while Zayle and Arabel danced together in the crowd behind them.

"This is my version of fun," Twist said, gesturing to the vista.

"I thought you didn't like heights," Aazzi said.

"I don't," Twist said thoughtfully. "I think Zayle might have gotten me a bit drunk after all. Either way, I just don't care at the moment."

"Good," Aazzi said, her smile apparent in her voice, though it was hidden behind her moon-shaped mask.

"Then I don't have to bite you."

Twist looked to her and narrowed his eyes. "Didn't you want to? I mean, isn't that how you eat, after all?"

"You probably wouldn't taste very good."

"Why not?" Twist asked, suddenly affronted.

Aazzi laughed. "You haven't lived enough yet, little one. But if you keep going to Carnivals and traveling around the world to bring myths back to life, I'm sure you'll be very tasty in no time."

"Naturally," Twist said. "I'm sure I'd already taste good now..."

Aazzi's form stilled suddenly, growing tight and poised in such a flash that it startled Twist. She pulled her mask away and turned slowly, looking over the crowd behind them with intent eyes.

"What is it?" Twist asked, seeing nothing changed in the crowd.

"I smell something," Aazzi said, her voice almost as soft as his. "We have to leave. Now."

"I don't smell anything," Twist muttered, still searching over the masked crowd. Aazzi took hold of the cloth at his collar again, pulling his face close to hers. Twist's numbed mind cleared sharply, feeling her breath on his skin, and he instantly pulled at her grip.

"Listen to me," Aazzi said, her voice still low. "There are dangerous people here. If they find us, they'll steal your lovely little clockwork girl away and sell her for parts."

"That's monstrous!" Twist gasped.

"Don't look at anyone, and come with me, quietly," Aazzi said, releasing his collar to grab his sleeve, and heading into the crowd.

Twist hurried to keep up with her, his heart beating quickly. His vision still swam slightly from the wine, but he kept his footing as he carefully made his way through

the dense crowds at Aazzi's heels. As they walked, a
small buzzing sensation began to tingle at the base of his
neck, growing stronger and taking on a high, electrical
whine. Twist shook his head to try to clear the strange
sensation, but it grew steadily, all the same.

Without explanation, Twist's head turned sharply—as
if on its own—and his eyes stuck on a single figure in the
crowd. Black-lensed goggles were pulled off eyes so like
Arabel's that for a moment in his confusion, Twist
thought that it was her. The moment Twist's eyes fell on
the stranger's, his senses flashed to a burning-hot
brightness that blinded him for an instant. The buzzing
sensation at the base of his neck exploded through his
veins like a lightning strike, before disappearing
altogether. Twist fell to the ground, gasping to catch his
breath as his senses flooded back to him.

"Twist, are you all right?" Aazzi was asking, standing
beside him.

"I tripped," Twist said, standing quickly. "I'm fine,"
he said, wondering why he felt so deeply that he needed
to lie.

"Come along," Aazzi said, scanning the masked faces
in the crowd but not apparently seeing what she was
looking for. Twist looked back to the figure he'd seen,
but now it was gone. He began to wonder if the person
had been real at all, as they continued on.

"Ara," Aazzi called, beckoning Arabel and Zayle
closer as they danced together.

"What is it?" Arabel asked. "Want to cut in?"

"Quay is here," Aazzi said quickly. Arabel pulled her
mask off, her face mirthless and intent while Zayle turned
quickly to look around. "I'm taking George, here, back to
the ship," she said, nodding to Twist. "It's getting late.
Go find the others." Zayle and Arabel nodded.

"Come on, George," Aazzi said to Twist, taking hold

of his sleeve. Twist was understandably confused about the sudden change in his name, but he remained silent and let her lead him on.

After a rather long walk through the throngs of party goers, they finally made it back to the docks and onto the ship. Aazzi took Twist up to the open third deck.

"Your name is George, you're my husband's nephew and the ship's cabin boy," Aazzi whispered to him quickly. "No matter who asks you, that's who you are."

"Sure, why not?" Twist asked dryly. "Who are you looking for?" he asked, pulling his mask off to see better.

"A captain named Quay, and his crew," she said, pulling her mask off too. Twist was slightly startled to see the intensity of her grim expression. She drew a small pistol from the back of her bodice and directed Twist to sit on the low railing behind the ship's helm. She stood before him, watching over the rest of the ship, and the docks beyond, from her vantage point.

"Who is he?" Twist asked.

"A cut-throat pirate," Aazzi answered bitterly.

"And you're a nice sort of pirate?" Twist asked.

"I don't cheat or steal against my own kind," she said, her silver eyes electric and cold when they snapped on to his. "And at the moment, I'm protecting you."

"And right well that you do," Twist said, crossing his arms. "If I were killed by cut-throat pirates, my mother would just about kill Uncle ..."

"Philippe," Aazzi said, bitterly.

"Uncle Philippe, yes," Twist said. "I'm drunk, not stupid, Aunt Aazzi."

"I think I like you better sober, after all," Aazzi said.

Before Twist could retort, Arabel and Zayle returned with Captain Davis and Dr. Rodés. They all boarded the ship quickly and Zayle disappeared instantly down the stairs to the engine room. Arabel began to climb into the rigging the moment she was aboard. Aazzi brought Twist to join the captain.

"Well, what say we call it a night?" Captain Davis said, looking over the edges of the ship.

"I don't sense anyone near," Aazzi said, softly.

"Better safe than sorry," Captain Davis said. "George, I think it's time you went to bed," he said to Twist.

"I'll see him to his room," Dr. Rodés said. "Can't have him walking into things in his state," he said, adjusting the fit of the five-shot revolver in his hand.

"Thank you, Doctor," Captain Davis said.

Dr. Rodés said nothing else to Twist until he had led him all the way back to his cabin, shut the door behind him, and looked out both windows.

"Did you tell anyone that you were leaving London, or where you were going?" he asked Twist, stowing his pistol under his coat.

"Who are you asking?" Twist asked. "George or Twist?"

"Don't be a fool," Dr. Rodés snapped. "Did you say anything about this trip to anyone in London?"

"No," Twist answered, sitting heavily on the closed chest against the wall. "I didn't speak to anyone after Arabel came to see me."

"It might not even seem important," Dr. Rodés said. "Did you say hello to anyone on the street, or tell the milkman that you weren't going to be round?"

"I didn't speak to a human soul after Arabel came to see me," Twist said. "I usually don't anyway. Why? Who is this pirate, Quay, and what makes him so dreadful? You all seem terrified of him."

"We're concerned," Dr. Rodés said. "We're not scared of that lowlife. He's a thief and a scoundrel. He's tried to steal finds from us before, and he's succeeded a few times, too."

"Aazzi said he and his crew would try to steal the clockwork princess if they found us. Does that mean he already knows about her?"

"I don't know," Dr. Rodés said. "He might not know anything. We're just being careful because this find is much bigger than our usual ones. Arabel really outdid herself this time," he added with a bitter touch to his words. "But if Quay finds out what we're up to, he'll definitely try to steal her from us," he said. "That man's greed knows no bounds."

"That would be bad," Twist said, his mind still too numb for anything more eloquent.

"Yes, very," Dr. Rodés agreed.

"So, what do we do now?" Twist asked. As if in answer, the soft rumble of the engines began to pulse through the wood of the ship.

"We're going to try to slip away," Dr. Rodés said. "If they haven't spotted the *Vimana* yet, then they'll never know we were here."

"And if they have spotted it?"

"We'll keep a good watch, and blow holes in any ship we catch following us," Dr. Rodés said with a smirk.

"Right, because you're nice pirates," Twist said. "Now I remember."

"Who said we were pirates at all?" he asked back.

"Whatever," Twist said with a dismissive wave.

Though he grumbled to himself a bit in what sounded to Twist like French, the doctor left it there. It was only a moment before the *Vimana* threw off her moorings and left Venice at top speed, flying silently through the night.

In the morning, Twist awoke to find a huge, sapphire sea stretched out below his windows while the airship sped quickly through a clear and empty blue sky. For many reasons, the events of the day before were a jumbled blur in his mind. Some of it was so strange to him that he wondered if it wasn't all just a fractured dream.

He was only partly dressed when Arabel knocked on his door. He quickly threw a waistcoat over his mostly buttoned shirt, and made sure his trousers were properly fastened, before he opened the door just enough to peer out.

"Are you only just getting up?" Arabel asked, looking at the sliver of him that she could see. "You missed breakfast, so I was coming to invite you to lunch."

"I'm sorry," he muttered, glancing down at himself. A draft at his throat caught his attention, and he reached up to finish buttoning his collar. "I've never been very good with time."

"You?" Arabel asked, almost laughing. "I thought you spent all your time with clocks."

Twist's mouth twitched with annoyance as he fastened the last button. No one ever missed that parallel. To his shock, Arabel seemed to take his moment of distraction as an invitation. She nudged his door open while his hands were occupied and let herself into his cabin. Twist backed away instantly and then turned his back to hurriedly tuck his shirt into his trousers. Arabel shut the door behind her.

"I mean, really," she went on easily, "I'd expect you

to be practically obsessed with time."

"I never read clocks," he said, running his hands through his mess of hair to little effect. He turned to face her stiffly, hoping that he now looked at least slightly presentable, and found her leaning against his closed door with a smile that looked somehow out of place on her face. "I just like the way they work. They're calm and constant."

"You're not having that much fun on this trip, are you?" Arabel asked, almost softly. Twist looked back at her silently and wondered why she was so intent on being in his cabin. He'd never read of a woman so brazen in any of his novels. She seemed to wait for his reply.

"I'm not here to have fun," Twist answered finally. "I'm just trying to stay somewhere near sane until we get to Nepal," he said and looked away to see where his scarf had gotten to. To his complete surprise, Arabel took hold of the front of his unbuttoned waistcoat and caught his full attention in the process.

"As much as you might like to think so, you're not a machine, love," Arabel said, her voice cold under tiring pleasantries. "Your heart doesn't tick, does it?" she asked, giving his chest a glance. Twist felt it beat faster under her attention.

"Mine probably does, actually" Twist said, jerking his waistcoat out of her grasp and taking another step away. "What difference does it make to you, anyway? We only just met. You don't even know me. Why must you demand that I enjoy myself?"

Arabel held his sharp gaze with a sternness of her own. "I hate to see anyone bottle themselves up. It doesn't matter who you are; it's not healthy."

"I'm quite all right," Twist said, buttoning his waistcoat. "I haven't been this far away from home in my life, and I'm letting you drag me around, to some extent.

Believe me, that's much more than I would usually allow."

"Then why are you *allowing* it now?" Arabel asked as if the words tasted sour.

Twist took a breath in silent pause. The world seemed to still in the light of his answer. "You are my only way to her."

"A girl made of clockwork," Arabel said coldly, nodding curtly. "I imagine she would be your vision of female perfection."

Twist stared at her clearly offended expression in bewilderment. He felt a confusion and fear that he couldn't identify, and sensed that he needed to do something, quickly. What needed to be done, however, was totally beyond his comprehension.

"Well, shall we go eat?" Arabel took an impatient breath and gave him a tight, thin smile.

Twist went with her and met the others, not wanting to anger her further. Today, everyone seemed to have returned to their usual carefree selves, even after the hasty flight from Venice. Though there had been light cloud cover through the night, and there was still a large bank of clouds sitting on the horizon to the north, there had been no evidence of any other airships following their path over the Black Sea. Aazzi had finally lifted the extra security, and the crew had begun to relax shortly after sunrise. By now, they seemed to have all but forgotten about it.

"Besides," Zayle explained to Twist over a hearty lunch, "it's likely that Quay was in Venice by sheer coincidence."

"Lots of people go there for Carnival," Aazzi said with a nod.

"If they weren't looking for us," Zayle continued, "then they might not have any idea that we were even there."

"We're too far away now, as well," Captain Davis said, inspecting his half-eaten chicken leg. "Quay has no idea where we're headed. Without that, all he could possibly know is that we stopped in Venice for the festivities and left."

"Why George?" Twist asked.

"What?" Zayle asked.

"Why did you call me George?" Twist asked, leaning forward on the table. "You all suddenly decided to change my name. Why?"

"In case someone heard us talking," Dr. Rodés said. "We decided on the story when we picked you up, in case we had to hide you."

"Why hide me at all?" Twist asked. "How would it be dangerous for someone to know my name?"

"Quay has powerful friends," Arabel said darkly. "Magical ones too." Twist gave her an incredulous look. Arabel leaned closer, speaking more earnestly. "They have ways of knowing things that they shouldn't. Simply hearing your real name could put you in danger. Besides, there are rumors about you all over," she added, as if he should have known.

"I have a reputation out of London?" Twist asked, frowning at the thought.

"Well, yeah," Arabel said easily. "But if anyone knew that we went all the way to London to get you, they might be able to figure out at least what we are after. Quay knows us too well. He'd certainly be able to figure it out."

"So, you frequently cross the world looking for mechanical people?" Twist asked.

"We hunt treasure of all kinds," Captain Davis said. "But mechanical people is a new one."

"Once I found out she was real," Arabel said, smiling

to herself, "I just had to see her."

"Ara usually brings us our best finds," Captain Davis said, looking at his niece fondly.

The lunch continued at a casual pace. Once everyone was finished eating, they drifted off to attend to various tasks, leaving Twist on his own once again. He took up his now-favorite place, at the bow of the ship, and watched as the Black Sea glided along underneath him. Eventually, the sea came to an end in a mountainous, green country. Clouds still lingered to the north, while vast copper-and-gold deserts stretched to the southern horizon.

Twist let his over-taxed mind drift in the cool air, gazing out at the next large body of water that approached from the distance. His thoughts found their way back to his home in London, now almost half a world away as the airship carried him over the western edge of Asia. His clocks must still be ticking calmly in the empty rooms, his mirrors reflecting nothing but the gray rain light that fell through the windows. While much of him yearned for the peace of his quiet, chilly rooms and London's soot-stained drizzling sky, part of him was rather entranced with the vista before him.

A great, green sea spilled slowly over the world below, stretching out to the north and south farther than Twist could see. The huge piles of white cloud to the north came to a point, almost reaching out to him from the pure-blue sky. As Twist watched, something appeared at the tip of the cloud—now close beside the ship—and it soon became clear enough to identify as another, much smaller airship. It was slim, two-decked, and fitted with large, vertical sails on either side of a single tall balloon hanging above the deck.

The *Vimana* suddenly plunged, turning to the south. Twist clung tightly to the rail as a siren bellowed and the

sound of shouting filled the air. Turning, Twist saw
Aazzi, Dr. Rodés, and Arabel all appear on the deck with
weapons in hand. Small, winged crafts flew from the
small airship, arcing through the air towards them.

"Twist!" Arabel yelled. "Get below decks!"

"What's happening?" Twist yelled, hurrying closer to
her.

"We're under attack," she said, checking her pistol
and watching the sky.

Twist looked to the smaller crafts. Streams of white
steam spewed out behind the winged things—coming
closer, Twist saw that they were people with wings and
steam engines strapped to their backs, flying like birds
and heading right for the *Vimana*. One of them crashed
onto the deck, tossing off the contraption and pulling out
a pair of pistols, while two other flying people streamed
around the ship in tight arcs.

"We want the clock maker!" yelled the landed
intruder. "Give him up!"

In answer, Aazzi started shooting at him, running
closer. Arabel yelled at Twist to run before turning to
join the fight herself. Noise and chaos erupted in all
directions: flaming fire began to rain down from the
smaller airship, the flying men fired pistols as they flew
by, the crew of the *Vimana* returned fire from the deck,
Zayle appeared with large wrenches in each hand to
strike at the fliers as they flew too close, Arabel took to
the rigging with her own weapons, Aazzi ran from target
to target at lightning and inhuman speeds as more fliers
appeared and tried to board the ship.

Twist ran for the stairs below decks, but one of the
fliers crashed onto the deck in front of him, blocking him.
The man didn't remove his wings, but he reached out to
grab Twist with both hands. Twist jumped away from
him, only to fall over a bit of debris on the deck. Aazzi

appeared out of nowhere and shot at the flier until he jumped over the side of the ship. She grabbed Twist's collar and hauled him to his feet, throwing him towards the stairs before turning to fire again.

The airship lurched to the left, throwing Twist to the railing. His vision fell to see the green sea now less than a hundred feet below the ship. He struggled to regain his footing and hurry below decks when he heard Arabel scream.

"No! That's Jon!" she yelled, grabbing Dr. Rodés's gun as he took aim.

Twist looked to see a man with wings running at him across the deck. The buzzing sensation at the base of Twist's neck reappeared, stilling him for an instant. The man wore black goggles that hid his eyes, but he pulled them off as he ran closer to Twist.

"Twist! Run!" Aazzi's voice yelled from across the ship.

Twist tore his eyes off his attacker and dove from the stairs. The other man was too fast and his hands caught Twist's arm. In the instant before his Sight took over, Twist looked up at the other man, meeting his brilliant green eyes.

The electric sensation in the base of his neck exploded into white-hot fire, throwing Twist off the deck and into the air with a strong concussion. The other man flew away from him while impossible light broke over them both and the force of the blast threw them apart. Twist's overwhelmed senses had only a moment to tell him he was falling through open air, before everything went black, silent, and still.

A throbbing pain at the base of Twist's neck came to him before anything else. The cold came next, and the shivering of his body. After some effort, Twist managed to open his eyes. A field of dull, deep green met his vision, as blurred shapes moved in the foggy darkness. Blinking brought the shapes into focus. Large, silver fish swam before him, through thick, murky, heavy green water.

Twist sat upright quickly, for an instant afraid that he was drowning in the sea, a scream escaping his lips. His voice came out clearly, and air returned to him without effort. Twist turned to look around him, taking in his surroundings with more coherence.

He was alone in a small, dark, metal room. A huge glass window filled the wall before him, showing a great depth of water outside. Twist, although drenched to the bone, seemed to be unharmed. He had been left lying on a stiff but soggy couch, and his pockets were empty. His first thoughts went to his watch, and a true fear broke to life in his heart. Looking about the room, Twist saw no sign of it. There was a metal door with a large valve-like wheel in the center of it, closed against the wall opposite the window, and a number of brass tubes hung out of the ceiling beside it.

Twist got to his feet, but found his legs weak and unsteady. He made his way slowly to the door and tried to pull it open to no avail. It seemed to be locked from the other side. Out of breath now, he pressed his back to the wall and let his legs go limp as he slid down to the floor. His fingers curled tightly in his damp hair, and

Twist closed his eyes to shut out the world. Utter confusion and total despair pounded heavily in the pain at the back of his head, threatening to swallow him whole. When losing his watch to the depths of the sea surfaced in his boiling thoughts, Twist felt his eyes begin to sting with tears.

The sound of strained metal came suddenly from the door, and Twist looked up to see the wheel spin on its own before the door swung open. A large man with dark skin and a long nose came into the room and looked around before his dark eyes fell on Twist.

"Ah, it's awake," the man said, in a thick accent Twist had never heard.

"Where am I?" Twist gasped to ask him. "What's happening?"

"You're under the Caspian Sea, little one," the man said. He came into the room as he spoke, flanked on either side by two even larger men with mirthless, expressionless faces. One of them closed the door behind them. "We found you floating near the surface, half dead. We brought you on board and got you breathing again."

"I stopped breathing?" Twist asked quickly.

The man laughed lightly. "You just about drowned, little one."

"Well, thank you," Twist said, smiling up to his savior. "I owe you my life."

"That you do," the man said, smiling back. "Where are you from? England?"

"Yes, London," Twist said, trying to get himself back onto his feet.

"Are you worth anything?" the man asked pleasantly.

"I'm sorry?" Twist said, still leaning heavily on the wall but relatively upright once again.

"About how much would someone pay to get you back?" the man asked.

"You mean, as a ransom?" Twist asked, his heart beating faster.

"There's a good boy," the man said with a wide smile. "How much can I get for you?"

"Well," Twist muttered, fear and confusion burning to life once again as he considered his situation more clearly. "I mean, I don't really ... I don't have any family."

"Friends then?" the man asked, still pleasant as ever. "An employer maybe?"

"No," Twist said darkly. "I'm alone. No one would pay anything for me."

"Oh, that's too bad," the man said with feigned pity. "No friends at all," he said to one of the two thugs. "Are you sure, little one?" he asked Twist.

"No one even knows that I left London," Twist said. He was surprised by how quickly his anger grew. "There isn't anyone for you to rob on my account."

"Well, then" the man said, taking a breath. "Welcome to the crew. I hope you're stronger than you look, because I need another boy in the engine room."

"Wait!" Twist said, holding up his hands as one of the two thugs reached for him and the other opened the door. "I don't want to join your crew!" he spat, moving away from the thugs.

"This just isn't your day," the leader said, shaking his head. "Throw him in with the coal," he told the thugs.

"Don't touch me!" Twist screamed, jumping away from them and into the dark, damp metal hallway outside the room.

"You really don't seem to understand," the leader said, following as his thugs continued toward Twist. "You fell into my hands, I saved your life, and I own it now."

"I'll do what you want," Twist said quickly, backing

away. "You don't have to touch me. I'll go wherever you want. Just tell me where."

The two thugs stopped and looked to their leader for orders. He considered Twist for a moment and then shrugged.

"Fine, just get him to the boiler," he said, waving them on.

"That way," one of the thugs said, pointing.

Twist did as he was told, walking through the tight, damp, metal hallways with the two thugs at his back. Steam burst out of valves and pipes here and there. Innumerable conduits and complex structures of pipes covered most of the walls. Twist pulled his arms tight against himself, trying desperately not to touch anything in the dark and cramped spaces.

Strong heat and a deep, rumbling sound grew louder as they walked, until the tightness of the hallways opened onto a large room filled with piles of black coal. The face of a huge boiler—easily three times the size of the one on the *Vimana*—filled the far wall. One young boy, not possibly older than fifteen, stood in the piles of coal with a shovel. He looked up when Twist walked into the room and his dark eyes widened.

The boy said something with a shuddering voice, in a language strange to Twist, and he backed away holding his shovel up defensively.

"He's just English," one of the thugs said. "Get back to work, and show him how." With that, the two thugs left the room and slammed the heavy metal door behind them.

"English?" the boy asked, moving closer to Twist cautiously. "I've never seen an Englishman so pale..." he muttered, reaching out a hand to Twist's face. "No one alive, anyway." The coal stains on the boy's face had masked his features, but up close they looked totally foreign to Twist. There was an accent similar to the leader's in his voice as well.

"I'm alive," Twist said, backing away from him. "I assure you. Though," he paused, looking around, "I'm not so certain that's a good thing right now."

"It must be better to be alive," the boy said softly. "Even here." He shook his head and put on somewhat of a smile. "I'm Halil," the boy said, holding out a hand. "What's your name?"

"Twist. Nice to meet you," Twist said nodding slightly but not accepting the handshake.

Halil looked at his hand as if to see what was wrong with it. "Don't Englishmen like to shake hands?"

"No, it's—" Twist said quickly. "I don't. I'm sorry."

"Doesn't matter," Halil said with a shrug. "How'd you get on board? Are we near the surface again?" he asked, his eyes going wide with wonder.

"Surface...?" Twist toned. He shook his head to clear his thoughts. "I'm sorry, I don't remember exactly how I got here. One moment I was on an airship, and then I woke up…here. Where are we, anyway?"

"Welcome to the *Hazar*," Halil said flatly. He wiped some of the coal dust from his forehead with the back of his hand as he looked around at the room. "It's a metal ship that travels deep under the water. I haven't seen the sky in many months. I'm not sure you and I ever will again." Twist swallowed his uneasy fear at the boy's words.

"Who were those men?" Twist asked, looking back to the closed door.

"Pirates," Halil said.

"More pirates?" Twist gasped, exasperated. "I'm sick to death of pirates!"

A loud siren bellowed off the metal walls. Twist looked around for the source, his hands over his ears, but the sound died again before he could find it. Halil immediately started to shovel coal into the small, glowing hole in the front of the boiler.

"Hurry," he said as he worked, "there are more shovels over there. Take one and help me. That sound means they want more speed. If they catch you not working, they'll beat you."

"Oh, this is not on," Twist said to himself as he searched for a shovel. He found one and fell into rhythm beside Halil, shoveling. "I get taken halfway around the world by pirates. I get attacked and thrown off an airship by pirates. Now I'm turned into a coal-shoveling slave by pirates. I'm not having it anymore!"

"You can't escape," Halil said in a hushed tone, stopping to stare at Twist in fear. "They'll beat you."

"Only if they stop me," Twist said, pausing in his work as well.

"They will," Halil said, nodding quickly. "No one escapes. If you try more than once, they kill you! Besides, we're under water. How can you get out?"

"I'll wait until the ship is on the surface," Twist said.

"They lock up the slaves before they go anywhere near the surface," Halil said. "And at night too, when everyone goes to sleep."

"And they keep you here otherwise?"

"Well, yes," Halil said. "There are other slaves too, but I only see them at night."

"Then that's when I'll escape," Twist said. "When they come to get us."

"But you…you can't!" Halil said, clutching his shovel fearfully.

"I'm not spending my life in this horrible place. I'm going to Nepal, I'm going to save her, and then I'm going home. That's final."

Halil stared at him in fear and wonder, his mouth

open but silent. The siren bellowed again, for longer this time. Halil turned with a frightened yelp and redoubled his efforts to shovel the coal into the boiler.

"Wait, no," Twist said, staring at the rumbling, bulging, furious steam engine. "Stop shoveling."

"But they'll—" Halil began.

"Beat us. Yes, I know," Twist said. "Just stop. They'll come in here if we don't do what they want, right?"

"Yes. And they'll bring things to beat us with."

"Just wait," Twist said, watching the door but standing close beside the metal face of the boiler. He held his shovel in one hand, and held his other hand close to—but not yet touching—the engine. "Do you know the way to the bridge of this ship?" he asked Halil over his shoulder.

"I think it's forward, on the level above us," he said. "I've only been there once."

"Lead me there, and you can come with me back to the surface," Twist said. "But whatever you do, don't touch me. Not for any reason. Do you understand?"

"No," Halil said instantly.

Twist smiled back at him. "Can you do it anyway?"

The siren bellowed for a long moment as the two stared at each other. Halil finally nodded to Twist, clutching at his shovel but remaining still.

It was only a few moments before the wheel in the center of the door began to turn. Twist pressed his palm onto the warm surface of the steam engine's face and let the enormous pressure, rage, pride, and blazing fire pour freely into him.

"What are you two doing?" growled one of the two thugs who opened the door and stepped inside. "This is no time to rest!"

Twist's blood pulsed fast and hot through his veins, his vision sharp and his body tight. He walked towards the thugs as they both came into the room. One of them smiled at him unkindly, holding a thick, baton-like stick in his hands.

"You need to learn your pla—" he began to say, before Twist swung his shovel at his head, swift and strong.

The thug let out a yell of pain as the unexpected blow connected hard against the side of his head. He fell to the coal at Twist's feet in a heap, and the other thug rushed with a growl to attack Twist. Twist thrust his shovel forward into the thug's stomach, the force of the blow pushing him back a step. The thug let out a grunt, his eyes glassing over as he dropped to the ground beside his fellow.

"Come on," Twist said over his shoulder to Halil, already heading out into the hallway again. "Which way is the bridge?"

"How did you...?" Halil gasped, stepping carefully around the fallen thugs.

"Halil," Twist snapped, stopping to turn on him with

a threatening fire in his bright, steel-blue eyes, "I have neither the time nor the patience. Are you coming or not?"

Though he jumped back at the sight of Twist's intent gaze, Halil nodded quickly and pointed. "Down that hallway, and take the stairs."

The two hurried through the cramped passageways with Twist taking the lead. Halfway along the upper hallway, a man appeared in a corridor to the right. Twist swung his shovel back without slowing his steps.

"Benny!" Halil yelped, hurrying to the new man. "Twist, don't!"

Twist backed away from Halil and glared at him like an angry dog.

"He's a slave, like us," Halil said, his voice shaking slightly. Twist glanced up to see a fair-skinned older man now behind Halil. He stared back at Twist with green eyes, edged with alarm. He was holding a tray of-wretched looking food and a metal cup of dark liquid.

"Halil, what are you doing?" Benny asked with an accent invisible to Twist's ears.

"Escaping..." Halil said, looking rather uncertain about it.

"Where are you going with that?" Twist asked, nodding at the tray of food.

"The captain ordered something to—" Benny began.

"The captain is on the bridge?" Twist asked, a wicked grin taking shape on his face.

"Yes, he usually eats—"

"Perfect," Twist said, nodding to himself. "Take the lead, Benny," he said, stepping back to let him pass.

"But...how do you plan to—" Benny began to ask.

"Now," Twist said, his voice quiet but sharp as a knife.

Benny stared at him for only an instant longer before

he hurried past him and on towards the bridge. Twist and Halil followed him silently until they stopped at another closed metal door with a wheel in its center.

"I'm supposed to announce myself and then enter," Benny said quietly.

"Get on with it then," Twist said with a heavy helping of indignation.

"I want no part of this escape of yours," Benny said, pulling himself up to his full height as he stared back at Twist. Twist looked up at him, unmoved.

"Afraid the pirates will beat you for helping me?" he asked, his voice even but acidic. "Open the door, or I'll beat you until you beg for them."

Benny only spared one more moment before he gave a sigh and turned to the door. He knocked and yelled through the metal that the captain's meal had arrived. After a pause, the door was opened. The man who opened the door didn't even look at Benny. Instead, he turned right around and walked away into the room.

"Why are we still only at half speed?" a voice said from within.

Twist pushed Benny aside with his shovel and leaped into the room. Large, flat windows filled the front half of the room, looking out into the green sea over consoles of varying design. A single brass chair with blue velvet cushions sat in the center of the room, the ship's captain sitting at the edge of it. Many other controls, pulls, and speaking tubes filled the back wall along with the now-opened door. Three other men stood at places inside the bridge, each concerned only with the consoles in front of them, as Twist swung his shovel back.

The first man was struck heavily across his shoulders from behind, and he fell instantly, motionless to the floor. The captain and the other two turned to look, but the captain was the first one to move. He got to his feet and lunged for Twist, who jumped to the side, turning to swing his shovel again.

"Mr. Twist!" Halil's voice yelled, drawing his attention.

One of the other men was rushing toward him too, from the side. Twist spun, striking his attacker and throwing him into the captain. Both men tumbled away while the last crew member leveled a pistol at Twist from across the bridge.

The shot rang out like a thunderclap in the metal room. Twist ducked down just in time and the bullet struck the metal behind him with a spark. Twist sprang back up instantly, leaping at the shooter with his shovel raised high. The man backed away, dodging the blow and taking aim again. Twist jumped quickly to his right, his eyes on the gun. The shooter followed him and fired again, but Twist fell to the floor on all fours. The shot rang loudly again, but there was no spark of it striking metal.

"No!" the shooter yelled, staring over Twist.

Twist lunged at the gunman's legs with his shovel, throwing him to the ground, before smacking at the side of his head with it. The man's body went limp on the floor and Twist sprang to his feet, turning.

"You little British bastard!" the captain yelled at him, gripping at a bleeding bullet wound in his side. Twist's eyes fell on a brass chain that hung from the captain's pocket, just below the wound.

"That's my watch!" Twist growled, taking hold of his shovel again.

In the instant of the captain's confusion, Twist lashed out at his face with the flat of the shovel. The blow came so fast, from so close, that the captain had no time to dodge it and he too fell to the floor. The last man stood behind his captain, his eyes wide with shock and his jaw already growing red from Twist's previous attack.

Twist took a solid grip of the shovel and stretched his neck slightly, pulled his shoulders back, and smiled at him.

"I'm just a mechanic!" the man said, holding up his hands.

"Get out," Twist snapped, nodding at the door.

"Right," the man said, hurrying to the hallway.

The moment the man was out, Halil slammed the door and quickly spun the wheel to lock it closed. "That was amazing!" he said, looking at Twist with wonder.

"They were all twice your size," Benny said, his face an image of bewilderment.

Twist leaned down to pluck his watch from the fallen captain's pocket by the chain. Seeing it again, he wanted nothing more than to touch it. But he knew this wasn't the time. He dropped his shovel on the floor and slipped the watch into his pocket, careful to touch nothing but the chain, as he looked over the consoles around the room.

"If any of them start to wake up, hit them again," he said, finding a central-looking section of the controls.

"But what are you going to do now?" Benny asked. "We're still under water."

Twist took a breath, already feeling the rage and confidence of the steam engine begin to fade from his mind. He pressed his hands against the brushed metal surface between a lever and a number of small wheels on the console. Cold, calm, methodical, mechanical simplicity rushed over him like heavy rain. It stilled his anger and pride, replacing it with the familiar, unemotional, rhythmic pulse of a complex machine.

His mind flew over the controls, mechanisms, and a multitude of systems at such a pace that he could hardly keep up with the rush of pure information. Many small things were wrong—loose welding, leaking valves, rust, age—but in an instant he also knew precisely where the ship was, exactly how deep and how close to port.

He opened his eyes and crossed the room, turning a wheel fully open, pulling a number of small levers, and then taking a seat in the captain's chair. A small copper wheel stood just in front of it on an articulated arm. Twist ran his fingers over its surface lightly, gaining another rush of detailed information. He closed his eyes and focused hard on his own breath to keep himself from getting totally overwhelmed.

"What are you doing?" Benny was asking. "How do you know how to pilot this ship? Who are you?"

"Leave him be," Halil said. "Look, we're nearing the surface."

Twist opened his eyes again, but they gave him little clarity as the senses of the ship flooded his mind: Heavy water pressed in on all sides, held back by strong metal and thick air. Currents pushed and pulled against his course as the huge, angry engine struggled against it all. Cold water outside and fire in its belly, the contradictions were more confusing than anything Twist had ever felt. It was all he could do to steer the ship back up to the surface.

The water outside the windows grew rapidly brighter and thinner. In an amazingly short amount of time, the ship burst up onto the surface under a rusty dusk sky, moments from full night. Twist heard Benny and Halil cheer. The ship fell into a restful mood as it sat easily on the surface of the silty water.

Twist got up, walked to the side of the bridge, and quickly climbed up a small ladder that was set against the wall. He threw the top hatch open to the cool night air outside. A gust of air rushed into the bridge, calling out more cheers from the other two within. Twist pulled himself out onto the top of the bridge just as Halil appeared through the hatch. There was a small flat area above the bridge, but the ship curved back into the water on all sides of it. Twist looked over the side into the dark water and realized that he hadn't thought through this final step.

"Benny, look!" Halil said, his arms open wide and his face full of joy. "It's the sky!"

"I can't believe it," Benny said breathlessly, getting to his feet on the top of the ship and staring up as the brightest stars began to shine in the darkening dusk.

"Any idea how we should get to the shore from here?" Twist asked, looking out at the nearest town along the coast, about a hundred feet away. "The sea is shallow here, and the ship didn't think it could get any closer."

"The ship had a thought?" Benny asked.

"We'll swim," Halil said. "It's not far."

"I've never tried to swim in my life," Twist said, staring into the water uncertainly.

"What happened to your courage, boy?" Benny asked. "Just a few minutes ago you took on four pirates with nothing but a shovel!"

"That wasn't me," Twist said curtly. "That was the boiler."

Halil and Benny stared at him for a moment. Sounds crept up from the hatch. Benny and Halil backed away from it, moving behind Twist.

"They're awake!" Halil whispered fearfully.

"Time to find out if you can swim or not," Benny said to Twist.

Twist's thoughts turned instantly to his watch; he'd almost lost it once. He took it from his pocket, and his Sight slipped into it before he could stop it. The confused details of the ship melted in the warm, comforting presence of his own memories, thoughts, and emotions that were still preserved flawlessly in the steady rhythm of the watch's tiny clockwork heartbeat. Peace and true relief flooded through him in an instant. The way forward was clear to him just as quickly. Whatever happened from here, he had to get to her somehow.

"Come on, then" Twist said, wrapping the watch chain around his wrist and making sure that there was no way it could get free. "Let's give it a try, shall we?"

The voices from below grew clearer and the sound of feet on the ladder rose quickly. Halil jumped first, diving expertly into the water. Twist took in a deep breath but his nerves seized, rooting his feet firmly in place. Benny saw the problem and shoved Twist hard on the back. Shock jumbled his mind enough to pick up nothing but a whisper of a vision from the quick touch, but his body reacted on its own, curling up as he fell gracelessly into the water.

Saltwater rushed instantly up his nose, and Twist was fully disoriented in the blur of deep, oily green. Another figure plunged in beside him, moving away again. He struggled against the water, fighting his way back to the surface. His head burst out into the air for only an instant before falling under again. Animal panic took him over as he thrashed up again. A hand grabbed his arm, pulling.

Twist's form stilled, floating limp just below the surface as his mind flashed through the images that flooded into it. A little boy, barely big enough to walk, splashing in shallow water. A crowd of boys yelling and shouting, daring him to jump from a high pier into the sea below, and the tight arc of his back as he did so in perfect form. A race through open water, pulling ahead of his friends and knowing he would win. Lying easily in the cool water on a hot summer night, staring up at the stars, in a moment of pure peace before something huge and metal burst out of the sea just beside him.

The desperate need for breath brought Twist back to himself. He pulled free of the grip and brought his head out of the salty sea, took a deep, full breath, and dove under again, flying easily and quickly for the shore. His limbs seemed to move on their own, while his lungs rationed the air to remain safely hidden beneath the dark water. He knew Halil was with him, swimming in exactly the same way, while Benny followed behind, splashing and kicking loudly at the surface. Twist came back up for another big breath and dived down again, before finally pausing to look back.

The pirate ship was still on the surface, but he couldn't see anyone following through the water. Benny caught up slowly. Not wanting to tempt fate, Twist turned back and swam for the shore as quickly as his body knew how, cutting through the surface like a knife. It felt like no time at all before he and Halil found ground beneath them and began to walk up onto the shore. Benny joined them shortly, all but collapsing onto the gray sand.

Halil went to him, but Twist only stood on the sand beside them, breathing heavily and watching as the ship slipped back under the surface, into the depths of the sea. He looked down to his wrist and saw a good amount of saltwater dripping out of his watch. He didn't even have to lift it to his ear to know that it had stopped ticking. He didn't have to touch it to know what the saltwater had done to the fine, intricate, mechanism. He unwound its chain from his wrist and ran a finger around its edge, silently promising to bring it back to life. Though it lay silent in his hands, he could still hear the soft murmur of London's rain on his attic window, wafting gently under the watch's tiny pains.

Once the pirate ship disappeared and Benny regained some of his strength, Halil couldn't seem to stop smiling even for an instant. He insisted that both Twist and Benny follow him into the city beside the shore to find his family home. He led them through the wide boulevards and tight backstreets of a large city, built in a style that felt at once familiar and foreign to Twist. Most of the pale stone buildings looked to be both Western— with flat, multistory faces and neat square windows—and also distinctly Eastern and medieval, with framed, onion shaped doorways and alcoves, adorned with red cloth awnings and intricate ironwork, fences and gates. Halil finally came to a stop before another stone-framed doorway. There was a woman in a long, embroidered gown just outside, sweeping the few low steps.

She looked up from her work, and her face blanked in total shock when her gaze fell on Halil. Her eyes then filled with tears as she rushed to him, wrapping him in her arms, laughing and crying, and talking quickly in a language Twist couldn't understand, all at the same time. Halil looked a picture of total bliss, hugging her and kissing her cheek, and talking just as quickly as she did. When he gestured to Twist and Benny, the woman looked up to them both with an enormous smile on her damp face.

"You will come in, and stay," she said with a much thicker accent than Halil's. "We will have a feast! My son is home!" she said, her voice breaking with tears of joy.

Twist and Benny were shown in, while Halil was

embraced by every person in the house—a man with the same eyes as Halil's, an older couple, and piles of children and young adults—each one overjoyed to hold him again. Twist watched the dispay curiously, and did his best to stay out of reach. None the less, as Halil spoke quickly, looking to Twist occasionally as he did, the others in the house turned to him with wonder and admiration filling their faces.

"You have saved my son!" said the man with Halil's eyes, coming closer to Twist with open arms.

"I saved myself," Twist said, his hands up as he stepped back, wide eyed. "He helped me, actually. I should thank him instead." He slipped around the man before he got too close, stepping quickly past a low, square, red-cushioned sort of couch and back into open space. Halil's father watched him with a curious smile.

"Mr. Twist is shy," Halil said as if it were a secret. "He doesn't like to touch."

Twist swallowed the implications against his pride, and gave Halil's father his best apologetic look. A few of the children giggled.

Halil's father laughed as well, but not apparently at Twist's expense, turning to the others with a wide smile. He said something with great declaration, calling cheers and happy words from the others. Halil's mother and many of the young girls hurried off, while Halil ushered Twist and Benny into another room.

The three of them, still dripping wet from their escape, were given warm towels and a change of dry clothes. Twist was almost as thin as Halil, and so ended up in a pair of his soft, dark, roomy trousers and a long tunic of blue linen, trimmed with an intricate, embroidered pattern. Benny was similarly attired before Halil finally took Benny and Twist to one of the low couches in the front room and told them to sit.

"We are having a party to celebrate," he said to them, excitedly. His father came to them with dark tea in thin, clear glasses, with a slice of lemon in each.

The festivities began quickly with sweets to start, and plenty of the hot, rich tea. The children played around the room while everyone else talked brightly together, laughing most of the time. Halil's attention was absorbed by his family at a furious pace, and he looked nothing but happy.

"So, what will you do now, Mr. Twist?" Benny asked. "Will you return to England?"

The thought of London was intoxicating in the exotic whirlwind that his life had become, and for a moment Twist wanted nothing more than the comfort of those soot-stained cobblestones under his feet, the chilly drizzle, and the quiet of candlelight and ticking clocks. He shook his head, steeling his courage once again.

"No," he said softly. "I have something I have to do first."

"Well, I'm headed straight back," Benny said. "I was here as an adviser for about a year before my survey ship was attacked by those pirates and I was taken. I started to believe that I would never see England again. Now, I want nothing more."

"What were those pirates doing, anyway?" Twist asked. "It seemed strange to go to so much trouble to hide underwater. Why don't they just use a normal ship?"

"They don't usually attack merchant ships, or anything like that," Benny said. "They're oil pirates. They tap into the pipelines on the sea bed, and steal the oil. They can't take too much at once, so the pumping companies, like BP and the others, hardly notice the difference. But split among a small handful of men, the prices they can get on the black market amount to small fortunes over time."

"Oil is that valuable?" Twist asked skeptically.

"They are finding new uses for it all the time," Benny said. "You watch. Soon, it will be one of the most valuable things in the world. Cities like this one will only grow richer and richer."

"What city is this?" Twist asked, slightly alarmed now by how little he actually knew about his situation. "I don't even know where we are."

"Baku," Benny said, a light laugh on his voice. "The capital of Azerbaijan," he continued as Twist stared at him blankly. "In the Caucasus. South of Russia, north of Iran, right in the middle of the Middle East. On the planet Earth..."

"How far are we from, say, Nepal?" Twist asked.

"Oh, that's the landmark you understand?" Benny asked, laughing again. "I don't know...we're about a day and a half away from India, on a fast airship. So, maybe two days from Nepal, depending on the transport."

"I see," Twist said, his mind working hard. If he was going to finish what he'd set out to do, he'd first have to get himself to Nepal on his own. Without the *Vimana*, though, he'd have a terrible time trying to find a forgotten myth in a country he didn't know in the least. It still seemed more reasonable to try it on his own—than to find the *Vimana* again—considering that he'd last seen her in the middle of an intense battle. For all he knew, she was lying at the bottom of the Caspian Sea.

"Mr. Twist?" one of Halil's relatives asked, entering the room from the entry hall. "There is someone here...to see you," he said, uncertainly.

"Who could possibly know you're here?" Benny asked, voicing everyone's confusion.

Arabel walked into the room, and her face burst into joy when her eyes fell on Twist. "I found you!" she said with a gasp, rushing to him. "Oh, I'd hug you if I knew it wouldn't cause you extreme discomfort!" she said, smiling brightly.

Twist stared at her in naked dismay. "How..." he breathed.

"I. Found. You," she said, sounding out each word slowly. Twist got it the second time: her Sight. "But where have you been? For two days, you were underwater. How ever did you do that?"

"Oil pirates," Twist said. "They enslaved me and made me shovel coal to keep their boiler running hot."

"You're having one hell of a week, aren't you?" Zayle asked, appearing in the room behind Arabel. "Look at this," he said, glancing over Twist's clothing. "Two days alone, and he's gone native."

"How charming," Arabel said, smiling at Twist. Twist instantly wished she wouldn't.

Halil jumped in to make the introductions after Twist explained that Arabel and Zayle were his traveling companions. Halil's family welcomed them as they had Twist, and insisted that they stay for a while and enjoy the celebrations. Halil and Arabel traded stories, explaining Twist to each other. Halil was just as delighted to hear of the mid-air battle that threw Twist into the sea, as Arabel was to hear of him fighting his way to the surface again.

"Seriously?" she said to Twist, smiling at him. "Five pirates, all by yourself?"

"Six if you count the one that ran away," Benny said.

"I didn't know you had it in you," Zayle said, shaking his head.

"They threw me into the engine room," Twist said with a shrug. "Steam engines are always angry."

"Of course!" Arabel said, clapping her hands with sudden understanding. "You touched it and *then* beat up the whole crew with a shovel. That makes so much more sense." Twist rubbed at his brow and prayed for strength.

"And then when you got to the bridge," Zayle said, "all you had to do was touch the controls. Am I right?"

"I don't get it," Halil said.

"He's got a Sight," Zayle said, hooking a thumb at Twist. "Touch something, and he knows exactly how it works."

"He takes on their emotions, too," Arabel said, sounding proud for some reason Twist couldn't imagine.

"Really?" Halil said, looking to Twist, wide-eyed with wonder yet again.

Twist shrugged and took a sip of his tea, hoping this conversation would go away if he ignored it.

"What about in the water?" Halil asked. "One moment you were drowning, the next you swam as well as me."

"You touched me," Twist said. "You probably saved my life."

"Amazing," Benny said, staring at Twist.

Much to Twist's relief, Halil's mother and the girls returned with large platters of food, drawing the room's full attention. Each dish was brightly colored with bits of meat and vegetables in a variety of sauces and forms unlike anything Twist had ever seen. While everyone dug in happily, eating off small plates with their hands and bits of flat bread, Halil's mother handed each of the visitors a plate piled with some of everything.

Not wanting to be rude, Twist tried a small bite of bright-yellow-colored rice and meant to smile back to her in thanks, but the flavors surprised him. Sweet fruits, nutty spices, the aroma of perfectly seared meats, and a multitude of flavors entirely foreign to him melded together into a level of deliciousness that he never knew existed. A true smile spread across his face instead, as he thanked her. Suddenly realizing that he was starving, he finished most of the plate very quickly, and each bite seemed totally different from the last.

Once Halil's mother was finally satisfied that everyone had eaten enough, the celebrations took a quieter turn. The girls disappeared again to clean up, while everyone else gathered for warm conversation over hot drinks.

"The *Vimana* is repaired from the battle," Arabel said, sitting beside Twist, "and we're ready to leave as soon as you are."

"What happened in the battle, anyway?" Twist asked. "I sort of missed the end."

"They were after you, actually," Zayle said. "Once you fell over the side, they didn't know what to do. We attacked them in full force while they were spread out."

"Most of their ship is at the bottom of the sea," Arabel said proudly. "What's left of it won't be flying again anytime soon." While Twist listened, his memory of the battle came back to him: the man with Arabel's green eyes, and the blast that threw him clear off the ship.

"That was your brother, wasn't it?" Twist asked. "The one who grabbed me."

"Jonas," Arabel said, looking at Twist carefully. "Do you know what happened? Between you two, I mean..."

Twist shook his head. "I've never experienced anything like it," he said. "He touched me, but I didn't see any vision. Everything just went white and hot, like my mind was on fire. I only remember falling after that, and then I must have blacked out. I don't even remember hitting the water. I just woke up later, under the sea on the oil pirates' ship."

"Jonas can't explain it either," Arabel said. "He was unconscious for most of a day, and when he woke up, he said kind of the same thing."

"We saw an explosion," Zayle said, leaning closer to

speak quietly. "When he grabbed you, there was this huge white flash and you both flew apart. The blast threw you right over the side and sent him flying to the other side of the deck."

"Wait, where is he now?" Twist asked.

"He's on the *Vimana*," Arabel answered. "Even if he is a traitor, he's still my brother. He's staying with us for now."

"The rest of Quay's crew scattered once their ship broke up," Zayle said.

"They didn't even try to take him back," Arabel said, her gaze distant.

"What did they want with me?" Twist asked. "I'm not important."

"It seems that Jonas got a look at you in Venice," Arabel said. "He admitted to telling Quay that he saw you and got a vision of you in Nepal, fixing the clockwork princess. Quay thought she'd be worth a fortune, so they left Venice right away and hid in the cloud bank, heading for Nepal and plotting the whole time to steal you from us."

"They seemed to think they could get you to fix the girl for them," Zayle said.

"Well, that was a bad guess," Twist said bitterly. "You might be pirates too, but at least you never attacked me," he muttered.

"I told you, we're not pirates," Arabel said sharply.

"My mistake," Twist said lifting a hand defensively. "The world seems to be full of them. No matter where I go, I always find myself surrounded by pirates!" he added, holding his head in his hand with a weary expression on his face.

"Poor Twist," Arabel said, barely stopping herself from reaching out to pat him.

When Twist and his companions left Halil's house, Twist was once again showered in thanks by the family. Try as he might, none of them let him refuse it.

"Every time I see the sun," Halil said to him on the doorstep, "I will know it is because of you, Mr. Twist."

Benny decided to accept the family's offer to let him stay with them until he could secure passage back to England. In the end, Twist had no choice but to leave the house with the family's undying gratitude and admiration. Arabel and Zayle took him through the winding backstreets of the city, to the airship docks along the shore of the Caspian Sea.

Dr. Rodés insisted on giving Twist a look once he got back on board the *Vimana*, but found nothing that a good meal and a night's sleep couldn't fix. Heedless of the advice, Twist immediately took his clockwork tools out of his luggage and set to work, mending his pocket watch.

While the airship pulled back into the thin clouds over the southern tip of the Caspian Sea, sailing quietly through the cold night air, Twist was totally absorbed with cleaning the tiny pieces of the watch. After everything it had just been through, his mind reveled in the calm and quiet of his work. Somewhere over the Durrani Empire, fatigue set in hard and unannounced. Twist awoke the next morning, hunched over the desk in his cabin with his tools still in his hands, and still dressed in Halil's old clothes. Sometime during the night, someone had left a blanket draped over his shoulders.

When he looked out the windows, he saw nothing but

sandy brown desert and huge, jagged, dry mountains below. The sky around the ship was clear and empty under the blazing sun. From the air, the land below looked inhospitable and desolate. For the first time that he could remember, Twist was thankful to be in the air, high above and out of reach.

It was Zayle who came to check on him that morning. Twist was putting the last piece of his watch back into place when Zayle knocked on his door and then let himself in.

"Hey, you fixed it already?" Zayle said as Twist snapped the back of the watch closed.

Twist held the watch up to his ear and closed his eyes. The tiny clockwork heart beat steady and calm, as if nothing had ever been wrong. "Yes I have," Twist said, smiling.

"What do you see when you touch that watch, anyway?" Zayle asked.

"It's mine," Twist said. "I only see my own memories."

"Isn't that kind of boring?" Zayle asked, as Twist slipped the watch back into his pocket.

"Sometimes, it's the only way I can be sure which feelings are mine," Twist said as lightly as he could.

"I wish I had a magic power," Zayle said with a huff.

Twist looked to him quickly. "No, you don't."

"Ara's is nice," Zayle said back, his arms crossed. "Well, sometimes it doesn't give her enough information, but it doesn't give her any trouble."

"Well, she's lucky then," Twist said, trying to bite back the bitterness in his voice.

"I just think it would be fun," Zayle said with a shrug. "Are you coming to lunch, then?" he asked brightly.

"I missed breakfast again, did I?" Twist asked, reaching for his short, black coat.

"Yep," Zayle said with a nod.

As he shrugged into his coat, the scent of the Caspian Sea wafted around him. Though Halil's family had graciously dried out his clothes, they still had a scent of salt water and silt to them. Twist tried to ignore it as the crisp wind of high atmosphere met him on deck.

As Twist walked to lunch with Zayle, a quiet, haunting fear crept into the back of his mind. He knew that Jonas was on board, but he hadn't seen him yet. He'd only laid eyes on him twice, but while both instances had been brief, they had been and staggering as well. He couldn't remember what the other man even looked like, except that he had Arabel's eyes. To Twist's relief, though, Jonas wasn't present for lunch.

"Your brother is on the ship, isn't he?" Twist asked Arabel when the conversation had slowed for a moment.

"Oh yes, he is," Arabel said. "He's just..." Her voice fell away, her gaze distant.

"He's avoiding people," Dr. Rodés said. "He's worse than ever, if you ask me."

"Philippe, please," Captain Davis said. "Give him some time."

"He's had months," Dr. Rodés said. "And years before that." The others looked at him silently. "I'm only saying what you're all thinking. He's not getting better."

"The boy is hurt," Aazzi said, her rich voice softer than usual. "So much so, that he cut himself off from his own family. He needs compassion, not ridicule."

"He was so sweet when he was young," Arabel said, as if to herself. "I miss him." The others looked away from her, each one quiet.

"So, how far are we from Nepal, then?" Zayle asked, pulling the group back into the light of day.

Twist asked nothing more about Jonas for the remainder of the meal. Once everyone was finished,

Twist returned to the open second deck with his book in hand. As he stepped into the light, the skin at the back of his neck began to tingle.

Lying on his back on the deck, his arms open at his sides and one knee bent casually in the cool air, a young man gazed up at the sky beyond the front edge of the balloon. His golden hair was cut short, standing away from his scalp in needle-like points, and his European skin was tanned from too much time in the sunlight. His form looked light but strong, and just as agile as Arabel's. He wore a simple white shirt and brown leather trousers, with high boots, and black-lensed goggles nestled in the front of his pointy hair. There was also a metal contraption over his ears that Twist couldn't identify, which looked something like complicated earmuffs made of brass coils and thin wires. They seemed to be connected to a small metal box that lay beside him on the deck by a thick, rubber-covered cord.

While Twist looked at him, his feet continued to take him slowly closer, as if compelled by some outside force. Twist's heartbeat sped quickly as a general sense of unease throbbed through him, and the buzzing at the back of his neck grew steadily more noticeable. No matter how Twist told himself to stop or turn away, his feet kept drawing him closer. The young man's uncovered, unblinking green eyes—or were they blue?—stole Twist's full attention.

For the first time that he could remember, the desire to touch another person burned to life in Twist's heart. Staggered by this, Twist's fear grew sharply. He approached to within only a few steps before Jonas reached back to rub at his neck. In the flash of an instant, his eyes flicked to Twist. Twist felt a shock of fire at the back of his neck and he struggled to keep his footing.

"Shi—!" Jonas hissed in the same moment. He sat up

like a shot, turning away from Twist and pulled the contraption off his ears. He was breathing hard, still holding his neck, as he pulled the black goggles on over his eyes. "What do you want?" he snapped.

"I'm sorry," Twist muttered, blinking his vision clear of the tiny star-like motes that seemed to swim in the air before him. "I didn't mean to..."

Jonas turned to him with an unreadable expression, his eyes hidden behind the black lenses. Twist pulled his gaze away instantly, but he felt no reaction as he had before.

"Can you...see through those?" Twist asked cautiously, glancing back to him. He'd taken a few steps closer still when he wasn't paying attention.

"No," Jonas said, still apparently looking right at him. "Don't come any closer," he said, lifting a hand as Twist's slow steps made a nearby board creak ever so slightly.

"I'm sorry," Twist said, forcing himself to step back and stop. "I can't help it," he said, shaking his head. The buzz at the back of his neck was reaching down his spine and up under his scalp. "Do you feel that too?" he asked, rubbing at his neck.

"What is that?" Jonas asked, shaking his head. "I feel it every time you get close to me."

"I had hoped you might be able to explain it," Twist said sorrowfully.

"No luck there, clock-boy," Jonas said unkindly, seeming to look to him again.

"You got a vision from me in Venice, didn't you?" Twist asked, catching himself leaning forward. The pull to touch Jonas's skin was becoming more and more difficult to resist, despite the fact that it was the last thing in the world that Twist actually wanted to do.

"I've never seen anything like it," Jonas said softly, his unseeing gaze slipping away to his thoughts. "It was fractured and chaotic, and I only got a glimpse." He turned quickly to look back up at Twist, seemingly looking him right in the eyes through the blacked-out lenses. "Who are you, anyway?"

"I'm just...Twist."

Jonas stared at him silently. Jonas's right hand had drifted slowly up toward his goggles. "I looked in your eyes. Twice. And I still don't know who you are," he said, his fingers brushing the leather strap that held his goggles in place.

"Don't!" Twist said, reaching out to stop him. Twist realized what he was doing only a moment before he touched Jonas. Twist was also now kneeling well within reach of him. He pulled his offending hand away, holding it to his chest while his heart thundered.

"What is this?" Jonas gasped, clenching his fingers into fists at his sides, his goggles still over his eyes. "Why do I keep wanting to look at you?"

Twist shook his head, all of his attention focused on not reaching out to the man so close in front of him. "We can't," he breathed. "Last time..."

"Did you see anything, last time?" Jonas asked, not moving.

"Nothing," Twist said. "Everything was washed out in whiteness."

"What's going on over here?" Captain Davis asked, walking closer.

"Nothing," Twist and Jonas said simultaneously. They both looked to each other suspiciously.

"Well, that sounds perfectly innocent," Captain Davis said, stopping beside them with a light smile on his face. "But, in case you didn't notice, the last time you two got close, you exploded. Do you really think it's wise to try it again?"

"You know, I really didn't miss you at all," Jonas

said, looking up at him through his black lenses.

It took all of Twist's will power to get back to his feet and to take a step away. "We were just talking," he said.

"What's going on with you two?" Captain Davis asked. Twist looked to him silently, pulling all meaning from his cold, steel-blue eyes and stilling his form completely.

"A normal like you doesn't have a prayer of understanding either of us," Jonas said, lying back on the deck again, one arm curled under his head.

Captain Davis looked down at him for a moment, before he reached down and, in a flash, snatched the goggles clean off of Jonas's face. Jonas was on his feet almost as quickly, his eyes closed tightly but his face otherwise a mask of rage.

"Not funny!" he growled. "Give those back! Now!"

"Tell me what's going on," Captain Davis said, backing away and holding the goggles behind his back. "I might just know more than you think, my boy. Maybe I could help you to understand it, yourself." Twist watched the two carefully, but held his tongue.

"I neither need, nor want your help," Jonas said, his voice low but vicious as he advanced on the captain. "And I am not your boy."

"Now, Jonas," Captain Davis said with false kindness, "be a good lad and stop lying."

As Captain Davis continued to back away from Jonas, Twist slipped closer. He gauged his moment carefully and then reached out, snatching the goggles out of the captain's unsuspecting fingers. Twist sprang away, behind Jonas, easily clearing Captain Davis's reach as he swiped out at Twist and gave a startled curse.

Twist's mind flared to light with countless faces. He saw Arabel and the rest of the crew in many different places across years of change and age. Each one looked to him, but none saw him; not one looked in his eyes. A deep, primal, sadness soaked into him with a level of lonesomeness that he had never imagined. Twist snapped back to himself not a second later.

"Jonas, here," Twist said, holding the goggles out to him by his fingertips.

Jonas spun, lowering his gaze before he opened his eyes and took the goggles back, careful not to touch Twist. The goggles went right back on over his eyes.

"Twist, you're not helping," Captain Davis said with a pained smile on his face.

"You don't understand anything," Twist said back to him, unable to keep the disgust from his voice. Jonas looked to him quickly, through the black lenses. "Don't do that again," Twist said to the captain.

"You're just as bad as him," Captain Davis said, shaking his head. "Fine. If you insist on blowing yourselves up again, then be my guest." He turned with his last words, stalking off.

Twist watched him for a moment, perplexed by his apparent lack of compassion, before the buzz at the back of his neck escalated sharply. Twist turned to see Jonas's black lenses trained squarely on him.

"Thank you," Jonas said, as if the words were foreign to him. Twist smiled, even if the other man couldn't see it. "But, what did you see?" Jonas asked, his voice suddenly fragile. "You had to see something when you touched my goggles."

"It was just a glimpse," Twist said after a moment. "I saw a rush of the things those goggles see for you. What you never see."

"People, then," Jonas said with a small smile on his lips. "Well, I suppose we're even now," he said more brightly. "I got a glimpse of you, and now you've had one of me."

To his complete surprise, Twist found himself still sitting with Jonas on the open deck, as twilight began to fall on the desert land below. The longer he spent with Jonas, the more accustomed they both became to the strange buzzing at the base of their skulls. After a while, Twist found it much easier to resist the compulsion to reach out to Jonas, while Jonas also seemed to have less trouble keeping his eyes away from him.

The strange metal earmuffs that Jonas had been wearing turned out to contain small electric speakers, connected to a mechanical device that played recorded music from wax cylinders. Jonas said he had picked it up in Vienna, and collected a handful of recorded cylinders from cities all over the world. He'd even recorded some, himself. The device seemed curious to Twist, but he began to understand why Jonas was so adamant that the technology would take the world by storm, as he listened to the disembodied, exotic music.

"Where is this one from?" Twist asked, pulling one of the earphones away. He was now sitting against the railing at the bow of the ship, watching the thin, high-atmosphere clouds stream by overhead.

"South Africa," Jonas said, now lying on his back, at Twist's feet. "I recorded that one. They are all local school children. Pretty enchanting, isn't it?"

"Wonderful," Twist said, putting the earphone back into place so that the angelic voices, singing words he found meaningless but beautiful, could fully encompass him again.

When the song ended, Twist pulled the earphones off,

letting them hang around his neck by the band that connected them, and looked down to Jonas. His goggles were sitting on his brow again, his eyes flashing gently in the failing light. For a moment, Twist thought he saw the color of his eyes change quickly from green to lilac.

"Twist..." Jonas's voice toned leadingly; he closed his eyes with what looked like an effort.

"Sorry," Twist said, looking away and absently rubbing at the buzz in his neck. He heard Jonas chuckle to himself. "But, you know, I haven't tried to touch you in at least half an hour."

"Very good," Jonas said, a light smile on his face as he opened his eyes to the sky again.

"What are you looking at, anyway?" Twist asked, trying his best to keep his gaze away from Jonas's eyes. "You're not just seeing the sky, are you?"

"Mars has been chasing us all day," Jonas said. Twist looked up to see it but, even as twilight began to darken the sky, the stars were all still well hidden in the deep blue. "I think it's amazing to look up and see another planet," Jonas said, reaching up to curl one arm under his head. "I never have seen anyone on Mars looking back, though."

"You can really see stars in daylight?" Twist asked, not bothering to hide his wonder.

"Sure," Jonas said dismissively. "And I see them in color, too. I can see the air patterns swimming around, as well."

Twist smiled lightly as he tried to imagine what colors the stars might be. He opened the cylinder player to switch to another record, but his mind flashed for an instant when he touched the cylinder that he'd just heard: hot sunlight, dry air, a handful of children with skin as dark as Aazzi's and smiles as bright as sunlight.

"By the way," Jonas added, "I don't think it's going to

be snowing when we get to Nepal."

Twist shook his head. "We really are strange people."

"Is this a revelation to you?" Jonas asked through a laugh, his eyes flitting away from Twist sharply as he made an obvious effort not to look at him.

"No," Twist said with a sigh. "Though it is new to find someone even stranger than me."

"Now just a minute," Jonas said, pulling his goggles on and leaning up on his elbows to look at Twist through his black lenses. "I'll admit I'm somewhat of a freak, but stranger than you? I'm not sure about that."

"I can't see planets in a clear blue sky," Twist said to his vision-less gaze.

"I don't think clocks are alive," Jonas said, unfazed.

"I can't see the future," Twist shot back.

"You took on a submersible full of pirates with nothing but a shovel," Jonas said, his voice gaining volume.

"The second time I met you, you flew at me!" Twist snapped back quickly.

"My word," Jonas said, looking away and shaking his head. "We're a proper pair of freaks."

Twist broke into a laugh, the tension of the silly argument breaking into the crisp, thin air. When he looked up, he saw Arabel standing farther off, leaning against the railing. She watched them with a quiet smile on her face for a moment longer before stepping closer.

"I have to say," she said, drawing Jonas's attention as well, "I never saw this coming."

Jonas sat up, curling himself against one knee with his back to her. His face lost its clever smile, and his form lost its ease. Twist stared at him curiously, shocked by how quickly and completely his manner could change.

"Jon, honey, are you honestly making a friend?" Arabel asked, her voice bubbly with glee as she reached down to pat his shoulder. Jonas jerked his shoulder out of her touch instantly, his head bowed. "Oh, don't be like that," Arabel said, putting on a false pout.

"How long have you been over there?" Twist asked, nodding to her previous perch.

"I got to see the 'who's a bigger freak' fight," Arabel said with a grin. "That was brilliant."

Jonas shot up to his feet, turning on her with his sightless gaze. "Shall I sing and dance for you too?" he hissed, his jaw almost too tight to let him speak at all.

"Jon..." Arabel said, as if scolding a pet. "You weren't being so mean a moment ago."

"And then you stuck your nose in where it wasn't wanted," Jonas replied. "Funny how that works."

Twist quietly got to his feet as well.

"Why must you always be so hostile?" Arabel asked, her voice losing all its kindness.

Jonas's jaw became visibly tight, but he kept it closed as he turned his back. He stormed away to the other side of the deck. Arabel scowled at his back and crossed her arms, while Twist struggled to figure out if there was something he should do in response to the now sharp-tension in the empty space Jonas had left behind.

"I seriously don't understand him sometimes," Arabel whispered to Twist.

"The way you're treating him isn't working," Twist said, his voice as small as ever, but certain. "Your uncle did the same thing and stormed off in less than a minute."

"What are you talking about?" Arabel asked, frowning.

"Do you think he's being stubborn?" Twist asked, still trying to work it out. "I don't think he's the one being childish."

"Of course he is," Arabel said, looking confused.

Twist took a breath. "You're wrong," he said, shaking

his head. "I've only had a glimpse of him from touching those goggles, but I can tell you that that is definitely not how he feels."

Arabel looked quietly at Twist, her thoughts working hard behind her uncertain eyes.

"Just give him some credit," Twist said, turning to walk over to where Jonas now stood at the railing across the deck, staring out over the horizon.

As he approached, he was almost sure he saw the color of Jonas's eyes change again as they looked out over the desert world below. The buzz in his neck tightened sharply with each step. Jonas began to look to him, but Twist looked off to the side quickly.

"Are you fond of meddling in personal affairs?" Jonas asked, slipping his goggles on again and putting on a tight smile. Though his words were taunting, his voice had smoothed out once again, and lost some of its vicious bite in favor of caution. "That's not going to make you very likable, you know."

"You heard that?"

"Well, I heard her," Jonas said darkly, looking away.

"Oh, well," Twist said, sounding as serious as he could. "I could never meddle. People make very little sense to me at the best of times."

"Weirdo," Jonas said, his smile growing. Twist stared back at him, at a total loss as to how such a word could be said in a friendly way.

"Isn't he, though?" Arabel asked, stepping closer from behind Twist.

Jonas's form seized instantly again, his black lenses turning to her sharply. "You're still here?" he asked flatly.

"I saw Twist first," she said almost teasingly. "You only just met him, and you've been hogging him all afternoon." Jonas seemed to watch her silently, as if unsure of her meaning.

"Heaven save me, I'm popular," Twist said gravely. Both Arabel and Jonas let out a tentative chuckle.

"Well, fine," Jonas said, walking away to collect his music player. "You can have him for now," he called to them over his shoulder. "I'm going inside anyway. The sun's going down and I'm already cold," he said as he headed for the stairs below deck.

"That's more like it," Arabel said proudly.

Jonas stopped just in front of Arabel and turned to look at her through the goggles. "But this is only a loan. I'm taking him back later."

"Do I get a say in any of this?" Twist asked.

"No," Jonas said with a clever smile before he turned to walk away.

Arabel watched him walk away with an amazed look on her face. Twist pulled his coat tighter around him, starting to feel the cold too, now that someone had mentioned it.

"That's got to be the most pleasant and friendly I've seen my brother in years," Arabel said softly at his shadow. She looked to Twist. "I haven't got a clue why, but you are really good for him."

"I didn't do anything," Twist said with a shrug. "Like I said, I'm no good at people."

"No, you figured him out," Arabel said, shaking her head. "You seem to know exactly how to make him civil. So, share. I haven't had a good conversation with him in...I don't know how long."

"Well," Twist said uncertainly, "I don't think he's trying to be mean to you. He's probably just defending himself."

"But why?" Arabel asked.

"I don't know," Twist said, giving a shrug. "Clocks are so much easier to fix than people."

"You've got that right," Arabel said with a sigh.

"Well, anyway, could you spend more time with him? I think it might help. He could use a friend."

Twist frowned at the thought of such an assignment. He couldn't remember ever having a human friend before, in his life. The prospect only seemed daunting to him now. As Jonas moved farther away into the airship, the buzz that Twist had all but gotten used to, dimmed to silence so complete that Twist clutched to his watch just to feel its tiny heartbeat in the back of his mind.

   Twist awoke the next morning to see towering, mist-
enshrouded mountains reaching up to the clouds outside
his porthole windows. The land below had turned
emerald green during the night, broken by jagged gray
stone. The peaks were all topped with white and
wrapped tightly in haunting, shifting wisps of fog. Twist
stared out at the mountains for a while, trying his best to
remember any other mountain ranges that might still be
between the *Vimana* and the Himalayas. By the time he'd
gotten dressed, he gave up trying and decided to go out
and ask someone. An unexpected knock at his door
stilled his hand, just as he was already reaching out to
open it. Twist felt the same nagging buzz at his neck.
Opening the door, he found Jonas outside with tray
holding a pair of plates and two mugs.
   "You were late for breakfast, so I brought you some,"
Jonas explained with a smile half obscured by his black
goggles. "I was late too. On purpose. Can I interest you
in a quiet, nonjudgmental and un-spiteful meal?"
   "Sure," Twist said, opening the door for him.
   They pushed Twist's trunk into the middle of the
room and set their small meal on it, sitting around it on
the floor. Jonas put his goggles on his brow and sat so
that his vision might not easily fall on Twist.
   "This is probably only the second breakfast I've eaten
on this ship," Twist said before taking a bite of buttered
toast.
   "They told me as much," Jonas said as he stirred
sugar into his coffee. "Ara said you usually sleep until
lunchtime."

"It's not by design, I assure you," Twist said.

"Of course, you're always getting yourself into some kind of trouble or other, wearing yourself out fighting pirates and what not. I understand."

"You have got to be the most sarcastic person I've ever met," Twist said, focusing on slicing up his fried tomatoes and sausage.

"No ... really?" Jonas said, laying it on thick with a wide smile. Twist fought the urge to glare at him.

"Oh, I wanted to ask someone," he said, pointing to the windows with his fork. "What mountains are those?"

"We're flying over the feet of the Himalayas," Jonas said. "I think we're technically in India right now, but Nepal is just across the next border."

"Then we're almost there," Twist said, stunned, watching as another crag of gray and green sailed by the windows, wrapped in the mist.

"Just about," Jonas said. "No one will tell me exactly where we're going to land, but Nepal isn't that big. We should reach our destination by tonight, sometime."

"Why won't they tell you?" Twist asked.

"They think I'm going to try to steal the clockwork girl and sell her for a load of money," he said calmly, and then took a bite of fried egg.

Twist stared at his face from the side.

"Twist, stop it," Jonas said around the bite, dragging his eyelids down.

"You're not going to, are you?" Twist asked, not looking away from his shielded eyes. The buzz at the back of his neck grew stronger as he stared at him, but he knew Jonas was feeling the same thing.

Jonas's eyes shifted toward Twist, while still staying low. "A walking, talking, life-sized puppet made of clockwork? It would be worth a lot."

"But she's not just a puppet, she's still a person,"

Twist said, his small voice tight. "So you're not seriously going to try to steal her away just to sell her off, are you?"

"According to the story," Jonas said, frowning, "the princess, whose soul haunted that puppet originally, died so long ago that the whole story is considered a myth. According to Ara, the puppet is lifeless now, and it's only Aazzi's guess that it's the princess's ghost that is still haunting the palace she died in. What makes you think you're going to find anything alive when we get there?" Twist's vision slipped away from Jonas, the buzz lessening instantly.

"Arabel brought me a piece of her," he said. "When I touched it..." He shook his head. "She's still alive. I'm sure of it."

"If you say so," Jonas muttered, rubbing at his neck. "Look, it's pointless to be worried about me at all," he said. "Uncle Howell is planning to do the same thing, and he has a ship."

"What?"

"Why else would they fly from Nepal all the way to London and back again?" Jonas asked. "Did you think this was a charity mission?"

"They told me they weren't pirates," Twist said as he felt his heart beat harder. "Repeatedly! They get mad whenever I even call them pirates."

"They're treasure hunters," Jonas said. "Pirates steal from people, treasure hunters steal from time and legend."

"Oh no..." Twist said, a cold lump of ice beginning to grow in his stomach. "What am I doing?" His breath came faster now, unbidden.

"Twist?" Jonas said, his hand stilled a breath away from a comforting touch. He took his hand away with obvious effort. "Calm down. It's all right."

"No, it isn't," Twist said, shaking his head. "I wanted to help her! She needs someone to help her, and I thought that I could."

"You can," Jonas said, stopping himself from looking into Twist's eyes to reassure him. "You will. I saw it. I can see the future, remember?"

"But then what?" Twist asked, his small voice ready to break.

"Twist," Jonas said gently, moving in so close behind him that Twist could feel the heat off his skin. The buzz at the back of his neck grew intense enough to take on its own heat. "It's going to be all right," Jonas said. "If you fix the puppet, and it actually does come to life and becomes a real person again, that will change everything."

"It will?" Twist asked hesitantly, turning to just see Jonas out the corner of his eye.

"Yes, it will. These people, while rather cold towards me, are not evil. In fact," he said brightly, "they are more cruel and heartless to me than they are to anyone else. And they never tried to sell me off for loads of money, against my will."

To Twist's surprise, the warmth of Jonas so close beside him became relaxing. He felt his heart calm despite the hum of energy running fluidly along his neck and down his spine. The simple fact that Jonas seemed to truly care that Twist was upset calmed him as well.

"Well," Twist muttered over his shoulder, "you wouldn't be worth as much," he said, forcing some level of brightness into his voice.

"Now, now," Jonas said, his words colored with a smile. "I sold myself to pirates, and got a pretty penny for me."

"Are you obsessed with money?" Twist asked, trying to give his words a snap.

"I'm not obsessed with it," Jonas said, backing off again. "I'm just saving up for freedom. It's expensive these days." The hum calmed back down to the usual buzz, leaving Twist's senses slightly chilled and hollow in its absence.

By the time they had finished eating, Twist's fears had quieted into a nervous murmur that hid beneath the rest of his thoughts. No matter what the crew planned to do, they were moments away from her now. After what felt like an eternity, after crossing countries, combating countless pirates, and pushing himself to new limits, Twist finally saw Nepal sail silently under the shadow of the airship.

The sun began to slip behind the mountains before the airship slowed. Twist stood at the bow, his chilled fingers clutching the wooden rail tightly as the ship nosed its way between the higher peaks in the thickening fog. His eyes focused hard through the mist and the blue lenses of his goggles, searching for an image he had never believed he would see. His imagination had built a palace on the top of these mountains, surrounded in snow and sunlight, bright and full of joy. Here, in the real, shifting, shadowed fog of Nepal, he could only sense foreboding.

After what felt like an eternity, the mist finally thinned before him. A cluster of buildings and small open gardens bound by winding stairs, clung precariously to the side of a peak of gray stone, nestled into a ledge-like crevice like a frightened child in her mother's arms. Small buildings and large halls of plastered white, topped with curving, wing-like roofs of once-vibrant red, fit themselves into the small nooks of the rock while the crumbling stone stairs and pathways wound along them like vines.

As they drew closer, Twist could see that many of the tall, glass windows were broken and that the gardens had overgrown into a truly wild state. Not a single white wall was clean or without a crack. Time and solitude had painted every inch of the once great, shining palace in shades of age and decay as it nudged closer and closer to the edge of the abyss.

"Not what you expected?" Aazzi's voice asked from close behind Twist.

He jerked at the sound of her voice, turning to find a light smile on her face. His eyes blinked to clear themselves and, for a moment, and he was glad that his goggles obscured them.

"The old stories make it sound so nice," Aazzi said when Twist made no response. "I'm sure it was, once. Nothing kills a nice dream like reality, wouldn't you say?"

"I just thought..." Twist's voice drifted away when he looked back, and he shook his head to clear it. "I knew she was alone, but I couldn't image her in this desolate place."

"Well, she's got you now," Aazzi said. "She won't be alone anymore."

Twist nodded, taking a heavy breath. It wasn't long before the *Vimana* came to a stop, floating at the edge of a hanging stone walkway that curved along the outside of one of the buildings. Arabel swung across on the rigging ropes and tied the ship securely to the broken railing before she and Captain Davis ran out a wooden plank to bridge the small gap between the walkway and the airship's deck. Arabel was the first to step across, followed closely by Twist. He already had his clock-mending tools, his candles, and the piece of clockwork that Arabel had given him, in the bag on his shoulder. He wasn't, however, prepared to look down over the side of the deck, into the impossible depths of jagged rock and mist below. Twist jerked, running back three steps before he could stop himself.

"You're kidding," Jonas asked, a wide smile on his face as he and the others gathered to disembark. "You're that afraid of heights?"

"We're at the very top of the world!" Twist snapped at him, still breathing hard. "Anyone who isn't nervous up here is insane."

"What are you doing on an airship at all?" Jonas asked, smirking at Twist from behind his black goggles. "No wonder you're jumpy all the time."

"Come along," Arabel said, crossing back onto the ship and taking hold of Twist's coat sleeve. "Just don't look down. You'll be fine," she said, dragging him back to the edge.

Twist's jaw clenched and his breath caught, but Arabel didn't slow her pace. She stepped easily over the little bridge while Twist scurried to keep up with her confident stride. Before he knew it, he was standing on the somewhat solid stone of the walkway, clutching the balustrade behind him and staring determinedly away from the drop.

"See?" Arabel said brightly. "That was easy." She then walked away to the open doorway, just off to the right. Aazzi and Captain Davis followed after her, leaving Twist to catch his breath.

"Lovely sister you have," Twist muttered when Jonas approached as well.

"If you want her, you can have her," Jonas said flatly.

"Are we moving on, or not?" Dr. Rodés asked with a tight tone when he came to meet them. Twist fell into step behind Jonas and followed the others in, through the open doorway.

A rotted, wooden door hung on one rusted hinge, on the inside of the dark room. The scent of musty fabrics and dust filled the air, while the failing light of day spilled in through broken windows to illuminate various forgotten items around the room. Twist's imagination gave him a glimpse of what this small sitting room used to look like, once upon a time: richly patterned rugs under the soft cushions on the floor, hanging drapes of red, purple, and gold at the windows, and tea served daily in bright glass teacups and silver, to the sound of the princess's favorite musicians. For an instant, he almost thought he could smell the long dissipated-scent of incense on the stale air.

Arabel led the procession out another door, into an open garden that might have been lovely once. Twist could just barely see the stone pots and low borders around pools of grass and flowers under the clawing roots of enormous trees. A single bird cage, torn and twisted by time and exposure, lay in the thick grasses, the only memory of the princess's once-large collection of exotic birds that used to fill this garden with their songs. Looking forward, he saw the face of the largest building. A huge doorway stood at the top of stone steps below a large circle of glass that was surrounded with thin windows that reached out from it like rays of the sun. The center glass was cracked nearly in half, and ivy grew over the white building like a thick blanket.

The moment Arabel stepped across the threshold, into the darkness within, Twist's heartbeat sped up and a cold wave of dread poured over him. A wafting, disconnected, sense of anger and fear danced at the edges of his mind without any cause or identity. Aazzi stopped before entering and gave a shudder.

"There it is again," she said softly.

"Is this place unbelievably creepy, or is it just me?" Jonas asked.

"It's the ghost," Aazzi said to him. "She doesn't like us being here."

"So, there really is a ghost?" Jonas asked her.

"Oh yes," Aazzi said, nodding as she stared at the doorway.

The others walked inside the palace, until Aazzi, Jonas, and Twist were left alone outside. Twist took out his watch and wrapped its chain around his hand, the back of the watch held firmly to his palm. The slow, emotionless ticking calmed him slightly and masked the feelings of anger and fear that threatened from the shadows. Aazzi looked back to him with a smile.

"Do you need a hand, dear?" she asked. "I can pull you inside if you want."

"No," Twist said, shifting the bag to sit more comfortably on his shoulder. He seized his faint courage and stepped forward again. Jonas followed beside him, and Twist felt the familiar buzz block out just a little more of the haunting emotions. They stepped through together into the dim, dusty, cold space inside the once-great hall.

A wide, open floor stretched out before them, rimmed with high stone walls. Tall, thin windows now lay broken on the floor. A balcony floated above the doorway, giving the front of the room a second level. Two curving staircases spilled onto the main floor from the sides, and a row of benches flanked a single throne against the farthest wall. This hall must have been a spectacle at one time, but now a fine blanket of dust and broken glass covered everything in it. Twist saw a few trails of footprints on the floor, with no other disturbances in the dust.

Arabel and the others were standing at the foot of one of the staircases, all silent as they looked down. Coming closer, Twist saw what had drawn their attention. Still lying where she must have fallen so many years ago, a body of tarnished metal lay twisted, broken, and shattered in the dust at the foot of the stair. The young female face was the least damaged, showing a look of horror and shock in the grayed copper and blackened silver of her metal features in a pool of long, tangled wire that fell from her metal scalp. One clear-blue jewel encased in silver sat in the place of one eye, while another lay farther away. Her broken limbs curled around her with the faded, thin, once-pink silk that still wrapped her body and swirled at her sides in long flowing wafts.

Looking down at the grotesque image before him, for a moment Twist didn't understand. The beautiful little princess of clockwork that he had imagined was so far from what he saw. He came within a step of her fallen hand—freed gears and cogs lay all around the ruined metal casing of the torn-open palm—and stooped down. He held out the piece that Arabel had given him in London, and found that it obviously would fit perfectly inside the broken hand on the floor. Tears burned his eyes, and his strength left him as he fell to his knees in the dust.

No one spoke for a long moment as Twist stared at her silently through his freely running tears and disbelief. Arabel was the first to move. She knelt close beside him and placed a gentle hand on his back. Twist shuddered at her touch, his senses overwhelmed by images of Arabel in many faraway places—laughing, running, flying through the air in the rigging of the ship, yelling in rage at her brother—but she pulled her hand away after only the merest instant, breaking the vision into glimmering dust motes in Twist's eyes.

"Sorry!" she said with a wince. "But, honey, are you all right?"

Twist blinked his vision clear, wiping at his eyes, and looked to her silently as if he didn't see her. His breath felt raw and ragged in his throat. Arabel's mouth opened and then closed again silently.

"You can fix her," Jonas said gently, standing beside him.

"She's so..." Twist's small voice quivered slightly as he spoke. "She's real," he said, looking back to the clockwork princess. "And it's horrible. I never thought the damage could be this bad. She could never have been harmed if she were only a myth."

The air in the hall chilled significantly, and far in the distance of the still air, Twist thought he heard the echo of a sorrowful voice. The others turned quickly, looking around into the shadows.

"Someone else heard that, right?" Jonas asked.

"It's the ghost," Aazzi said darkly. "She doesn't like us being here."

"The ghost..." Twist breathed, feeling the chill soak into him, carrying unbidden sorrows with it. He shook his head and got shakily to his feet. "This whole place is haunted!" he said, clutching tightly to the watch in his hands. "I can feel it."

"You mean, you can *feel* it?" Jonas asked, moving closer to Twist, his goggles shielding his eyes as he seemed to look at him. "The ghost is affecting your Sight?"

"Of course, you idiot!" Twist snapped savagely at him. Jonas's eyebrows shot upward over his goggles as he stepped away slightly. "Oh, I'm sorry," Twist muttered, shaking his head again as a wave of his own fear washed over him. "That wasn't me."

"Outside," Jonas said, pointing to the door. "Now."

"No," Twist said, shaking his head.

"Twist, you can't—" Jonas began.

"I can't leave her!" Twist said as defiantly as he was able, without letting the sorrow that wasn't his take control again. He opened his bag quickly and pulled out one of the white candles that he had brought with him.

"Clever lad," Aazzi said with a smile, coming to him.

Aazzi held the candle for Twist to light, and muttered something under her breath as the flame came to light. The moment the golden glow of the candlelight fell on Twist, he felt a release of tension, and the disembodied emotions faded from his heart. The others moved closer as well, into the light.

"I don't get it," Zayle said, staring at the flickering flame.

"The candlelight is pushing the ghost away from us," Jonas said, looking into the light with uncovered eyes as he held his goggles off his face, just an inch. "How does that work?"

"It's an ancient trick," Aazzi said. "But it still works. The light of a white candle cleanses the air of spirits. That's why people burn them at funerals and wakes."

"If I could only explain somehow," Twist said softly, looking out into the shadows. "I'm here to help her. If I could just tell her, I wouldn't need to push her away."

"Explain it to her once you get that puppet to wake up again," Jonas said, looking at him through his black lenses. "It'll be much easier."

"Then I should get to work," Twist said with a heavy breath.

Twist decided to start with her hands. With his candle burning beside him, he carefully took the broken clockwork hand in his own. The moment his fingers touched the tarnished copper, his mind flooded with hundreds of tiny fractures, loose gears, broken springs, and many other points of damage. For a moment he only waited, letting the information settle in his mind and fall into order. Unlike other clocks and watches that he'd repaired before, memories started to echo at the edges of his vision as well. He saw the hand clapping happily, holding a cup of tea, petting a beautiful bird with brilliant green feathers, and running through soft silks. Twist pushed those images away and focused on what needed fixing.

He set to work by first removing the damaged pieces and then carefully repairing the outer case of the hand. As he worked, Aazzi sat silently near him on one of the stairs, her eyes closed and her form still. When a distant sound echoed in the shadows or the air changed temperature outside of the candlelight, she would look up and mutter something in a language Twist couldn't recognize. Finally, curiosity took hold.

"Aazzi," Twist said softly in the echoing quiet, "what are you doing?"

Aazzi smiled slightly. "The candle is helping," she said, "but I'm afraid it's not enough. I can feel a lot of anger on the air."

"What am I doing to anger her?" Twist asked, looking up to her quickly.

"You're meddling, I guess," Aazzi said with a shrug.

"But I'm trying to help," Twist said, frowning bitterly into the shadows.

"Maybe she can't see us clearly," Aazzi said. "She may be trapped in her memories and unable to see our reality."

Twist gave a sigh. "I wish I could just explain."

"Don't worry, little Twist. I'll watch out for you and keep the ghost at bay."

Twist wasn't sure about this new pet name, but he did his best to ignore it for the sake of the added protection. By the time night fell completely on the chilly, crumbling palace, Twist had fully reconstructed the clockwork hand in all its minute and intricate detail. The copper, silver, and fine pale gold now gleamed in the candlelight, inside and out. When Twist did one last test of the finger articulation, there were no problems with the mechanism to hold back the flood of images and flashing sparks of disembodied emotion.

Twist lost himself for a long, timeless moment, drowning in a sea of tiny sensory memories that didn't belong to him. There was no continuity, no sense, and nothing strong enough to shock him or show him a way out. After what could have been years or an instant, an electric murmur grew loud enough to hear. Twist clung to it instantly, pulling hard to drag his attention closer.

"Twist?" Jonas asked, kneeling close beside him, looking at him curiously with uncovered eyes.

With a sharp breath, Twist threw his eyes open and looked to Jonas quickly. Jonas reeled back onto his feet, turning away before their eyes could meet.

"Watch it!" Jonas snapped.

"I'm sorry," Twist said on his still-ragged breath, pulling his eyes away. He could still feel the memories trying to pull him back in. He put the clockwork hand carefully down and got to his feet, backing away. The pull dissipated instantly, leaving behind only the buzz of Jonas's presence at the base of Twist's neck.

"Are you all right?" Aazzi asked, watching him from her seat on the stair.

"You were glowing again," Jonas said, looking at him with his goggles back on.

"I was just—" Twist began, gesturing to the clockwork girl. He paused and looked to Jonas. "Wait, what?"

"You know," Jonas said with a shrug. "You were glowing. Like you do whenever you get a vision off of something. But you weren't moving at all. I thought you might be stuck."

"What do you mean I was glowing?" Twist asked.

"I've never seen him glow," Aazzi said with a frown.

"Sure you have," Jonas said to Aazzi. "Whenever he uses his Sight. His skin glows a little." Aazzi and Twist shared a confused glance.

"What color?" Twist asked slowly.

"Blue or purple mostly," Jonas said, sounding a little tired of this charade. "But it changes."

"So, it's like when your eyes glow, then," Twist said.

"Jonas's eyes never glow, either," Aazzi said flatly. "What are you two on about?"

Twist and Jonas looked to each other, despite Jonas's goggles, each one coming to the same conclusion.

"Same as the buzz then," Twist said, nodding.

"That's just bloody strange," Jonas decided.

"Well, thank you anyway, Jonas," Twist said, looking to the clockwork girl. Her right hand and wrist were now complete and cleaned, gleaming brightly in the candlelight, while the rest of her still lay in ruins. "I did get sort of stuck."

"You'd best be careful of that," Jonas said with a sigh. "But you haven't eaten in a very long time," he said, changing his tone. "Join me for dinner?"

"That's not a bad idea," Aazzi said, stooping to extinguish the candle with moistened fingertips. "I'm hungry too," she added, stepping close behind Jonas silently.

"I've gone anemic!" Jonas said quickly, spinning and taking three steps away from her. "It just started after I left. I'd taste just terrible, I'm sure."

"Such a poor liar," Aazzi said, shaking her head with a wicked smile.

"Can we go now?" Jonas asked Twist, already stepping closer to the door as he kept his covered eyes trained on Aazzi intently.

"Certainly," Twist said, watching Aazzi as well as he followed after Jonas.

Aazzi laughed lightly at the both of them and walked easily past, into the deepening night. The moment Twist crossed the threshold, out into the chilly air, he felt an enormous weight lift from him. The haunting emotions that had been peering at him from the shadows inside the hall fell so quiet on his senses that he wasn't sure he could feel them at all anymore. There was only the briefest echo of past memory in the shadows of the overgrown garden, and no anger or fear in the still night air.

"I'll bet you're glad to be out of that place for a moment," Jonas said, giving the black doorway behind them a disapproving glance.

"I hadn't realized how oppressive it was," Twist said softly, shivering slightly against the chill. Ahead of them, Aazzi stepped easily into the darkened sitting room on her way to the ship. "Jonas, can I ask you something?" Twist asked, slowing his steps.

"Something about the vampire we live with?" Jonas asked, keeping his voice low.

"I have yet to see her…feed," Twist said carefully.

"You're not likely to see it," Jonas said. "She fancies herself above all that."

"But she needs to eat, doesn't she?" Twist asked, coming to a stop at the edge of the garden. "Or can she live on food like we can?"

"Have you seen her drinking wine?"

"Yes, many times," Twist answered. "She seems to have it with every meal."

"It's not wine."

"Oh…" Twist toned.

"She keeps her own supply with her, on the airship," Jonas explained. "I don't know where she gets it, or from what creatures, but she always has it."

"That's highly disturbing."

"Oh yes," Jonas said with a nod and a smile. "Shall we talk of nicer things now?" he asked, gesturing for them to continue on.

"What do you have in mind?" Twist asked, walking with him again.

"Something that doesn't have to do with grotesqueries or death," Jonas said brightly.

The two boarded the ship in brighter spirits, speaking about whatever pleased them, and found the others just finishing with their own meals in the main common room of the airship. Upon seeing Jonas, many of them readied to leave. Arabel and Captain Davis said nothing as they left the room, while Zayle remained, seemingly only halfway finished with his dessert. Dr. Rodés excused himself shortly afterward, leaving Twist, Jonas, and Zayle alone with the last of the meal left out on the table.

Jonas didn't appear at all distressed with the coldness of his reception, lazily taking a seat and immediately helping himself to the leftovers. Twist followed his example and poured them each a cup of still-warm tea.

"I'm telling you, Twist," Jonas continued from the previous conversation, "it's the absolute best place for surfing."

"Surfing?" Twist asked as he reached for a roll. "What's that?"

"Surfing!" Jonas said with a bright smile. "Come on, it's the best sport on earth! Well, unless you count swallow racing. But seriously, don't tell me you've never even heard of it."

"This is the first time he's been out of London," Zayle said to his mulberry pie.

"Wait, you've never been anywhere with warm water?" Jonas asked Twist gravely from behind his black-lensed goggles.

"Why is it such a shock to all of you that I haven't traveled?" Twist asked back. "There are plenty of people around the world who never stray beyond their own neighborhoods. It's perfectly natural."

"But it's so..." Jonas paused, grasping silently at adjectives.

"Weird?" Zayle offered. "Boring? Soul dissolving?"

"Yes, exactly!" Jonas said. "I've spent my whole life traveling. I can hardly imagine what it would be like to live in just one place," he said, sounding wistful.

"Isn't that exactly what you want?" Zayle asked him.

"Not at all," Jonas said. "I'm not looking for a house or a piece of land. I just want to be able to be alone when I want to be." Zayle made a slightly bitter face and returned his attention to his pie.

"You want to be alone?" Twist asked Jonas. "But you're the most social person I've ever met." Zayle gave a sudden, sharp laugh.

"Social? Jonas?" Zayle asked Twist with an astonished expression.

"He spends an awful lot of time with me," Twist said.

"You seek me out whenever I'm not with you," he added
to Jonas.

"Really?" Zayle asked Jonas.

"Well he's a reasonable human being," Jonas said
quickly to Zayle.

"And no one else on this ship is reasonable?" Zayle
asked.

"Not in my experience," Jonas said with a falsely
even tone, staring sightless at Zayle. Zayle looked back
at him bitterly.

"Oh dear," Twist said with a heavy sigh, drawing
their attention. "I don't even like people, but you'd still
rather spend your time with me than anyone else on the
ship," he said sympathetically to Jonas. "That's very sad."

"You see?' Jonas said to Zayle, gesturing to Twist.
"This man gets me."

"Yes, you're a wonderful match," Zayle said flatly.
"You're both bloody strange."

Twist gave a shrug, having been called far worse in
his past, while Jonas puffed slightly with a show of pride.
Zayle shook his head and got up from his now-empty
dessert plate.

"I'm going to go talk to the engine," Zayle said as he
headed for the door.

After a pleasant dinner together, Twist and Jonas
parted to retire for the night. Twist found himself gazing
out the windows in his cabin, watching as the stars turned
slowly through the blackest night sky he had ever seen.
Here in the mountains of Nepal, so far from any city
lights and so close to the sky itself, there were so many
brilliantly bright stars that Twist couldn't find a single
familiar constellation. The sky was filled to the bursting
with light, even on this moonless night, that every
familiar point was surrounded and confused beyond all
recognition, and bathed in the full light of the galaxy

around them.

Twist opened his pocket watch and set it on the windowsill near him. Its familiar heartbeat ticked gently in the quiet, calling out now-distant memories of his home. London felt like a universe away. Twist had been through so much just to get here, and had traveled so far in such a short amount of time that even the thought of home was starting to feel foreign. A new fear crept slowly into the back of his mind. It was a thought that he had never imagined, and for a long while he was too confused by it to recognize it at all.

What if he didn't want to go home at the end of this journey? What would he do if he grew and changed too much out here, in the rest of the world, to feel comfortable in London again? The unexpectedness of the fear itself put him more on edge than anything else.

The next morning, Twist returned to his work as soon as he could. Arabel insisted that he eat something first and refused to let him off the ship until he had. Having finally forced down a piece of toast and a half cup of coffee, Twist managed to get himself back into the palace.

The ghostly emotions that had threatened him the night before seemed diminished in the light of day. He re-lit his candle and set out his tools before Aazzi came to join him. She retook her post, sitting on the stairs, and Twist resumed his work.

He took apart the rest of the right arm, cleaning and repairing every piece before reassembling it. Next, he moved on to her other hand, and then her other arm, until both lay in gleaming perfection at her sides. He then carefully lifted her head, placing it in his lap as he began to repair the damage there, sweeping the tangled mass of her wire hair to the side. Gazing down into her beautiful young face that was frozen in terrible fear and horror, Twist had to focus very hard on not letting his mind wander to the emotions that surrounded his thoughts. This was much harder as he realized that many of the worst feelings of sadness and lament were actually his own.

Once he had finished repairing her glimmering, silver-encased, blue-jewel eyes and closed them to give her face a more peaceful appearance, it became steadily more difficult to keep his focus where it needed to be.

"Twist, dear," Aazzi said, drawing his foggy attention to her. She was rubbing at her temple, her face showing weariness. "It's been four hours. Shouldn't you have a break?"

"Four hours?" Twist asked, finding it hard to find meaning in the thought.

"Almost four and a half," Aazzi said, glancing at her own small silver pocket watch.

"Time and I have never really gotten on," Twist said with a sigh. He carefully took the clockwork girl's head from his lap and placed it gently on the floor again before he got up. The moment he got to his feet, he realized that his back was stiff, his neck was beginning to ache, and a headache was blooming brightly behind his eyes.

"Oh heavens," Twist said softly, holding his head to keep it from spinning.

"Are you all right?" Aazzi asked.

"I shall be," he said with a heavy sigh. "Thank you. I do need a break."

Aazzi left the hall with Twist, pulling the black hood far over her face before she did, and she hurried quickly back to the ship the moment the sunlight fell on her. Twist walked slowly through the overgrown garden, pulling at his tight muscles and letting his mind wander aimlessly through the rich, untamed green expanse.

There was something beautiful about the way the leaves of the single, huge tree in the center of the garden fluttered in the sunlight. The thin atmosphere made the colors seem brighter, sharper, and deeper, even with the occasional waft of mist that wandered through the open spaces. For a moment, Twist could perfectly understand why the princess and her family had wanted to build this palace in the first place. If it were in its original condition, Twist would want to stay as well.

Twist sat on a block of stone that had once been part of a low wall and let the cool, damp air soothe his exhausted senses. Fragments of thoughts, images, and distant emotions ebbed and flowed like ocean waves in the back of his mind. For a long while, he just let them dance as they willed. It seemed like an enormous effort to push them away, and his strength was hard to find. After a few minutes, though, his own thoughts came back to him.

Getting up again, Twist headed to the airship. Just as he expected, Jonas was on the open deck again, lying on his back and gazing up at the sky. He was listening to his recorded music again as well. Twist stepped closer, careful not to watch his eyes too closely. Sure enough, Jonas glanced in his direction once the buzz in Twist's neck grew prominent.

"Twist, you look awful," Jonas said, taking the headphones off his ears.

"I knew you would cheer me up," Twist muttered, coming close and sitting down on the deck beside Jonas.

"Am I mad, or are you learning the subtle art of snark?" Jonas asked brightly, looking away with his uncovered eyes.

"Too much time with you, I'm sure," Twist said, rubbing at his neck. The vibration of Jonas's presence seemed to be helping his tired muscles to relax.

"So, what brings you out of the horrible haunted palace?" Jonas asked, lying back again to look up at the sky.

"A break," Twist said with a shrug.

"Wonderful idea," Jonas said. He held the headphones out to Twist. "Here, I've got Beethoven's Ninth playing now. The good part is just getting started."

Twist took the offer, put on the headphones, and let the familiar "Ode to Joy" wash over him with the warm sunlight. He leaned back, lying beside Jonas on the deck, and watched the high, thin clouds pass slowly by in long streams of silver-white. The low, constant electric murmur of Jonas ran gently down his spine and drowned out every thought of his work on the clockwork princess.

By the time the recorded symphony had come almost to its close, Arabel's curious face came into Twist's vision. He pulled one earphone off slightly and frowned up at her.

"What?"

"You two certainly know how to relax, I'll give you that," she said with a smile.

"You're mussing up my calm," Jonas muttered with a whine on his voice. "Don't you have a hobby yet?"

"Just the same one as always," Arabel said, crouching down to tussle his hair.

"Oh, bothering me, you mean," Jonas snapped, swatting at her.

"Of course!" Arabel said, almost laughing.

"You're mussing up my calm now, too," Twist said, disappointed to hear the music fall into nothing at its end. He pulled off the headphones and handed them back to Jonas. "Do you need something?" he asked, leaning up on an elbow to look at Arabel properly.

"Uncle Howell would like to know how much longer it will take you to finish your work," Arabel said with a sigh. "I told him it would take a while, just looking at all the damage."

"I'm not sure," Twist said, sitting up. After the rest, he noticed he really did feel much better. "I haven't begun on her core or her legs yet. The head is going to take a while on its own. There are a lot of intricate pieces in her neck as well. Did you know that her face is actually a layered collection of plates that can slide over each other to allow her to have real expressions like a human face?"

"So, a few more days then?" Arabel asked.

"At least," Twist said, nodding.

"Are you going to be all right for that long?" Jonas

asked, looking concerned.

"What do you mean?" Twist asked.

"It's obvious that working on her is taking a lot out of you. It hasn't even been a full day yet, and you already look a bit ragged."

"I'll be fine," Twist said with a dismissive wave. "I've worked on complex mechanisms before. It's tiring, but it's not a problem."

"Have you ever tried to fix something with its own soul before?" Jonas asked. "You got stuck last night, and you were almost overcome when you touched her the first time. There's no telling what the added strain of her personality is doing to your Sight."

"But he's the only one who can do this," Arabel said to Jonas.

"That doesn't mean it's safe for him to rush it," Jonas said instantly.

"I'll be fine!" Twist said, drawing both of their attentions. "Really. It's not a problem. Aazzi is keeping the ghost away, and working is helping me to keep everything else at the back of my mind. It's just going to take a while."

"If you say so," Jonas said on a heavy breath as he lay back down. "I just don't think there's anything wrong with taking your time."

"If it's going to take more than a week, we'll need to leave to get provisions," Arabel said. "It's all right if we need to," she said, seeing the look on Twist's face. "We just need to know."

"Let me see how far I can get tonight," Twist said, feeling his headache kick back up again. "I'll try to assess how much work there still is to do and then let you know."

"Sounds like a plan," Arabel said brightly.

Not wanting to waste time, Twist headed back to

work shortly after that. With Aazzi back at her post and the candle lit, Twist returned to working on the clockwork face, head, and neck. By the time the light began to fall again, he had finished cleaning and adjusting the thin plates of the face, and left it in a peaceful expression.

Aazzi all but dragged him away to have something to eat, but Twist returned instantly afterward to finish working on the neck. His headache became a constant pressure behind his eyes, and his neck continually tightened no matter how he tried to remember to move it once in a while. Twist's senses also dulled slowly over time until he simply grew accustomed to finding his mind wandering onto thoughts that had nothing to do with his work. Slight memories and feelings that didn't belong to him wafted through his thoughts regardless of how he tried to focus.

After a while, Twist lost the strength to notice or care.

Twist worked on as time dragged long and silently around him. The ghost seemed to grow more active, drawing more and more of Aazzi's attention, as the night deepened. Twist eventually stopped paying attention to anything beyond the detailed and delicate work of repairing the extensive damage. He didn't notice at all as the air around him grew cold, and the light of the candle dimmed below that of the late, thin, new moon that poured through the broken windows.

A hand, small and gentle, fell to rest lightly on his arm with a frigid cold that soaked through his coat to chill his skin. Twist braced against the vision he expected from the touch, but nothing came. His mind remained still, drowned as it was in the tiny visions he got from the clockwork in his hands.

"What are you doing?" a voice asked from close beside him: young, sweet, and deeply familiar to his imagination.

Twist looked up to see a face his heart knew well, but his eyes had never seen. Barely more than a child, beautiful and untouched by time, the fairytale princess of his imagination looked at him curiously through shining black eyes as she sat at his side. Her delicate, pale fingers lingered on his arm, and still no vision came. In his total astonishment, it took Twist far too long to realize that the girl beside him was human, and not the clockwork puppet that lay on the floor. He stared, mesmerized by the childlike beauty of her face, the long, soft tail of shining black hair that hung from the crown of her head to the floor, and the glittering pink silks that wrapped her slight form in flowing wafts.

"Do you speak?" she asked, smiling slightly.

"I, well…yes but," Twist muttered as his thoughts struggled to grasp some form of meaning. He looked down to see the still-unfinished clockwork puppet on the floor before him. "I'm trying to fix you," he said softly.

"That puppet is broken," the princess said coldly. "It's not me."

Looking back up, Twist began to understand. "You're the ghost."

"No, I'm me," the girl said as if he were being silly. "To be a ghost, you have to die. I never have."

"But you're haunting this place," Twist said, trying desperately to hold his thoughts together in the face of her enchanting smile.

"You're funny," she said, smiling deeper. "Who are you?" she asked, reaching up and toying idly with the soft curls behind his ear. The chill of her touch sent a shiver down Twist's spine, but still no vision came. For a moment, he lost himself in the foreign sensation of her harmless touch.

"Twist," he said, finally. "My name is Twist."

"That's a nice name. Where are you from?" she asked, a curious expression on her face as she wrapped a lock of his hair around her finger.

"London," he said, holding utterly still for fear she might take her hands away from him.

"Where's that?" she asked brightly. "Is it far away?"

"Very far. It's on the other side of Europe."

"Europe?" the girl asked with a wide smile. "Oh, that is far away. And you came all this way just to fix my puppet?"

"I have," he said, surprised at his own pride. "I should be finished soon. Then you will be able to return to it."

Her smile faded and she leaned closer still, staring

into his eyes and holding very tight to his arm with both hands. "You mean that I will be able to dance again?" she asked softly, her eyes pleading with his.

"I'm sure you will," he said, his heart now racing under her intense attention.

"That's wonderful!" she cried in glee, wrapping him in her arms. Stunned and reduced to nothing but pure instinct, Twist's hands found her slight waist and he held her gently. Her body felt real and solid in his arms, but her skin was as cold as ice.

"You are wonderful, too," the princess said, pulling back just enough to smile at him with her cold arms still around his neck. "I can't wait to dance again!" she said, falling into a happy, bubbly laugh.

Twist watched silently, totally lost in her. He no longer cared how she was here. He didn't care if this was real or a dream. All he wanted was to stay in her arms and watch her joy. It seemed sweeter to him than any happiness he had ever felt before.

"*Twist?*" another voice called from far away, echoing off the walls. It sounded frightened, but Twist couldn't imagine why. The princess jerked, looking around.

"What is that?" she asked, pulling herself close against Twist and fitting her head into the crook of his neck. "Is it the others? I don't like them! Make them leave!"

"It's all right," Twist said, holding her. "They won't hurt you."

"*Twist!*" the voice called out again, still sounding frightened and frantic. "*Wake up!*"

"Make them leave!" the princess said again, her voice edged with tears. "I won't give you up. You're not like them. I want you to stay with me."

"This is a dream," Twist said, mostly to himself. "They are worried for me," he said gently, pulling his lips closer to her ear. "Let me tell them that I'm all right. I won't leave you. I promise."

The princess pulled away to look in his eyes, searching them uncertainly.

"Trust me," Twist said, stroking the soft silk on her back. "I've crossed half the world just to help you. I only need to talk to them for a moment."

"You promise," she said, still uncertain. "If you lie, I'll never forgive you."

"I'd never lie to you," Twist said, smiling softly. "It would break my heart."

She smiled slightly, looking somewhat convinced. She got to her feet and stepped away as the rest of the world fell totally black. In the absence of her, a familiar electrical sensation burned to life, far away in the unknown blackness. Twist caught it and pulled hard, following it back into the light.

"He moved!"

"Is he coming around?"

"He's stopped glowing."

"What does that mean?"

Twist followed the frantic voices back to consciousness, clawing his way out of the darkness. He finally found out how to blink his eyes open to find his vision blurred in stark, sharp light. Many figures were crowded close around him, and the growing buzz of Jonas's presence grew clearer than any other sense.

"Oh thank God," Jonas's voice said with a relieved exhale.

"That's it, come back to us, Twist," Arabel said from close beside him.

"I'm fine," Twist said on a voice that felt far weaker than usual.

"Really, stop saying that when you don't mean it," Jonas snapped.

"I'm so sorry," Aazzi's voice said, sounding weak as well.

Twist pushed himself up on his arms and sensed the others moving back to let him sit up. Everyone was crowded closely around him on the dusty floor of the main hall, and they all looked seriously concerned.

"What's the matter?" Twist asked, looking around at them all.

"You wouldn't wake up," Aazzi said, standing now with her arms wrapped tightly folded over her chest. "I stopped watching for only a moment. When I came back... I could hear your heart beating, but I couldn't wake you up." To Twist's shock, she seemed terrified.

"You were glowing like crazy," Jonas said. "What happened to you?"

"I saw the princess," Twist said, looking down to the clockwork puppet. "I talked with her. Touched her."

"You must have fallen asleep," Arabel said. "It's almost midnight."

"Then the ghost took control of your dream while I wasn't watching," Aazzi said.

"It's all right," Twist said to Aazzi, giving her a light smile. "It was a wonderful dream." Looking up proved to be a significant drain on Twist's tired muscles, and his head fell as his vision blurred again. He tried to blink it clear.

"This is way too dangerous," Jonas said darkly. "Come on, let's get him out of here."

"I'm just tired," Twist tried to say, but his voice barely made it over his lips.

"You're pushing your Sight to its limit," Jonas said, kneeling down and leaning close enough to push the electric buzz into a high, whining pulse down Twist's spine. "You're a wreck. Stop saying you're fine!"

Twist's resistance failed entirely and he wrapped both hands around his neck, curling up against the pulsing, screaming energy. A small moan escaped him before everything fell back into blackness.

It felt like a very long time before he woke up again. He found himself in his cabin, bathed in sunlight and covered with warm, soft blankets. This time, his vision came back to him clearly, and his thoughts were calm, easy to control, and understandable. Looking around, he found Zayle sitting at his desk, reading a small book. The motion of looking around the room pushed his hammock to sway ever so gently. Zayle looked up at the motion.

"Oh good!" Zayle said, coming closer. "I was starting to wonder if you'd ever wake up. How do you feel?"

"Don't tell Jonas, but I feel fine," Twist said, running a hand over his brow.

"Humor. That's a very good sign," Zayle said with a smile. "Any pain or dizziness?"

"No," Twist said, searching his senses to be sure. "Honestly, everything just feels sort of numb. And quiet."

"Are you hungry? Thirsty?" Zayle asked as he held his fingers up close to Twist's forehead. Twist readied himself to jerk away, but Zayle was careful not to actually touch him and then pulled away quickly.

"I am a bit thirsty, now that you mention it," Twist said, relaxing again when Zayle took his hand away.

"You're not warm anymore," Zayle said, reaching for a glass and pitcher that sat nearby. "You were for most of yesterday. Philippe said it wasn't dangerous as long as you didn't get any warmer, but he was worried about it."

"Wait, yesterday?" Twist asked, automatically taking the offered glass of water as he propped himself up on one elbow in the curve of the hammock. "How long have I been asleep?"

"A day and a half."

"What?" Twist asked, staring at him in shock.

"Philippe has been checking on you the whole time," Zayle said quickly. "He said it looked like you were simply exhausted and that you'd wake up when you recovered. And you have!" he added brightly.

"Why would I be so exhausted?" Twist asked, frowning into space.

"Jonas thinks it's because you're overusing your Sight," Zayle offered. "Ara says it's because you never eat or sleep like you should. Aazzi said it could be the result of everything that's happened to you since you left

London with us."

"Damn..." Twist sighed, before he took a long drink of water. It was the most delicious, most refreshing thing he'd ever tasted. "I've been busy, haven't I?"

"I'm going to tell Philippe you woke up," Zayle said. He took the empty glass from Twist. "Just take it easy. I'll be right back."

Twist lay back again and gave a sigh once Zayle had left. It felt like it had been a long time since his mind was this empty. There were no visions lurking in the back of his mind, and no haunting emotions in the sun-warmed air of his cabin. The silence felt hollow and unnerving. He was relieved to see Dr. Rodés return with Zayle.

"Welcome back," Dr. Rodés said, looking at him critically. "How do you feel?"

"Honestly?" Twist said, putting on a thoughtful face. "I haven't a clue. Just numb. I think I'm all right."

"Are you in any pain?" Dr. Rodés asked. "Do you feel dizzy or weak at all?"

"Not a bit of it," Twist said with a shrug. "Are you sure I've been asleep for over a day?"

"That's the only thing about your condition that I am sure of," he said, reaching out quickly to Twist's forehead. Twist jerked away instantly, looking at the man wearily. "It's very difficult to treat a patient whom I can't even touch," he sighed.

"We all have our cross to bear," Twist muttered, still watching him.

"Jonas's theory seems reasonable," Dr. Rodés said. "You should avoid using your Sight for at least another day."

"But I can't work on the puppet without using my Sight," Twist said, frowning.

"Then you will have to put off your work until you

are recovered."

"No, no, I can't do that," Twist said quickly. "I told her I wouldn't leave her. I've been gone a whole day already. If I'm not back soon she'll think I broke my promise."

"The machine will understand, I'm sure," Dr. Rodés said flatly.

"The *princess*," Twist said, sitting up now. "I talked to her in a dream. But it was really her. I'm sure of it. I have to get back to her as soon as possible."

"Lay back down," Dr. Rodés said, reaching out a hand. Twist leaned away from his touch, but the effect was the same. "You're to stay in bed for the rest of the day, or at least here on the ship. Tomorrow we'll talk about when you're getting back to work."

"Why?" Twist snapped back. "Have you forgotten that this is why we're all here?"

"We'll all be here for nothing if you kill yourself by pushing too far, too fast," Dr. Rodés said, his voice strangely unemotional. "Don't let him out of the room," he said to Zayle as he turned to leave. His absence left the room silent again.

"This is madness," Twist said after a moment of staring at the ceiling.

"He's probably right, though," Zayle said softly. Twist gave nothing but a sigh in response. "You shouldn't spend so much time with Jonas," Zayle added. "You're turning into him."

Twist looked indignantly at Zayle. Zayle seemed somehow disappointed with Twist's response, and so turned away and returned to his seat at the desk without retort. After another hour of doing nothing at all, restlessness set in hard. Twist finally convinced Zayle that he wouldn't make any attempts at escape if Zayle left for a moment to call Aazzi to see him.

As soon as Zayle was out of the room, Twist got himself relatively respectable. Being dressed again in a clean, cool, white cotton shirt and his simple black trousers, felt better than he'd expected, but Twist was surprised to find his feet somewhat unsteady on the floor. Though his mind was clear and ready, his body seemed to still be fatigued somehow.

He was sitting in the chair at the desk and rubbing at his stiff neck when Aazzi opened the door and stepped into the room. She stayed well back from Twist, and kept her eyes away from him. Her expression was as hesitant as her manner.

"You wanted to see me?" she asked, her voice braced against his answer.

"Yes," Twist said slowly as he tried to make sense of her. "I need your help."

Aazzi gave a mirthless laugh. "Are you sure you really want mine?"

"Next to me," Twist said, "you are the most aware of the ghost in the palace. She may listen to you. I need you to explain to her what happened to me, so that she won't believe that I've broken my promise and abandoned her." As he spoke, Aazzi's silver eyes finally found him.

"Then it was the ghost that hurt you," she said, hollow and soft. "It used your Sight to..."

Twist frowned. "How many conversations are we having? Because I'm only aware of the one." Aazzi seemed to snap out of her thoughts and looked away from him again. "Please, Aazzi, can you help me?" Twist asked. "I know it sounds mad, but I actually spoke with the princess. I barely got her to trust me when you all tried to pull me back. She didn't want to let me go, but I promised I wouldn't leave her for long. I just don't want her to misunderstand."

"So, you want me to tell the ghost that you're coming

back?" Aazzi said.

"Yes, exactly."

"That you'll be at her mercy once again, even after what she did to you."

"Well..." Twist muttered.

"I should tell the ghost that you'd be back there right now if we weren't all afraid for your life," Aazzi said before he could finish.

"Now, just a minute," Twist said, getting to his feet.

"I told you I could hear your heartbeat," Aazzi said, locking Twist's eyes in her own cold, silver gaze. "But it was not stable. I've never heard a heartbeat that weak. Not one that didn't fail immediately afterward. Do you understand that she was killing you?"

Twist stared back at her silently, stilled now.

"Yes, she is a wonderful treasure," Aazzi said, visibly trying to soften her words. "A myth become real. But she is already dead. Is it worth your life to bring her back into this world?"

"Aazzi, what is this about?" Twist asked softly. She stared back at him silently. Looking in her eyes, it was obvious to Twist that her mind was raging. "I didn't ask you to protect me," Twist said, playing the most likely gamble. "I'm thankful that you did. It gave me a chance to make some real progress."

"But I didn't," she replied, sounding hollow again. "I failed utterly."

"Far from it," Twist said, relieved at his lucky guess. "You did me a great service. Honestly, I'm even thankful that you left when you did."

Aazzi bristled and opened her mouth to respond, but Twist stepped closer quickly, with a wide smile on his face.

"That moment with the princess, it was worth it all, just to speak with her. I could touch her in my dream," he said, looking to the memory of the princess on his hands. "I've never touched anyone in my life. Not without fear. Not even in my dreams. She was exactly as I knew she would be," he said, smiling up to Aazzi's uncertainty. "Thank you for giving me that."

It took a moment for Aazzi to accept this before she finally nodded.

"So, please," Twist said, pulling himself back to normal, "go and tell her that I'm still here, and that I'll be back to finish her puppet as soon as I can."

"All right," Aazzi said. "I will. But..." She paused, still watching Twist carefully.

"I'll be careful," Twist said. "I promise."

Still looking somewhat uncertain, Aazzi left Twist in his cabin. He sat down again heavily, having found it increasingly difficult to stay on his feet. Silence set in once again, setting his nerves on edge. Thankfully, Arabel appeared soon after, with a plate of food. She sat with him as he ate, talking brightly about many things that had little to do with anything important. Twist nodded or made encouraging tones occasionally, happy to have something to chase away the silence.

"Where's Jonas been?" Twist asked as he stared at the terrible hand of cards he was holding in the gaslight. "I haven't seen him in a while."

"He's been in his cabin all day," Arabel said, rearranging her own cards.

"I raise you two," Zayle said. He tossed a pair of dry beans into the pile on the floor between them all. "You in, Cap?" he asked, looking to Captain Davis, who sat to his left.

"No, I fold," Captain Davis said, putting his cards down and looking to Twist.

"Jonas usually seeks me out by now," Twist said as he tossed two more of his beans into the pile. "Is something wrong with him?"

"I call," Arabel said, tossing in her own bet. "Zayle, what have you got?"

"Pair of fours," he said with a shrug, turning his cards for the others to see.

"You bet on a pair of fours?" Captain Davis scoffed. "That was a silly bet."

"I'm a silly person," Zayle said as if Captain Davis should have known.

"I've got three tens," Arabel said brightly. "Twist?"

"What's wrong with Jonas?" Twist asked, tossing his useless collection of random cards into the pile of beans.

"Nothing. He's fine," Arabel said, collecting her prize while Zayle reshuffled the cards.

"Then what's wrong, in general?" he asked. "Something's going on here."

"Maybe he just wants a little space," Zayle offered,

not looking at Twist.

"What's wrong with your nephew?" Twist asked Captain Davis.

"Where would you like me to start?" he asked back with a chuckle.

Twist leaned his head back against the wall. "This is why I don't like people."

"He's just worried about you," Arabel said, taking her turn to deal. "He's staying away because he doesn't want to stress your Sight."

"He said he felt something strange when you passed out in the palace," Captain Davis offered as he re-ordered his cards. "He thinks he might have caused part of the problem."

"But if he hadn't been there, I wouldn't have gotten out of the vision," Twist said. "I followed him out."

"See?" Arabel said. "Everything's fine."

"And I'm the one with a skewed vision of reality?" Twist asked sharply. Arabel shot him a quiet, but warning look.

"Just leave him," Zayle said, pointing to the new hand of cards that lay untouched at Twist's feet. "Jonas will be fine. He always is."

"I'm going to talk to him," Twist said, halfway to getting up.

"No, sit down," Arabel said, reaching out to block him. Twist stopped short before her hand, still on one knee.

"Don't worry about him, Twist," Captain Davis said. "Worry about yourself."

"I'm no better off if he thinks he did something to hurt me," Twist said. "If none of you are going to talk with him, then I will."

"He doesn't want to talk with any of us," Arabel said, her face bitter. "He's alone because he wants to be."

"We've lived with him before, you know," Zayle said. "This is the only way to deal with him when he gets in a mood."

Twist shook his head. "That man is starved for compassion. I don't have to touch him to know that. He doesn't want to look weak, and so he lashes out. It's what wounded characters always do in novels. But that doesn't mean that this is what he wants."

"This isn't a novel. It's real life, Twist," Arabel said, more sharply than Twist had expected. "What makes you think you know my brother better than I do?"

"Because I used to do the same things," Twist said. "I finally just gave up on people entirely. Neither of us can get close to anyone." The moment the words left his mouth, Twist felt the echo of their meaning with a solid concussion.

The others all paused to look at him, while shifting thoughts played behind their eyes.

"If you'll excuse me," Twist said when the others made no obvious response. He got to his feet, with no resistance this time, and left the room.

It was easy to find Jonas as Twist walked down the halls, following the buzzing sensation at the back of his neck. More than before, he found the feeling strangely comforting. He stopped outside one of the cabin doors and reached up to knock, but the door opened before he could. Jonas stood inside, his eyes covered with his black lenses and his hand still on the door.

"You shouldn't be here," he said coldly.

"I'm fine, damn whatever you say."

"Stay away from me," Jonas said, pushing the door closed again. Twist glared at the door.

"If I'd wanted to stay perfectly safe and unharmed, I never would have left home!" Twist yelled, as loudly as his small voice would allow.

"Go away!" came Jonas's voice through the closed door.

Twist leaned his back against the opposite wall and slid down to sit on the floor. He waited silently for long minutes, his eyes closed as the buzz wandered around the base of his skull like a trapped alley cat. Eventually, Jonas's door opened slightly.

"What is wrong with you?" Jonas asked through the crack.

"Stop it," Twist said flatly.

"I'm not the one stalking you!" Jonas snapped.

"Stop blaming yourself for everything. It's not your fault."

"Get the hell out of my head," Jonas said, dark and deadly, as he opened the door a little wider to lean out menacingly.

"You first," Twist said with a smile, rubbing at his neck.

"What do I have to do to get you to leave me alone?" Jonas asked, sounding fatigued.

Twist got back to his feet and stared directly into the black goggles. "Mean it."

Jonas didn't move, staring back sightlessly for a long moment. "Remind me not to play poker with you," he muttered.

"Actually, we're in the middle of a game right now," Twist said, nodding to his cabin. "Care to stop torturing yourself and join us?"

"Look," Jonas said, pointing a finger at Twist's nose, "I got close to you, the buzz got worse, something gave, and then you hit the ground and didn't wake up for a day. We have no idea what's happening, or what it's doing to either of us, and you're already pushing your Sight too hard as it is!"

"Fine," Twist said, holding his arms out. "Have a

look then. I'll close my eyes. You tell me if being in
your presence is killing me."

"Don't be an idiot," Jonas said, shaking his head.

"Stop being so scared of yourself," Twist snapped.

"Keep that up and I'll touch you, all right," Jonas said,
brandishing a fist.

"Look at me," Twist said, closing his eyes.

It took another moment before Jonas gave an
exasperated sigh. An instant later, Twist felt a noticeable
increase in the electric tension at the back of his neck.
He had to focus hard to keep his eyes closed and to keep
his hands at his sides. Every fiber of his being screamed
for him to reach out, to look into Jonas's opened eyes.
The knowledge that Jonas must have been feeling the
same thing did little to calm him.

"You're not fine," Jonas said finally, as the buzz in
Twist's neck died down slightly and the compulsions fell
quiet. "You're mentally and physically exhausted."

"Is that all?" Twist asked, chancing a glance up.
Jonas's goggles were back over his eyes, and he was
leaning against the door frame like he needed it.

"That, and someday," he said, smiling lightly, "you're
going to go somewhere tropical and you will simply love
lychee."

"What?"

"It's a kind of fruit," Jonas said. "Little white things
in a hard red shell. I like them too."

"What?" Twist asked again.

"You think I only see people's future when I look in
their eyes?" Jonas asked back. "I can see random bits
from the future whenever I look at anyone. I can only see
your death if I look in your eyes."

Twist stared at him until the enormity of the
implications fully sank in. "Oh my God."

"Ah, so I still have some secrets from you, then?"

Jonas asked back with a grin.

"Well, did you see any point in the future when this buzz is going to kill either of us?" Twist asked, trying to shake off the cold dread.

"No."

"And is it obviously harming me now?"

"No," Jonas said, shifting slightly.

"Then are you going to continue blaming yourself for whatever madness happened to me in the palace?"

Jonas looked up at him through the black lenses. "I would if you'd let me, you pushy little twit."

Twist shook his head. "Too damned bad," he said with a note of satisfaction. He took a heavy breath, feeling the strain of standing begin to weigh on him. "I'm going to sit down again." He took two steps away, felt the buzz ease again, and looked back. "Are you coming?"

Jonas made a show of being inconvenienced, but he followed after Twist with the tension of a hidden smile at the edges of his cool expression. When the two of them returned to Twist's cabin together, the others looked up at them in stunned silence.

"Told you," Twist muttered to Arabel, taking up his place against the wall again.

"You're a magical being, Twist," Zayle said, still wide-eyed as Jonas sat beside Twist.

"Who won the last round?" Twist asked as Captain Davis began to deal the cards out once again. Jonas grabbed a handful of dried beans from the sack to the side of the circle.

"I did," Arabel said brightly.

"I know she's cheating, I just don't know how," Captain Davis said.

"That's hardly fair," Arabel said with a pout. "Maybe I'm just a lucky person."

"We'll see about that," Jonas said, pulling his goggles

up to sit on his brow as he looked over his cards. Glancing from the side, Twist saw the faintest glimmer of blue light dance in the color of his eyes.

"Am I the only one not cheating?" Twist asked.

"You're not cheating?" Zayle asked, aghast. "How do you expect to win?"

"Sorry, I forgot where I was," Twist muttered, shaking his head. "I'm playing poker with nice pirates. I don't know what I was thinking."

"We're not bloody pirates!" Captain Davis said.

"Not today, especially," Arabel added.

Jonas laughed quietly to himself.

"Yes, yes," Twist said with a dismissive wave. "So who's going to start the bet?"

When Twist made it through the day without more than mild fatigue to complain about, Dr. Rodés had no choice but to let him return to work again the next day. As soon as the sun was peeking out over the surrounding hills, and Arabel had gotten him to eat something, Twist walked back into the cool echoes and dust of the palace hall. The moment he stepped over the threshold, the air tightened sharply around him. This time, he knew exactly who it was.

"Damn, she's wide awake today," Jonas muttered, standing beside him as Aazzi spoke softly to herself in her own language. His eyes were glowing softly as he looked over the space.

"Princess," Twist said to the throbbing, full air. "I came back, just as I promised. Please, leave me to work. I'll be finished much faster if you do."

The tension in the air wavered for a moment, but then it lessened, drawing back into the depths of shadow that lingered even in the sunlight. Jonas frowned, watching it.

"That's downright spooky," he muttered.

"I told you," Twist said, walking forward. "She's quite reasonable."

"She's still watching us," Aazzi said, following close.

"Naturally," Twist said as kindly as his impatience would allow.

He stopped at the end of the stair, and looked over the work that was still left to do. She looked much better already: her hands, arms, face, and neck were all repaired and shining while her long wire hair lay untangled under her head, polished back to its natural dark-maroon color.

Twist sat beside her and began working on her legs. The moment he touched the metal, his Sight leaped up to fill his mind just as readily and clearly as it ever had. Twist let out a silent sigh of relief and resumed his work.

Hours passed namelessly to Twist. Jonas and Aazzi spoke occasionally, but they both stayed at his side throughout. The soft, warm, electric hum of Jonas's presence served as a touchstone for Twist. Whenever his Sight began to wander off into the ghost's memories, he followed Jonas back to himself and to his work.

Before long, Arabel arrived to insist that Twist take a break for lunch. When Jonas and Aazzi joined her cause, Twist had no choice but to acquiesce. While he was out of the palace hall, Dr. Rodés gave him a quick looking over as well, much to Twist's annoyance. Once the others were convinced that he was rested, well fed, and not overstressed, Twist returned to work while Aazzi and Jonas resumed their posts.

When the light started to fail outside the glow of Twist's candlelight, a soft rain began to fall as well. The thin air chilled with the moisture, dragging in wafts now and then while the remaining sunlight fought its way through the clouds. When Twist looked up to stretch his stiff neck, for an instant he thought he was back in London. He jerked, looking around, but the confusion passed just as quickly.

"What? Are you all right?" Jonas asked instantly.

"No, no, it's nothing," Twist said, shaking his head. "It's just…the rain. It sounds like London. I thought…" He smiled meekly and looked away. "Never mind."

"Are you going to take a break any time soon?" Jonas asked, pulling up his goggles to rub at his eyes. "It's been hours. We talked about this," he added, glancing towards Twist under the edge of his goggles.

"I'm almost done with this whole limb," Twist said.

"Just let me finish it."

"Aazzi?" Jonas said with a sigh. "You going to back me up?"

"Give him ten more minutes," Aazzi said. "Then we'll drag him out."

"Sounds good to me," Jonas said, smiling at Twist through his goggles.

"That's not funny, you know," Twist muttered.

"Is too," Jonas assured him with a nod.

Twist gave his sightless gaze a nasty look and then went back to his work. He finished with the last leg of the puppet as quickly as he could and then moved on to the last part of her, the core of her metal body. He reached out to gently stroke below the dip in her slender throat, and let his Sight run through her. He took in a sharp breath and pulled his hand away quickly, a decidedly concerned expression on his face.

"What?" Jonas asked. "What's wrong?"

"Her heart," Twist said, ever so softly.

"What?" Aazzi asked, moving closer.

Twist reached out to the puppet's shoulder. His fingers instantly found the latch and he pulled off the front casing, revealing the infinitely complex clockwork beneath. In the center of innumerable fine, thin copper gears and tiny levers, where a human heart should have been, was a single, large, crimson crystal in the shape of a perfect sphere. There was an ugly crack running through it at an angle, almost shearing it in half. "It's broken," Twist said, looking up to the others.

"Can you fix it?" Aazzi asked after a moment.

"That crystal is the source of every movement in the rest of the body," Twist said. "Every other part leads back to it. If it can't resonate at the exact, perfect vibrations, then the body won't respond. She would be paralyzed."

"But, you can fix it, right?" Jonas asked slowly.

Twist looked up at his covered eyes. "I can't mend a broken crystal. It's impossible."

"No, no, that can't be," Jonas said, shaking his head. "I saw the two of you together—talking, laughing—like nothing was wrong. You will complete her, eventually."

"Is your Sight never wrong about the future?" Twist asked.

"Never," Jonas said, his tone darkening.

A high, slight cry seemed to echo off the palace walls in the depths of the slowly encroaching shadows. Aazzi turned instantly, following the sounds with her silver eyes, and muttered to herself quickly.

"Has she been listening?" Aazzi asked them.

"I'll find a new crystal," Twist said to the darkness, as loudly as he could. "Jonas is right, I'm sure," he added with a gesture to him.

"Is it just me, or is it getting colder?" Jonas asked quietly, watching the shadows with softly glowing eyes.

"Princess, please," Twist said, getting to his feet to address the entire hall. "Trust me. I will bring you back into this world. I swear it."

A sharp blast of wind rushed in from a broken window and snuffed out the candle flame. The cold grew deep enough to turn Twist's breath into silvery clouds, and the shadows seemed to reach out from the walls toward him. Jonas and Aazzi both got quickly to their feet, standing close to Twist, with their backs to him. The darkness before Jonas grew so black that it almost appeared to take a solid form in the matter of an instant.

"Holy..." Jonas breathed, staring into the shadow, now with much more brightly glowing eyes and a decidedly alarmed expression. "She's taking shape!"

Aazzi moved to stand beside him, between Twist and the blackness, speaking quickly and clearly with her hands held out before her. Twist peered between them as the blackness seemed to pause in its approach, as if it had run into some kind of wall. His body began to tremble in the sudden cold, his heart racing in his chest.

"I can see her," Jonas said. "She's yelling, trying to say something, but I can't hear it." He paused, frowning. "Ah hell..."

Jonas braced as if expecting an attack, and Aazzi's voice rose in volume. In a flashing instant, the blackness flooded forward, washing over them like a wave and then crashing down onto Twist. To him, the others disappeared like smoke before the wind, and the princess appeared in their place, standing before him as real and solid as she had before. The darkness around her lifted as well, bathing them both in a haunting white light.

"Princess," Twist said, his voice all but lost to his shock.

"There are others now," she said to him, taking his hand in hers. Once again, Twist twitched when her cold skin touched his, but no vision came. "They say they will take you away. Can't you see them?"

"Who?" Twist asked, alarmed to find fear on her gentle, childlike face.

"They arrived last night, on the other ship," the princess said. "They say very bad things. They just said they will kill the others if they stand in their way. I tried to tell you, but you couldn't hear me, could you?"

"Where is the other ship?" Twist asked, his mind struggling to catch up.

"Here," the princess said, placing a hand on his back to lead him away, to one of the windows. As they approached, Twist saw that the glass was now repaired, and gleaming like new. "It's drifting beyond that mountain top," the princess said, pointing through the window to a green-and-gray bluff not half a mile away. "They jump to my palace like birds, on mechanical wings," she said, staring out as she took an absent grip of Twist's arm. "They hide and watch you," she added, looking to him intently.

"There, there," Twist said softly, disturbed by her fear. He could remember seeing people reaching out to hold a frightened child, and tried it himself, hesitantly putting one arm around her slender shoulders. She responded instantly, wrapping both arms around his waist and fitting her head into the crook of his neck. "Don't be frightened," he said gently, fighting to keep focus as he held her cold body in his arms.

"I don't like them," she muttered bitterly. "They say such bad things about you."

"*Twist!*" a distant, echoing voice called from very far away.

"No!" the princess yelled, holding him even tighter. "I won't let you go. I want you to stay here with me! I'm frightened."

"There, there," Twist said again, rubbing her back softly. "They are only worried about me. They think I'm in danger because they can't wake me up."

"Don't wake up," she said, pulling back just enough to look up to him with her shimmering, dark eyes. "Stay with me."

Twist knew that his heart was barely beating, that he was likely on the verge of death as she overstressed his Sight. He knew he needed to wake up to tell the others that they might all be in danger from the newcomers. He knew that there were many reasons to break out of this dream. But as he looked into her eyes and held her in his arms, very little of him cared.

"*Twist, please!*" called another voice, still far away in the distance of light.

"My dear, I want nothing more than to stay with you," he said finally, surprised by how easily the words left his lips. She smiled slightly. "But I have to go. Just for a moment," he said, this time fighting for each word. Her smile faded away. "I have to tell my friends what you told me. They don't have any idea about the other ship. If we're attacked, we'll be defenseless. They could take your puppet away and trap you here forever."

"I don't want to be alone anymore," she said, pain coloring her face and dampening her eyes. "I've been all alone for so long!"

"I don't want you to ever be alone again," Twist said quickly. "Please, let me make sure of it. Let me protect you."

She pulled him tighter again, pressing her cheek to his shoulder as she looked away. "I like you," she said, ever so softly. "You're not like anyone else. You're so sweet to me. I watch you work so gently on my puppet. I like to watch you."

"You know I don't want to cause you any pain," he said, stroking the long tail of black hair that hung down her back. "You can trust me, princess."

"Myra," she said.

"I'm sorry?"

"My name," she said, looking at him again. "Servants call me 'princess.' I want you to call me by my name."

"Myra," Twist echoed, tasting the name with a smile. He couldn't stop himself from reaching up to stroke the side of her lovely little face, but she only moved into his touch with a smile of her own. "Let me go, please. I need to make sure that you will be safe. I would never forgive myself if I let something happen to you."

She looked down slightly and took a heavy breath, letting it out to run over the skin at his throat. "All right," she muttered.

"Thank you, my dear," Twist said gently as she pulled away from him.

"I'm trusting you," she said sternly to him.

"You can trust me to the end of the world," Twist said.

Myra smiled and took a step away. The white light burned in from the distance and enveloped her completely until Twist was alone in a pure-white space. He reached out with his senses and found Jonas's electric resonance wafting indistinctly in the air. He caught it and pulled, dragging himself closer and closer.

"Twist!" Jonas's voice called, pulling Twist into consciousness.

"Jonas..." Twist tried to say, but his voice barely made it out of him as he struggled to open his eyes. Somewhere close, rain was falling gently on stone.

"Come back to us," said another voice—maybe Arabel's. It was cold now, out of that white light. Tiny, chilly, drops fell on his face and hands. It took him a moment to realize that he was no longer in the palace, but outside in the gentle rain. Figures circled him, but he could feel Jonas very near. He could feel himself slipping into the soothing darkness of sleep, but he fought to hold on.

"Jonas..." Twist said again, more loudly this time, and he reached out as the electrical buzzing sensation grew.

"Careful," Jonas's voice said in the foggy, indistinct rain, and the buzz calmed.

"No, he's reaching for you," said Aazzi's voice. "Look at him."

"But last time..." Jonas said hesitantly.

"Just do it!" Aazzi said sharply.

Jonas made a reluctant tone, but the buzz grew again, bathing Twist's dull senses in warm, sparkling, energy. Twist snapped his eyes closed before he could find Jonas's eyes, and pulled on the sensation of his gaze as hard as he could, letting it run through him. His mind cleared quickly. He pushed himself up to sit on the wet stones and blinked to clear his vision. His breath came more strongly, and his skin prickled in the chill.

"We're not alone," he said, forcing his voice out as

strongly as he could.

"What?" Arabel asked, kneeling beside him.

"There's another airship," Twist said, feeling like he was yelling at the top of his lungs.

"Here?" Aazzi asked, standing close by. She looked around through the mist.

"The bluff behind the palace hall," Twist said, fighting to remember the dream. "They are hiding behind it."

"Whoa!" Jonas gasped, turning away sharply as he stood quickly. He threw his hands up to cover his eyes. The buzz in Twist's neck all but died, but he hung on to what little was left as unconsciousness drifted alluringly at the edges of his mind.

"What?" Arabel asked instantly. "What's wrong?"

"I see it!" Jonas said. "I think..." he paused, lowering his hands to reveal an astonished expression. "I think I just saw what he was thinking."

"I don't sense anything," Aazzi said with a sigh. "Twist, are you sure?"

"Yeah, he's sure," Jonas answered, pulling his goggles down over his eyes. "The princess was trying to warn us, but we couldn't hear her. They've been there all day, hiding behind that mountain top," he added, pointing. "She just took over his Sight so that she could tell him. And..." his voice drifted off as he turned his unseeing gaze to Twist. "She wanted him to stay in the dream. Twist, she wanted to kill you."

"She didn't want to hurt me," Twist said, shaking his head. "She doesn't understand."

"How do you know?" Jonas asked instantly. "I'd bet that ghost knows exactly what she just asked of you. She has to be perfectly aware that she's dead." Twist stared back at him skeptically, wholly unable to imagine it.

"Disturbing as that may be," Arabel said, "if there

really is someone else up here with us, we need to know who they are and what they want."

"They may be using a spell to block my senses," Aazzi said softly, still staring out into the rain and mist.

"Who would know to do that?" Arabel asked.

"Let's get him back on board the *Vimana*," Aazzi said, gesturing to Twist.

"Can you walk?" Arabel asked him.

"I don't know," Twist said. His limbs felt weak and heavy, but he tried to get himself back onto his feet. It proved difficult indeed. A hand gripped the cloth of his coat, behind his neck, and pulled him up to his feet. Twist held still, afraid to move into a solid touch. The grip released him, and Twist swayed for a moment on his feet before catching his balance.

"I think I can make it," he said, trying a few steps.

He took them one at a time. The others stayed close to him, but thankfully no one reached out to help him. Jonas was silent, but the buzz in Twist's neck remained strong. Twist held to it as much as he did the walls and banisters that he passed.

Once finally back in his cabin, Twist collapsed against the wall and let his weak legs go limp under him as he slid to the floor. The effort of walking back to the ship had left him so fatigued that he felt he could easily sleep for a week. Arabel had left him, as soon as his feet had touched the deck, to tell the others of Myra's warning, but Jonas and Aazzi had followed him. Jonas watched silently from beyond the doorway as Aazzi looked Twist over critically. Twist felt Jonas's gaze dance at the edges of his own perception.

"I'm going to get Philippe," Aazzi said finally, turning to leave. Jonas moved aside to let her pass, but he remained in the hallway outside.

"Jonas?" Twist called, his voice still just loud enough

to be heard.

"Yeah?" Jonas responded, not moving.

"Can you come closer?" Twist asked, finding it almost impossible to keep his heavy eyelids open at all.

"Are you sure that's a good idea?" Jonas asked, drifting only one step closer.

"I can't afford to sleep for another day," Twist said, forcing his lips to cooperate as his words struggled to form themselves. "Not now. If I can feel...well, *you*, it helps."

Jonas paused for another moment, but then he entered the room. He knelt down on the floor, just beside Twist. Twist took in a deep breath as the electric warmth flooded down his spine, and he closed his eyes to savor the feeling. Jonas's eyes were covered, but Twist could still feel them from behind the black lenses, gazing at him blindly.

"Last time, I thought I pushed you over the edge," Jonas said, his voice quiet.

"I wasn't ready then," Twist said, his voice finally steady now. "If you hadn't been there this time, I never would have stayed awake long enough to warn anyone. I followed you out of the dream."

"Is it just me, or is that buzz a lot more pleasant than it was before?" Jonas asked.

Twist gave a tone and a nod in response. "We're growing accustomed to it." His hands itched to reach out to Jonas, and for an instant, he had a wild desire to take Jonas's goggles off and look into his eyes.

"It's still bloody strange, though," Jonas said, dropping his sightless vision to the floor and taking a calming breath. One hand was clenched tightly on his knee. Staring at it, Twist couldn't stop himself from wondering how warm Jonas's skin would be to touch. Myra's was always ice cold in his dreams. But Jonas...

Footsteps in the hallway drew them both out of their private thoughts. Dr. Rodés appeared with Aazzi and looked down at the two of them skeptically.

"Should you be that close?" he asked Jonas.

"It helps," Twist said. "I'm feeling better already." Jonas stayed put, not moving at all.

"Last time—" the doctor began.

"This time is different," Twist said, cutting him off. "Can you give me something to help me to stay awake?"

"I could," Dr. Rodés said slowly. "But I won't do anything until I've had a look at you."

Twist stared back up at him silently for a moment. "Are you finished now?"

The beginning of a choked-off laugh escaped Jonas. The doctor's jaw tightened but he said nothing. He knelt down on the floor before Twist and reached out to his neck. Twist jerked away from his advance, wide eyed.

"Are you mad?" Twist gasped. "I don't care if you're a doctor, don't touch me!"

"Let me do my job," Dr. Rodés said, his voice flat and calm. "It'll only be an instant."

"But—!" Twist yelped, watching the doctor's fingers reach for him again. He was faster this time, though, and Twist's back was already against the wall. Twist turned his face aside and snapped his eyes closed at the doctor's cool fingertips pressed against his throat, just below his right ear.

Twist felt the vision come, felt it burn across his perception like fire. Without thinking, his attention retreated to the heat at the back of his neck—to the electric rush of Jonas, so close beside him now—and his mind remained there. Brilliant, startling chaos raged behind his closed eyes, but Twist wrapped the warmth of Jonas around his mind until the vision from the doctor's touch became muffled and dim.

Twist took in a smooth breath as the pressure of Dr. Rodés's touch pulled away, leaving his mind empty save for the still, constant, pulse down his spine. He blinked his eyes clear, finding a bitter tightness and concern on Jonas's face. The doctor was peering at Twist's eyes carefully, like he was inspecting an insect under glass.

"What just..." Twist breathed, his gaze flying between the doctor and Jonas.

"Is something wrong?" Jonas asked quickly. "Was the vision too strong for you?"

"No, it..." Twist said, searching for the right words. "It never came. Not really. I held it back."

Jonas's eyebrows lifted. "How?"

"I haven't a clue."

"Do you mean that your Sight didn't work?" Jonas asked, fear sharpening his voice.

"No, it worked like always," Twist said, shaking his head. "I just held the vision back. I didn't look at it." In his confusion, Twist almost gave in to the urge to pull closer to Jonas for comfort. The notion was so foreign to him that he wondered if it had been his thought at all.

"Well," Dr. Rodés began. Both Jonas and Twist looked to him sharply as if they had forgotten that he was there at all. "Your heart is beating quickly, but it's steady. You don't feel warm either, as you did last time. How do you feel, exactly?"

"Tired," Twist answered. "Like I could fall asleep any second. Jonas is all that's keeping me awake." Aazzi and the doctor both glanced at Jonas, and then back to Twist.

"It's nothing," Jonas muttered to them.

"I can give you a stimulant," the doctor said, standing as he looked down at Twist. "But I'm not sure if I should. You may very well need to rest."

"We could be attacked any minute," Twist said, shaking his head. "Myra—I mean, the princess, told me that they are talking about stealing her body and then killing us. How do you expect me to rest at a time like this?" Twist's anger and impatience surprised him. It didn't feel like his own.

"Just give him something, Phil," Jonas said tersely.

Dr. Rodés muttered something to himself in French as he left the room. He returned quickly with a small cup of strange-smelling tea for Twist. Not ten minutes after drinking it, Twist felt just energetic enough to stand again.

Try as she might, Aazzi could catch no sign of the intruders on the chilly, thin air. She and the rest of the crew armed themselves anyway. Not wanting to arouse suspicion in anyone who might be watching, however, they took casual positions around the ship. The rain lightened into a fine mist while Arabel busied herself in the high rigging near the balloon, which happened to give her a wonderful view of the surrounding mountain tops. Zayle and Captain Davis took a stroll around the edges of the open deck, seeming to talk pleasantly about the weather as they watched the sky. After a small rest, Jonas, Aazzi, and Twist returned to the palace hall. Both Jonas and Aazzi kept their weapons concealed.

"Myra?" Twist asked gently of the dusty air. As the sun began to fall, the shadows seemed to fill the palace hall to bursting. Something stirred in the air in response to Twist's voice. "Thank you for your warning," he said, keeping his voice low enough that only he and his companions could hear.

A soft murmur, almost too low to hear at all, rippled out from the shadows. Though none of them could pick out a word, the distant voice sounded pleasant.

"My dear, we may have to move your body, to keep you safe," Twist said. "But I'm not sure you will be able to return to it if your spirit remains here."

Jonas shifted nervously beside Twist, while Aazzi muttered something under her breath.

"What is it?" Twist asked them quickly.

"She's moving," Aazzi said.

"I think she's trying to appear to us again," Jonas said,

his uncovered eyes peering into the seemingly empty air before them.

"My dear," Twist said to the air, "I have a plan, but I need you to trust me again." The air chilled sharply around them, sending a shiver down Twist's spine, despite the warm buzz of Jonas's presence in his neck.

"There she is..." Jonas toned, staring with glowing eyes at nothing Twist could see. Aazzi made a gesture over herself with another soft murmur. "She's staring at you, Twist."

"I need you to return to the crystal now," Twist said. The coldness in the air took a sharper, more biting turn.

"Oh, she doesn't like that..." Jonas said. "She looks angry."

"I know," Twist said to the air. "You won't be able to move. You'll be trapped. But it's the only way I can protect you. Please, trust me."

"She's still angry," Aazzi muttered.

"She's crossing her arms and glaring at you," Jonas said to Twist. Twist took a moment to reorder his thoughts.

"You said you wanted me to stay with you," he said finally. "Did you mean it?"

"She nodded," Jonas said. "But she still doesn't look happy."

"I'm asking you to stay with me," Twist said gently. "I don't want to be without you."

"She's coming closer," Jonas said quickly, stepping in front of Twist as Aazzi did the same.

"No, it's okay," Twist said, reaching out a hand to hold them back. They both stilled before he had to touch them. A frigid breath wafted between them, to Twist, and he held his hand out to it.

The cold licked at the tips of his fingers, and his Sight burned to light. A dim, translucent image appeared in the air before him, building like smoke into the shape of the princess. This time, however, nothing else changed and Twist was still completely aware of Jonas and Aazzi as they watched beside him. Myra's tiny hand rested lightly in his as she stared into his eyes.

"They said you were dying," she said, her voice half whisper, half echo, to his ears. "They said I was killing you when I touched you before." Her childlike face darkened with confusion as she spoke. "Why do you keep coming back? Why do you trust me?" she asked, looking to the hand she held ever so lightly.

Twist smiled when she looked back to him. "Because I don't care what happens to me, as long as you are safe and happy."

Her eyes opened wide, but her little mouth took on a smile. "Oh," she said softly, as if only to herself.

"Twist..." Aazzi said, her tone warning. "Your heart is slowing down."

Myra looked to her quickly and snatched her hand away from Twist. The moment she did, his vision of her wafted away to nothing, and he suddenly found it incredibly difficult to stand. He fell to one knee, breathing hard, and his eyes drifted closed.

"You have really got to start caring about yourself, Twist," Jonas hissed, as Twist felt his gaze pour over him. Twist let the feeling flood through him, wrapping the warmth around his mind again.

"The princess," Twist said, keeping his eyes closed. "What is she doing now?"

The warmth of Jonas's attention chilled for an instant. "She looks very scared."

"I'm all right," Twist said, looking up to where her apparition had been. "Don't worry. But please, will you do what I ask?" He and the others all waited for what felt like a long moment, in silence.

"Yes," Jonas said, a relieved smile on his face. "She's nodding."

"Thank you," Twist said, smiling in her direction as well.

The darkening dusk outside, blurred with thick mists, had slowly stolen the last of the daylight away. Nevertheless, the shadows inside the palace seemed to lighten and draw back. Jonas stepped forward, toward the clockwork puppet, and the others followed after him. Aazzi watched the shadows recede around them, her eyes sharp as starlight. Twist knelt down beside the puppet and placed a hand on the cracked crystal heart. As the biting chill in the air faded away, he felt the crystal chill instead. A peaceful, gentle, sleep filled the crystal in his Sight, and it began to vibrate ever so softly under his hand.

"That had to be the strangest thing I've ever seen," Jonas said, staring down at the crystal as well.

Aazzi turned slowly, peering into every shadow that was left behind. "This air is empty," she said. "She's gone."

"She's asleep," Twist clarified, drawing his hand away. "She'll be safe now, no matter what happens."

Not ten minutes later, Twist chided himself sternly
for saying something so final. The mist thickened to such
an extreme that it was difficult to see more than an arm's
length away, and a strange, shifting wind picked up only
to confuse them more. The crew of the *Vimana* drew
back the ship's sails, fearful that they could be damaged
in this bizarre weather. Arabel came to take Jonas,
Aazzi, and Twist back to the ship, but Twist refused to
leave Myra for an instant.

"Aazzi and Jonas are the only ones who can see in
this mist," Arabel persisted. "If one of them wants to
stay, then fine. But what can you do by staying? It'll be
much safer on the ship."

"I'm not leaving her alone," Twist said flatly.

"You're insufferable sometimes, you know that?"
Arabel snapped at him. "You said yourself, she's asleep.
Trust me, no one can even move in this mist. No one will
be able to bother her at all until it clears."

"Ara," Jonas said, his tone calming.

"What?" Arabel snapped at Jonas. "Am I wrong? Or
are you just siding with him for the sake of it?" Twist's
attention drifted for a moment onto the mist that was
creeping in through the broken windows.

"That's hardly fair," Jonas said instantly. Twist
couldn't identify the cause, but the mist and the wind
seemed wrong, somehow. It was as if they didn't belong.

"Stop it, you two," Aazzi said with a heavy breath.
"I'll stay with the puppet, and Twist can go with you."

The mist seeped close enough to prick at Twist's skin.
In an instant, his Sight flew through the mist at enormous

speed: through the windows, past the palace, across the gullies, around a mountain top, onto the deck of another airship, and right up to a man with pure-white skin, full golden eyes with no whites in them, and glowing tattoos across his face and bare scalp. The man's face took on a surprised expression and he muttered something in a language that sounded ancient and savage to Twist. In response, the wind picked up to a much stronger gale.

Twist forced his eyes closed in his vision and he reached out for Jonas, pulling himself back. He shot to his feet—a little too quickly, making him teeter—and shook his head to clear away the vision. The mist still stung at him, but he wrapped the warm sensation of Jonas's presence around his mind until he couldn't see it any more. The vision in the mist danced chaotically before him, but he managed not to look.

"What is it?" Jonas was asking.

"The mist," Twist said, struggling to hold the thought long enough to voice it, with all that his attention was busy doing. "It's not real. A man is making it."

"What?" Arabel asked. "How can that—"

"Twist," Aazzi said sharply, cutting her off. "Did you see this man?"

Twist nodded. The effort it took to keep the vision at bay was staggering to him, but the vision felt like it was drifting steadily farther away.

"Were there tattoos on his skin?" Aazzi asked.

"Yes, on his face," Twist said. "They were glowing. His skin was white as a lily, and his eyes were...very strange. They were fully gold."

"A djinn?" Arabel gasped. "Then it has to be Quay's crew! They've got the only djinn I've ever seen. But how did they managed to follow us from Baku?"

As Twist's attention grew easier to control, he began to notice something in the warm buzzing that he was using as a shield. There was an uneasy tension in it that hadn't been there before. He looked to Jonas, whose eyes were turned away as if he were lost in his own thoughts.

"This is the attack," Aazzi said, drawing the silver pistol from beneath the back of her bodice. "We have to move the puppet to the ship. Now."

Jonas and Arabel both moved to the puppet, but Twist got there first. With fast, effortless skill, he removed the crystal from the delicate cage of clockwork.

"What are you doing?" Jonas asked.

"Now that she's in here," he said, looking to the crystal, "it doesn't matter what happens to the body, or how far away it is. She's safe in here."

"Good idea," Arabel said. "Even if they manage to steal the puppet, we'll still have the most important part. Here, hide it," she said, handing him a cloth handkerchief from her pocket.

Twist wrapped the crystal and tied the ends of the cloth off in a knot. The wind began to howl through the windows with such a force that it made it almost impossible to stand against it. The mist chilled so fast that it was as if the air had turned to ice. Everyone ran for the doorway of the palace, leaving the puppet behind. Pistol fire rang out at them through the mist from the garden outside. Aazzi, Arabel, and Jonas all blindly returned fire with pistols of their own as they protected themselves behind the edges of the stone doorway.

"Twist, we'll cover you," Jonas yelled over the sudden din. "Run for the ship!"

"I can't see!" Twist protested, peering around him into the solid, freezing mist. "I could run right over the edge and never know it."

"Jon, go with him," Arabel yelled to them. "Aazzi and I can hold them off for you."

Twist began to protest again, but the two women both

leaned out into the doorway to fire randomly into the mist. The attacking fire died for an instant, and Jonas took hold of Twist's sleeve as he dove outside.

More alarmed by the fact that Jonas was holding his sleeve—Jonas's hand so very close to his own—than by the reality of running blindly into the freezing mist and bullet fire, Twist hurried to keep in step with Jonas as they both flew through the indistinct darkness. A flick of metal shot by them from the side, striking the wall that was hidden by the fog, with a sharp sound.

"What was—?" Twist began to ask.

"Quiet!" Jonas hissed, jogging quickly to the side.

Twist followed his motion, but unwittingly stumbled over a loose block of stone. His hands both shot out to break his fall, and he heard the crystal fall to the ground beside him, rolling to the side as Jonas lost hold of him as well. Twist sprang to his feet and followed the sound, blocking out the gun fire behind him, until he saw a dim shadow of the small, rolling mass not two steps ahead. He dove for the bundle just as it fell silent in its motion.

His fingers caught the tied handkerchief in open air, and his feet lost their footing as the ground disappeared beneath him. It took far too long for Twist to realize that he'd run off the edge of the walkway, through a broken balustrade. His open hand flew back for some purchase in the disorientation of frozen mist and sudden gravity.

Another hand took hold of his arm just before he dropped over the edge. Twist's Sight screamed through his mind like fierce lightning, burning with an electric fire so intense that all he could see was impossibly white light. For only an instant, he saw Jonas's uncovered eyes in the blinding light, staring down at him in fright. Then, the whole world went totally white, silent, and empty. The last thought Twist managed to have was the will to cling to the cloth in his fingers, to Myra's heart.

A sweet, spicy, thick, and wholly foreign scent was the first thing to return to Twist's senses out of the depthless emptiness of unconsciousness. He wrinkled his nose reflexively, and found his shallow breaths vastly insufficient to clear his lungs. He sat up quickly, coughing, as his head swam and struggled to identify his current situation. He was wrapped in soft, cool, silks, on a wide bed. Opening his eyes, Twist saw nothing but color.

Vibrant red carpets lay over slate-gray wooden floors, while rich red paint covered every wall of the large, open room. Shining black bars created intricate, decorative designs in the large, circular windows in one wall. Deep green, blue, and pink light flooded through them from the bizarre mess of colors outside, below a black sky. Square, shiny-black, wooden furniture—a pair of chairs and a long couch around a low table—padded with gold-and-white cushions were clustered before the windows, while softly glowing paper lanterns hung from the ceiling. The four-poster bed he was in was low to the ground, with white, red, and black silks layered over him, as soft, translucent red curtains hung open around it, swaying gently in the cool, humid breeze that streamed in through the windows.

Silver smoke wafted through the air from the smoldering ends of long, thin sticks set in a bowl of dry rice on the table near the window. What looked like a wardrobe of more shiny black wood etched in gold was placed against the wall across from the bed beside a closed black door. A few simple brush paintings of birds and leaves hung on the walls, while small vases sat in the corners of the room with a single twig of tiny pink flowers in each one.

After taking a moment to give the scene time to reveal itself as a dream, Twist finally pushed himself to the edge of the bed. A pair of slippers waited for him there, so he slipped his bare feet into them. Standing up on stiff legs, Twist realized that he was wearing completely new clothing. His thin form was draped in bright-azure silks, in the general shape of loose pants and a long, collarless, buttoned shirt. The cuffs were trimmed in black brocade, and the same black stitching surrounded the buttons of his shirt in intricate designs.

Stepping to the windows, Twist looked down from the third floor, onto a chaotic mess of strange wooden shops, tall Western looking buildings, and brightly colored signs on every story—hanging out over the street as numerous as leaves in a forest—all written with complex symbols that made no sense to him at all. More paper lanterns, each of a different, vibrant color, hung zigzagging over the street. Looking up over the curving tile rooftops of the obviously immense and crowded city around him, Twist couldn't see a single star in the black sky. For a long moment, he wondered if he was still on planet Earth at all.

"Welcome to Hong Kong," said a voice behind him.

Twist spun quickly to see a man smiling at him widely as he closed the door behind himself. He was tall and obviously well built, judging from the smooth brown skin that showed through the loose tan shirt and emerald vest, that hung open to his stomach. He wore gray cotton slacks, but his feet were bare in roped sandals. The man was heavily decorated in jewelry—a collection of bracelets made of what looked like cloth, bone, and metal, a long string of silver hanging round his neck on which hung a number of small keys, rings by the handful on his fingers, and even a number of metal pieces pierced through his ears and one through his right nostril—but Twist was most highly distracted by the man's hair, which seemed to be made of bits of black rope and sat on his head like a ragged lion's mane.

"What?" Twist managed.

"Hong Kong," the man said again, his dark eyes gleaming in the low light like a cat's. He stepped to a set of three long ropes that hung halfway down the wall beside the door. Each one seemed to be marked with a wooden tag bearing a different, complex symbol like those on the signs outside. "Would you like some tea?" he asked in what Twist now heard as a light, rolling, rich version of an American accent, as the man reached for one of the ropes.

"Isn't Hong Kong the name of the British colony in China?" Twist asked, frowning.

"You're a smart one, all right," the man said, still smiling. He tugged at the rope, which responded with a little bounce and a soft jingle of tin bells, before he moved toward the long couch. "Have a seat, Mr. Twist," he said as he sat. "I'm sure you have loads of questions you'd like to ask me. We can get started while we wait for the tea."

In the brighter light of the lantern near the table, Twist saw a number of thick black lines that wound an interesting pattern in the gently wrinkled skin around the man's left eye. Up close, he looked a bit older.

"Who are you?" Twist asked instantly, not moving from the window.

"My name is Adair Quay," the man said pleasantly. "Next?"

"You're the pirate who's been chasing me since Venice!" Twist said with an accusing finger and an alarmed expression.

"My goodness," Quay said with amusement. "This isn't going to take long at all, if you're always this quick."

"What do you want from me?" Twist demanded. "Where is Jonas? The rest of the *Vimana* crew? How did we get all the way to China? How long have I been asleep?"

"Please, please," Quay said, raising a hand. "One at a time, Mr. Twist. And you really should sit down. You have been unconscious for over two days now. Best to take it easy."

"Two days?" Twist breathed, falling onto the white cushion of one of the chairs. "What happened?"

"You don't remember?" Quay asked. "One of my associates brought you to me after you had fallen out of consciousness. I was honestly hoping that you knew what had happened."

Twist looked up to him with a darker light in his steel-blue eyes. "You attacked us, didn't you?" he asked softly.

"That's a matter of opinion."

"Well, it's my opinion that your associates were shooting at us in a mystical fog that one of you created, and that you sent your ship to attack ours in the air above the Caspian Sea, which resulted in me being thrown into that sea and then captured by oil pirates in a submersible."

Quay smiled, a deep, rich, warmth in his dark eyes. "You've had quite a trying experience, haven't you?"

"I thought you were going to answer my questions," Twist snapped.

"I never said that," Quay said evenly. "I merely acknowledged that you might have several. I will gladly answer any that will help you to understand your new situation, but I will not bow to pointed attacks from you without cause."

Twist stared at him silently while a cold certainty
gripped his spirit. "Do you plan to kill me?" he asked, his
voice calm.

"Certainly not," Quay said on the edge of a laugh.

"Well, at least there's that," Twist said with a sigh.

At that moment, the door opened and a girl dressed in
shining pink silk entered the room, holding a black
wooden tray. Her round face was alarmingly pale against
her gleaming black hair, which was bound up complexly
on top of her head and adorned with an array of colorful
pins, combs, and hanging beads. Twist stared at her first,
though, for her eyes: the same shape as Zayle's and as
black as the starless sky above the city outside.

She walked silently to the table between Quay and
Twist, and knelt down in her tightly wrapped silk dress to
place the tray on it. There was a small white teapot and
two perfectly round white cups with no handles on them.

"You should have no fear for your safety, Mr. Twist,"
Quay said pleasantly. "Your Sight is one of the rarest and
most valuable I've ever heard of. Only a fool would try
to do you harm. I myself, hope to be your friend."

Twist watched as the girl poured golden tea into the
two cups and placed them down before Twist and Quay.
She seemed to pay him no attention, until she was
finished. Her dark eyes flitted to him only for an instant
before she rose to her feet and left just as silently.

"Mr. Twist?" Quay said.

"What?" Twist asked, looking to him blankly.

"I was saying, that I had hoped we could be friends,"
Quay said, a knowing smile playing about his mouth. "I
think we can help each other greatly."

"Can you give me back my friends and let me go
home, then?" Twist asked, taking his cup of tea from the
table.

"You deserve so much more than those idealistic fools can offer you," Quay said flippantly. "You should be properly appreciated for your talents, don't you think?"

Twist nodded vaguely, sipping at his tea. "So you're going to make me very rich and famous, I'm sure," he said with very little interest. "Oh, this tea is wonderful."

"It's the finest in China," Quay said before taking a sip himself. "Only the finest for my newest ally, I should think."

"I haven't yet sold my soul, Beelzebub."

Quay laughed as if it were a joke. Twist didn't.

"Where is Jonas?" Twist asked.

"He's been asleep just as long as you have," Quay said, sounding concerned. "He's staying in another room in this hotel. I just checked on him, though, and he was still sleeping. I'm sure, now that you're awake, he will return to us as well, very soon."

Twist looked into his tea, but he let his mind open itself to the air. He focused on the area at the base of his neck, where he could usually feel Jonas if he were close by. There was no feeling there now, probably because Jonas was too far away, but he pushed at it gently with his mind, searching for any sign of him. After a moment, a faint, almost imperceptible buzzing began to appear on the farthest horizon of his perception.

"I'm surprised, though," Quay said while Twist's mind was still elsewhere, "that you have yet to ask about the clockwork girl."

Twist's eyes shot to him: sharp, cold as ice, and just as blue.

"You were clinging to a crystal when we found you," Quay said with some satisfaction. "It's broken, but my associate says that it has the most curious signs of energy within it."

Twist clenched his jaw to keep himself from

speaking, and slowed his own breathing as he held his body in perfect stillness, staring at Quay as unemotionally as he could. A flicker of discomfort flashed to light in Quay's eyes, but he blinked it away and looked to his tea.

"I don't mean to steal her away from you," he said evenly, "if you are afraid of that. I'm not sure what Davis and his crew might have told you," he said, chancing a glance at Twist, who didn't move a muscle. "You've done a wonderful job of repairing her thus far," Quay continued, looking away again. "I don't imagine it will take long at all to complete the work."

Twist took a sip of his tea.

"Mr. Twist, can we discuss terms?" Quay asked gently.

Twist looked back at him impassively. "Discuss all you like."

"Won't you join me?" he tried, a hopeful smile on his face now.

"I'm not very social," Twist said, looking to his tea again.

"Clever as a lightning strike," Quay breathed, admiringly. "That's what they say about you. I see now that they are quite right. I had hoped that the coldness they spoke of had been a lie, though."

"I want to see Jonas," Twist said.

"When he's awake, of course. But for the moment—"

"Now," Twist said, his voice even and impassive.

"Perhaps—" Quay began, but Twist stood up quickly and put his tea cup down.

"Never mind. I'll find him myself," he said, heading for the door.

Twist got to the door and opened it before Quay could get near him. Hurrying his pace, Twist strode out into a red-and-black hallway, carpeted with dark pinks and gold on the same slate-gray wood, and lit by more white paper lanterns mounted on the walls. Twist pressed at the spot at the back of his neck again, and followed the buzz easily down the long hallway and around the first right turn while Quay came to follow him, speaking imploringly on various subjects that didn't matter to Twist in the least. Turning the corner, he found a figure sitting in a chair outside one of the many black doors.

Coming closer, Twist realized that Jonas was certainly behind that door. The man in the chair looked up at Twist, as he approached, with large, almond eyes as black as shadows. Although his smooth, clear-featured, pale face appeared young and only slightly foreign to Twist, something in those deep black eyes was undeniably ancient, strange, and inhuman. His nose seemed a little too pointed, and his ears a little too long as well, in the fluffy cloud of short, thick black hair that stood up all over his head. He was dressed in a wide-sleeved, silver-trimmed, deep-purple tunic that crossed over his chest, a wide, gray, richly patterned belt around his waist, loose black trousers, and simple wooden sandals on his otherwise bare feet. It took Twist only an instant to recognize Jonas's black goggles sitting snugly on his brow.

"Vane, block him," Quay said around Twist.

In an instant, the strange young man was on his feet, holding a long, single-edged, slightly curved, and gleaming silver blade before Twist, with his back to the door. In his rush, Twist managed to stop only a step away from the end of the sword.

"Now please," Quay said, stepping beside Twist. "Can we speak now?"

"Call off your dog, and let me pass," Twist hissed to him. A wide smile broke onto Vane's face and he laughed lightly under his breath.

"You don't even know where Jonas is," Quay said, sounding like he was near the end of his patience now.

"He's in that room," Twist said, pointing past the sword-bearing sentry. "I want to see him this instant."

"You need to understand something—" Quay said quickly.

"Twist! In here!" Jonas yelled, his voice muffled by the wooden door.

"Damn it all to hell!" Quay bellowed, all his pleasantness disappearing instantly.

Vane glanced to the door for an instant, and Twist dove past him. He heard Quay yell Vane's name as he felt a concussion of sliced air fall over him. He leaped, throwing his body fully at the door. It burst open onto a room almost identical to the one in which Twist had woken up. Jonas was dressed in the same sort of silk clothing, though his was a bright lime green, as he stood beside his bed. His right wrist was securely chained to one of the bedposts by a set of silver handcuffs.

"Wow!" he breathed, smiling widely in Twist's direction as he struggled to retain his footing. "I didn't know Vane was out there. Did you just take on a bloody samurai to save me?" he asked in delighted wonder. His naked eyes flitted quickly around the edges of the scene, while carefully keeping away from everyone else's eyes.

"Are you all right?" Twist asked him, coming closer. Behind him, Vane and Quay simply watched from the doorway. Quay's face showed nothing but frustration.

Jonas shook his chained wrist. "No. I'm tied to the bed. That's very rarely a good thing."

"Please, Twist, let me explain," Quay was saying, while Twist carefully reached out to touch the cuffs. "Jonas and I have a history, you see," Quay continued. "I'm not sure where his allegiances lie at the moment, and I don't want him running off until we've had time to talk."

"You just love to talk, don't you," Jonas said acidly to Quay. Vane snickered again.

Twist tapped at one point on the edge of cuffs with a knuckle while the others talked, and then pulled sharply at the bolt that held them closed on Jonas's wrist. The cuffs unlocked instantly with a bright little click.

"Blimey," Jonas said, rubbing at his newly freed wrist. "Twist, you're a good man to know," he added seriously.

"Do you know where the others are?" Twist asked back, careful not to look into Jonas's eyes.

"No idea," Jonas said. "But we're in Hong Kong. We don't need them to escape."

"We don't?" Twist asked.

"I know half the city, personally," Jonas said brightly. "All we need to do is get away from Quay."

"Now, just a minute!" Quay said, making sure that he was solidly in the way.

"Vane, look!" Jonas said excitedly, pointing down the hallway, "A mouse! I just saw a mouse!" Vane's black eyes snapped to the floor, looking after Jonas's indication. "Now," Jonas said to Twist, lunging forward at Quay.

"Wait!" Quay yelled an instant before Jonas threw his shoulder at him, with his whole body weight behind the blow. Quay fell back against the other side of the hallway but hung onto Jonas's arm tightly as he struggled to catch his balance. "Jonas, knock it off!"

"Let go!" Jonas snapped, jerking at his grip and kicking. Twist watched perplexed, utterly unsure about what needed doing.

"Damn it, Vane, there is no mouse!" Quay yelled angrily as the samurai continued to focus on the floor despite the struggle. "Pay attention, will you?"

Vane looked up in the exact instant that Jonas managed to free his arm. Jonas only had time to turn and take one step away before he came flying back into the room as a black shape—lightning fast and indistinct as a shadow—slammed him down against the floor, face down. The shadow solidified into the shape of Vane, holding his sword across Jonas's neck as he crouched over him, now wearing a wide grin. To Twist's renewed shock, there seemed to be a very fluffy, white-tipped, black fox tail hanging from under Vane's tunic.

"Down, boy," Jonas said soothingly, his arms struggling to gain some kind of leverage. "Let me go and I'll scratch your ears like you like..."

"I'll let you go if you give me a mouse," Vane said to his ear, his voice flavored with an accent that only seemed to affect his vowels and 'L's.

"I don't usually walk around with a mouse in my pocket."

"Too bad," Vane said, enjoying the phrase far too much. He changed his grip on the sword, readying it to strike. Twist froze, his heart racing and his mind swimming. He couldn't conceive of a single way to help, or to stop this attack.

"Good boy, Vane," Quay said, appearing in the doorway. "Don't hurt him, just keep a grip on him." He looked to Twist, who still stood in place, thanks to his complete confusion. "I trust you're smart enough to know now that you can't escape."

Twist didn't respond, but he didn't protest either. He watched as Vane pulled Jonas up to kneel on the floor, still holding him securely from behind as Quay stood in front of Jonas. Quay stared at him with a sigh, his arms crossed over his chest.

"Did you seriously think that would work?" he asked flatly.

"Oh, anything to get this close to Vane," Jonas said with a purr and a luscious expression on his face, his eyes tightly closed now.

"I thought you didn't like me," Vane said quickly, though his grip loosened as he pulled away slightly to peer around at Jonas's face. Jonas used the instant of distance to throw his elbow back into Vane's ribs.

"So get off me!" he yelled as Vane jerked to avoid the blow, but didn't release him.

"Excuse me," Twist asked softly, drawing Quay's attention. "Have I finally lost my mind, or does that man have a tail?"

Quay nodded. "He's a fox."

"A fox?"

"Yes, a fox," Jonas answered as if it made some sort of sense.

"Aren't foxes…you know, small woodland creatures?" Twist asked stiffly. Vane smiled over Jonas's shoulder at Twist, as if enjoying his confusion.

"Not according to Japanese legends," Quay said, as if it were a reasonable answer.

Jonas's eyes opened wide with a sudden thought. "By the way, never say your own name in front of him," he said, hooking a thumb back at Vane.

"Don't tell him that!" Vane whined, slapping at Jonas's head from behind.

Twist fell silent rather than spend any more time in such a ridiculous conversation.

"Come on," Quay said with a heavy breath. "Let's get ourselves back into some sort of civilized situation, shall we?" He glanced at Twist. "Then we can continue our conversation."

"This is hardly necessary," Jonas said as Vane finished re-cuffing Jonas's wrist to one arm of the chair he was now sitting in, in Twist's room.

"You've just proved that it is," Quay said.

"Did you not see Twist snap these open?" Jonas asked with a sigh. "It's pointless to try to lock me up."

"No, it's pointless to lock him up," Quay said, pointing to Twist, who now sat in the chair beside Jonas with his heavy head in his hands. The flight to find Jonas had taken up the bright moment of energy that had come from his long rest. Now, Twist began to feel the weight of his fatigue again.

"If one of you is tied up, it will slow you both down, at least," Quay explained coolly.

"Then, if you do get away, I can pounce on you again," Vane said with a happy grin.

"You enjoy that too much," Jonas said, looking concerned.

"Do I nag at you about your nature?" Vane snapped back.

"Do you think we could get back to the point of this meeting?" Quay asked the room.

"Seriously, you're not talking about an animal, right?" Twist said, looking up to Jonas. "When you say he's a 'fox,' you mean it metaphorically."

"No, I mean it literally," Jonas said instantly. "He. Is. A. Fox," he added, taking extra time for each word. "Well, a kitsune, anyway." Vane grinned at Twist.

"Now, Mr. Twist," Quay began.

"But he looks like a person," Twist said to Jonas.

"Because he likes to," Jonas said. "Foxes are shape-shifting spirits."

"All of them?"

"Can I just ask—" Quay began again.

"Why is this so hard for you to understand?" Jonas asked Twist.

"I'm sorry," Twist said, his voice sharp. "I didn't live in a world of magical weirdness until your bloody sister came into my home and handed me a tangible piece of my favorite fairytale. I've never left London in my life, and now I'm sitting in Hong Kong with a pirate who's hardly even dressed,"—Quay looked down at his own attire quickly but didn't seem to find anything amiss—"a fox that looks like a person, and a man whose eyes I can't look into without exploding!" The others waited quietly for Twist to get his breath back.

"Feel better?" Jonas asked.

"Marginally," Twist muttered, holding his head in his hands again.

"So, tell me, Mr. Twist," Quay said, his voice still smooth and calm as he sat patiently across the small table from Twist. "What is it that you really want?"

"A bloody quiet day," he said flatly, not moving.

"Jonas wants something like that," he said, looking to Jonas. "Don't you?"

"At the moment, I'd really like my goggles back, actually," Jonas said, staring pointedly at his own feet. Vane smiled silently, pulling the black-lensed goggles off his brow and over his own eyes. He then waved his hand in front of the opaque lenses with an amazed expression. Quay rolled his eyes and looked away from Vane.

"Win back my trust, and I'll give them to you, gladly," Quay said pleasantly.

"Where's my pocket watch?" Twist asked, looking up suddenly.

"Your what?" Quay asked.

"I had a watch with me," Twist said. "Where is it?"

"I assume it's with your things," Quay said, gesturing to the wardrobe. Twist got to his feet instantly, heading for it. "But honestly, you and I need to have an undisturbed conversation," Quay said imploringly.

Twist opened the wardrobe and found a small collection of clothes that he'd never seen before hanging neatly inside. A small shelf held the key to his home which had been in his pocket, along with his small brass watch. The instant his fingers touched the watch, the gentle echo of London rain whispered to his ears. He took hold of it tightly as he turned back.

Vane was sitting on the end of the long couch, his feet folded under him, as he continued to entertain himself by trying to see through Jonas's goggles. Twist walked up to him and reached out quickly, plucking the goggles off his eyes and over his head without touching him. Vane blinked in the sudden light just long enough for Twist to jump out of reach.

"Now, come on," Quay said to him, grinning imploringly. "Just let me—"

Twist sat down beside Jonas again and held the goggles out to him while Quay bit his lip with obvious effort not to let his anger overrun him.

"Sweet heavens above!" Jonas gasped in sudden joy. He took the goggles and instantly placed them over his eyes as he took in a deep, relaxing breath. "You're a good man, Twist." Vane glared at Twist darkly, while Quay rubbed at his temple and sighed.

"Vane was playing with them," Twist said as he wrapped the chain of his pocket watch around his hand.

"I'm going to skin you alive and use your pelt for a throw rug!" Jonas said savagely in Vane's direction.

When Twist glanced at Vane, he was wholly

astonished to see a second Jonas sitting exactly where
Vane had been. He was wearing the same clothes that
Jonas wore now, though without the goggles, and was
otherwise a perfect copy in every aspect save one: this
new Jonas had a fluffy black fox tail curled up on the
couch beside him.

"*I'm gonna kill you dead*," the new Jonas said in
Jonas's voice, but with a childish, over exaggerated sneer.
"You're such an angry person," he sighed, in Jonas's
normal voice.

"Knock that off!" Jonas yelled at himself from behind
his goggles.

The new Jonas laughed back at him with Jonas's
laugh, but through a grin that looked somehow predatory
and very alien on his face.

"What the blazes is going on?" Twist asked in a
hollow voice as he looked quickly between the identical
twins.

"I've surrounded myself with silly fools, apparently,"
Quay muttered.

"This is exactly why you never say your own name in
front of a fox," Jonas said, looking toward Twist from
behind his goggles. "If they hear your name from your
mouth, they can put on your face. Disturbing as hell, if
you ask me," Jonas added with a shiver. "Just knowing
your name will let them track you down, too."

Vane smiled wickedly at Twist with Jonas's face.
Twist twitched his vision off of Vane's eyes, but Vane
didn't flinch at all. Twist looked back and, for the first
time, saw Jonas's full face, unobscured. His eyes were
bright and green, round and keen, set in his sun-kissed
features like gleaming, precious jewels. In his wonder at
this forbidden image, Twist stared for a moment too long.

"Do you see something you like?" Vane asked in
Jonas's voice, with a wicked smile and a playful wink.

"Vane, will you stop it?" Quay sighed.

Vane clicked his tongue disapprovingly, but then gave his body a shake. For an instant, his form blurred into a shadow, but then just as quickly returned to the form he had worn before. Twist watched the transformation, not believing an instant of it.

"Now, please, can I have your attention for a little longer than the merest moment?" Quay asked Twist.

"So that you can get me to agree to sell you something I can't afford to lose?" Twist asked him back instantly. Jonas and Vane both looked to Quay silently.

"Whatever do you mean?" Quay asked, looking honestly astonished.

"You have her, you've made that clear," Twist said. "But she isn't yet finished. You want me to complete the repairs."

"Well, yes," Quay said, watching him carefully. Twist pulled himself still once again, staring at Quay with all the unnerving energy that he could muster beaming out of his steel-blue eyes. This time, Quay didn't look away, but held his gaze steadily, albeit uncomfortably.

"To what end?" Twist asked coolly. "Why would you go to any trouble for some strange old clockwork toy, left forgotten for so long?" To Twist's amazement, he managed to make it sound like he might have actually believed a word of it.

"A walking, talking, self-aware mechanical woman would be amazing to anyone," Quay answered. "Amazing things are always worth something."

"So you would sell her?" Twist asked, holding his voice even.

"Of course," Quay said. "Royals tend to like toys like this one. I'm sure I could find a prince somewhere who might want it. And royals are never careful with their money. Then there are the Rooks, of course. I could offer you a large percentage of the takings if—"

"No," Twist said, as solidly as any other undeniable fact.

"But—"

"No amount of money is worth that girl's soul," Twist said before Quay could say anything else. "You forget, she is still very much alive. You can't expect to sell a human being for money."

"I think you forget," Quay said quickly, leaning forward, "people have been selling each other as slaves since the beginning of time. My own father was born a slave in Kingston."

"Then you should know better!" Twist cut in quickly. "Do you now honestly mean to sell an immortal princess into slavery?"

"I mean to make a living," Quay said flatly. "We do what we have to do to survive."

"You could always get a normal job, you know," Twist said. "I have a nice little clock-fixing business back in London and I never want for money."

"You are squandering your talent!" Quay snapped, his anger showing on his face now.

"I'm using it as I see fit," Twist answered evenly.

"With the Sight you have, you could be one of the most powerful men in this world," Quay said, his words biting. "But instead, you lock yourself up in a tiny little shop, never even touching anything but ruddy clocks! Touch the right people, learn the right secrets, and your Sight could be used to rule nations!"

"Is it just me, or does he sound jealous to you?" Twist asked Jonas lightly.

"Don't get me into this," Jonas said back quickly. "I've never seen him actually show anger before." Vane was also watching Quay with an alarmed expression.

Quay sat back in his seat, taking a moment to breathe

slowly and calm himself. "I'm sorry," he said, his voice smooth once again. "I just hate to see something so valuable wasted."

"I'm happy, thank you," Twist said. "I wouldn't want to rule anything."

"Everyone wants power," Quay said, shaking his head.

"I don't."

"Of course you do," Quay protested. "You just don't see it that way."

"All I want is to spend the rest of my life tending to the needs of the clockwork princess," Twist said, silently amazed by the ease by with which the words flew from his lips. "She is a beautiful and impossible myth become real. Nothing in this world could ever be more valuable to me than she is. And I'll never give her up to something like you."

Quay stared back at Twist with frustration smoldering in his eyes. "The *Vimana* is in pieces, hanging off the side of a mountain top more than two days flights from here," he said, his voice smooth as silk, curling into the vowels on the gentle Caribbean-colored accent. "You are now halfway around the world from anyone else you might know, and last I checked, your pockets were empty except for one old, uninteresting watch that isn't even telling the right time. If you leave me now, you'll be lost, alone, and destitute. Instantly.

"Now," he said, smiling slightly, "I, on the other hand, have a ship, a crew, and most of my not-inconsiderable wealth stockpiled in banks here in Hong Kong. I also have your precious clockwork toy and her crystal heart. If you agree to work with me, I'm willing to not only make sure that you are fed well, paid for your work, and made very comfortable, but I'm also ready to make sure that you are able to finish repairing that toy.

You're a clever boy," Quay said, his dark eyes gleaming above his wicked grin, "so you tell me, Mr. Twist. Which path suits you better?"

Twist's eyes slid away, into the reality of the situation. His watch ticked softly in his hand, echoing the silence, simplicity, and comfort of the life he'd left behind in London. It hadn't felt final when he'd shut the door to his shop. It hadn't felt like an ending when the *Vimana* had carried him up out of the London rain, and into the painfully bright sunlight. For the first time in his life, Twist truly didn't know if he would ever see his home again.

The ground seemed to dissolve under his feet, falling away to leave him hanging by the tiniest possible thread: the fickle whim of a man he didn't trust. All he could do now was try to buy himself some time.

"Do I have to sign anything in blood?" Twist asked softly, still looking away. Though he said nothing, Twist felt Jonas take a heavy sigh beside him.

"Not at all," Quay said gently. "You can stay with me for as long as you need to. All I ask is that you don't run away," he added, glancing at Jonas, "and that you help me when your skills are needed."

"That sounds quite reasonable," Twist said, finding the words heavy on his breath.

"Wonderful," Quay said with a reptilian smile.

"You're awfully good at getting what you want," Jonas said suddenly to Quay. "Are you sure you don't have a Sight of your own?"

"I'm just a business man," Quay said lightly. Dread tickled up Twist's spine, sending a shiver through him.

Once things had been settled to a point, and Jonas had eventually promised not to try to run away again, Quay took Jonas back to his room and left Twist alone to rest. Quay sent for some food to be brought to Twist's room, but Twist wasn't very interested. Instead, he sat on the couch and turned the watch over slowly in his hands.

He could still sense the memories of his home within it. After everything that he had been through, after all the miles he'd traveled, the quiet moment that he'd locked inside the watch hadn't changed in the slightest. He could still hear the rain falling softly on the thick windows. He could still sense the slightest aroma of a snuffed-out candle, metal polish, and damp wood. The gentle, constant ticking of all his clocks still pulsed in time with the beating of the watch's own clockwork heart. Even the thin, gray light falling through the soot-stained sky was still reflected in the silence between tick and tock.

The door opened suddenly when the serving girl entered with another tray, the items on it clinking together noisily. Twist was so wrapped up in his thoughts that he jumped at the sudden sound of her entrance and the watch slipped through his fingers. He tried to catch the chain as it fell, but missed. The watch fell to the wooden floor with a wretched crack, its delicate inner workings jolted violently.

Twist gasped in the moment that the damage rushed to his awareness. Just as suddenly, the watch was in his hands once again, undamaged and perfect, and he was alone in the room. He looked around quickly, searching for some explanation for this. He had no memory of picking the watch up again, or of the serving girl leaving. He absently wrapped the chain around his hand as he struggled to figure out what had just happened.

The next moment, the door opened again and the serving girl entered with a tray, the items on it clinking together just as noisily as before. Twist was on his feet in an instant, turning to watch as she entered. The girl started slightly at his quick motion, but when he said nothing she walked around him to place the tray down on the table. Twist looked down to the watch, as it still ticked away softly, safe in his grip.

"Did you just come in, a moment ago?" Twist asked her hesitantly.

She looked to him quietly.

"I know it sounds mad, but..." he began, not yet sure how to finish the sentence.

"*Shen ma?*" she said softly to him.

"What?" Twist asked.

The girl shook her head, the beads hanging in her hair tinkling softly as she did. "No ... English," she said stiffly, with a thick accent and an apologetic smile.

"Oh, I'm sorry," Twist said quickly, putting on an apologetic smile of his own. "Never mind," he said, waving his hands dismissively.

The girl nodded and turned to leave with no further response than the soft sound of her pink silk dress brushing the floor as she walked. With the door closed again, Twist fell back into his seat and held his head in one hand as he stared at his own confusion.

"That's it," he said to no one. "I'm losing my mind now. I suppose it was bound to happen eventually, with all the madness in my life these days."

Though he didn't feel hungry, he looked over the meal that the girl had brought him. Small pieces of meat and vegetables were drowned in a thick sauce on one

small dish beside a bowl of broth-like soup, while another
bowl held nothing but simple white rice. There were also
a few rolled tubes that appeared to be fried, along with a
few tiny dishes of sauces in varying bright colors. There
was a spoon placed on the tray beside two long pointed
sticks, but Twist found no knife or fork with them.

After much deliberation, Twist hesitantly plucked a
piece of the meat out of its thick sauce with his fingertips
and gave it a sniff before placing it in his mouth.
Succulent and tender, drowned in a tangy, smooth,
buttery sauce, the morsel pleased his tongue just as much
as the strangely colored food in Baku had. As he
swallowed the first bite he also came to realize that he
was actually quite hungry indeed. Once the tray was all
but licked clean, Twist leaned back on the couch and let
out a happy sigh.

"Remember that, Twist," he said to the ceiling,
"China has great food."

"Do you always talk to yourself?" asked a man's
voice from close behind him.

Twist turned quickly to find a woman also standing
not a foot away from him. Twist had not heard her enter,
nor the man who stood behind her. The woman was not
tall, but her body was very slender and wrapped totally in
sapphire-blue cloth—loose trousers that gathered at her
ankles and waist, with a tunic not unlike Vane's that had
tightly wrapped long sleeves, and a collar that crossed
low over her breastbone. Her black hair was cut very
short for a woman, and was in such a sharp style that it
seemed like it could cut the bright amber skin at her
throat. Her face reminded Twist instantly of the serving
girl's, but the woman appeared to be twice her age. She
looked down at him through cool eyes, as narrow and
judgmental as a wild beast's.

Glancing to the man behind her, Twist leaped to his

feet and backed away almost to the wall. "You made that mist in Nepal!" he said, pointing at the man.

The man's face was pure, snowy white and covered in black lines that wove together and up over his bare scalp. He wore a long, white cotton coat of a European design, buttoned tightly over white trousers, and there were spats over his shining black shoes. Though his clothes looked to be Western, his features and his solid, muscular build were wholly foreign to Twist: the man seemed to be made of nothing but sharp angles that only accentuated a sense of power in his form. Certainly the most striking thing about him, however, were his eyes. They were fully gold, with no whites in them.

"You saw me?" he asked, grinning with a mouthful of gold teeth. His deep, dark voice was colored with an accent not unlike Twist had heard in Baku.

"How did you get in here?" Twist asked. "I didn't even hear you open the door."

"We didn't use the door," the man said with a shrug, while the woman simply watched Twist silently. "My friend Jiran, here, is a shadow assassin, and I am not human at all," he offered as clarification. Twist decided to pick his questions carefully.

"What do you want?" Twist asked slowly.

"To ask you about this," the man said, holding out one pure-white hand. To Twist's amazement, sourceless smoke pooled in his open palm and shaped itself quickly into the solid form of Myra's cracked crystal. "As far as I can tell," the man said, examining the crystal as he spoke, "this is a critical piece of that clockwork puppet. I assume that it is meant to vibrate correctly to allow the ghost to control the rest of the puppet. Of course," he said, smiling at Twist for a moment, "I'm no expert in these things."

"That is generally the idea," Twist said, still trying to

figure out how he'd manifested the crystal in his hand in the first place.

"Is there any way to fix this?" he asked Twist.

"No, it has to be replaced."

"Ah, I see," the man said looking to the crystal again. "Well, this appears to be a cave crystal from somewhere in south east Asia. It's lucky Quay decided to come here to Hong Kong. We shouldn't be far away from the place where this crystal once grew."

"How could you know that, just looking at it?" Twist asked.

The man smiled at him, his unnerving, golden eyes gleaming in the lantern light. "I'm a magical being. I understand magic."

"Who are you?" Twist asked, finally unable to hold the question back any longer.

"You may call me Idris," he said pleasantly. "To answer what I'm sure is your next question, I'm an earthbound djinn. And to answer your next question, no, I will not grant you any wishes unless they sound like fun."

"Wait..." Twist said, grasping at the loose threads of his understanding. "Do you mean, like a genie? Aladdin and his magical lamp, sort of genie?"

"Whatever," Idris said, looking somewhat disappointed at the sound of Aladdin's name.

"But that's just a story," Twist said, desperate for some sense of reality.

"Weren't you the one to pluck this out of a fairytale princess's chest, not two days ago?" Idris asked, gesturing with the crystal. "Your real problem is that you don't believe the stories."

Twist gave a sigh and shook his head before he looked to the still-silent Jiran. "And what about you?" he asked her. "A 'shadow assassin,' was it? Then are you a magical shadow creature of some kind?"

She smiled slightly and shook her head.

"She is human," Idris said. "Perhaps you've heard the term 'ninja' at some point?"

"Oh, of course," Twist said spitefully, crossing his arms. "Pirates, vampires, people made of clockwork, shape-shifting foxes, a genie, and now a ninja. I should have guessed. What shall we have next? Creatures from outer space? A mermaid or a flying horse perhaps? No! I have it," he said, snapping his fingers. "We need a dragon! A proper fire-breathing one."

Idris looked at him with a concerned expression. "Are you all right?"

"No. I'm going mad, obviously," Twist said irritably. "I'm sure I'll be chasing after white rabbits and playing croquet with flamingos in no time at all."

"Perhaps we should leave you to rest," Idris said slowly. Jiran nodded silently. "Thank you for helping me to understand this," he said, closing his hand over the crystal until it ceased to be in his hand at all. "I'll tell Quay, and we should be able to head out to find a replacement as early as tomorrow."

"Whatever," Twist said, rubbing at a new pain between his eyebrows. When he opened his eyes again a moment later, Idris and Jiran were both gone, though he had not heard a single sound of their departure.

Twist awoke the next morning to a muffled concussion about his head. Blinking his eyes open quickly, he found a woman standing over his bed with the corner of a pillow in one hand and a bland expression on her face.

"Come on, get up or I'll whack you again," she said with an American accent as she brandished the pillow as if to strike him with it. "I haven't got all day, sugar."

Twist pushed on stiff arms to sit himself up, as he struggled to make sense of the woman before him. She was tall and her form looked capable and firm, with wide shoulders. She was standing in the way only a man should, and wearing clothing that looked entirely male as well. Her blond hair—flecked gently with a hint of gray —was hanging in a braid down her back under a wide-rimmed leather hat. Brown eyes in a face that bore evidence of many hard years stared down at Twist without even a hint at pleasantries.

"Who are you?" Twist asked her. "What are you doing in my room?"

"I sure as hell ain't your damn babysitter, you limey little whelp," she snarled. "But Jiran is invisible like always, Vane's an idiot, and the other two are too bloody high and blooming mighty—as you limeys might say—to bother with getting you out of bed. So, here I am," she added with a mirthless smile.

"You're a member of Quay's crew?" Twist asked slowly.

"Ding, ding, ding! Give the boy a prize."

Twist pushed himself to the edge of the bed to put his

slippers on again. "Madam, I—" he began pleasantly. He didn't finish, however, because the pillow she'd been holding flew and struck him suddenly.

"I ain't running a brothel either!" she bellowed angrily. "The name is Cybele, thank you very much. Call me 'madam' again and I'll have your skin for a new pair of boots." She looked him over critically as he stared back at her in shock. "Well, one boot anyway. God you're tiny."

Twist realized quickly that it would be much better not to argue with her. He did as he was told, and hurried to get himself ready to leave, no matter how groggy his head still felt from his fitful sleep. When he went to the wardrobe to get dressed, however, he had to pause as Cybele was still in the room, watching him impatiently.

"What's the matter, sonny?" she asked with a nasty little grin. "You think you've got anything I'd want to see? Get your britches on and let's go!" she snapped, examining her fingernails idly.

Having no other option, Twist turned his back and got himself dressed as quickly as he possibly could. The clothes inside the wardrobe were all new to him, but they fit better than anything he'd ever worn before. Well-tailored, heavy black trousers, a soft white cotton shirt, and a waistcoat of a deep-blue silk that shined in the light, all fit him as if they had been made only for him. He found a pair of sturdy and tasteful black boots as well, which fit right up his legs almost to his knees with a number of silver buckles on the sides. There was also a long, thin, scarf of silver cotton, which he looped hurriedly around his throat.

He took the black jacket off the hook quickly, as Cybele continued to huff impatiently behind him, but he paused when he saw the color of the lapel; the same exact color of his own eyes. Silver buttons ran up the front, while a blue cord laced up the back, pulling the fabric in down to the waist, where the ends of the cord hung over the long black tails of the jacket. Slipping the garment on, Twist was astonished by how good it felt to wear—not clumping or pulling anywhere, but clinging to his small form perfectly. There were two last pieces inside the wardrobe: a black silk top hat and a pair of silver goggles with a black leather band and deep-blue lenses that were almost as dark as Jonas's. Looking through them for a moment, Twist saw that while they were not opaque, they blocked out most of the light.

Slipping the goggles on to hang around his neck and popping the top hat onto his head, Twist left the silks that he'd been wearing in a mess on the bed. He snatched his pocket watch off his pillow, stuffed his house key into his pocket, and headed out of the room with Cybele drastically in the lead. After all but running down three flights of stairs after her, he finally caught up to her in the lobby of the hotel, on the ground floor.

The lobby was decorated just as lavishly as the rooms had been, with more of the same brilliant reds, shiny black wood, gold, flowers, and intricate designs spilling over every inch of the large room. Sets of couches and chairs sat in small circles around the lobby, and Twist recognized Vane and Jiran sitting together not far off.

"Go wait with Vane," Cybele said to him quickly. "I'll check you out of the room."

Twist did as he was told and took a seat opposite Vane and Jiran in their circle of couches and chairs. Vane's half-reclining form lay limply on the couch, his legs crossed lazily over the edge of the seat and his head resting on the back while he spoke to the ninja, who looked his total opposite; Jiran sat with such stiff posture and stillness that she looked more like a statue than a living person. To Twist's mild surprise, Vane's fingers wound through Jiran's playfully.

"How about Sabang then?" Vane said sweetly to her, smiling gently. "Let's have a tropical drink with exotic fruit in it, and walk the beach. You know what they call that beach, just outside Sabang? *Pantai Kasih*, that means 'Love Beach'." Jiran seemed to giggle at that, but no sound left her smiling lips as her dark eyes gleamed, looking down at his.

"Oh no, are they flirting again?" Jonas said, beckoning Twist's attention.

"Then, we can watch the sunset over the far western tip of the island," Vane said to Jiran, as if he hadn't heard Jonas at all. Jonas perched himself on the armrest of Twist's couch and made sure that his opaque black goggles were securely in place.

"Sometimes, blindness in a blessing," Jonas said seriously to Twist. Twist noticed that Jonas was wearing new clothes as well, though all in shades of soft copper and white, with pale-green accents that attracted the eye. "Who went to get you this morning?" Jonas asked Twist. "Don't tell me you've been stuck with these two all morning."

"It was a woman named Cybele," Twist said, shaking his head.

"Are you all right?" Jonas asked quickly. "Did she hurt you? Don't tell me she touched you! God, I could only imagine..."

"I'm fine," Twist said, putting on a smile and raising a hand to calm him. "She just...hit me with a pillow a few times."

"Wow, you got off light," Jonas said. "She gave me a black eye the first time we met."

"Then she's always that charming?" Twist asked.

"Only on the good days," Jonas said with a sigh. "Or if she is simply bored to death of you. Otherwise, she's far worse than I'm sure you saw. I mean, you're not bleeding, so I can assume so."

"Saying nice things about me again?" Cybele asked, appearing beside Jonas like a cold, sudden wind.

"Always," Jonas said brightly, smiling widely to her. "You know I love you, right? And might I say, you're looking simply ravishing today."

"You asking for trouble?" Cybele snapped.

"Have you lost weight?" Jonas asked, with a pleased gasp.

"Oh knock it off," Cybele snapped, though her fists seemed to unclench. "Can't even see, and he's giving me compliments..." she muttered to herself.

"Good morning, everyone," Quay said pleasantly as he walked towards them. "I hope you all rested well, because we are off again, to Indonesia, if you haven't heard."

"I hate humid weather," Cybele grumbled.

"Idris has found the origin of the broken crystal that we need to complete the clockwork doll," Quay continued. "Once we finish this last leg of the trip, we're all going to be very rich men and women, I assure you." Twist's jaw tightened but he kept it closed.

"Tell me again, how much we're going to get for all the trouble this job has turned into?" Vane asked, still lounging lazily beside Jiran as he spoke.

"Enough for you to buy yourself a lifetime supply of mice, to entertain yourself with," Quay said lavishly.

"You know I'm immortal, right?" Vane asked back.

"Well you'll be full up on mice until you get your second tail, then," Quay said, almost impatiently. When Vane's face took on a grin at the news, Quay turned to Twist.

"Ah, I'm so glad they got that blue right," he said with a smile, pointing to Twist's jacket. "How does that all fit?"

"Very well, actually," Twist answered. "How'd you do that?"

"It's called tailoring," Quay said with a wink. "I thought that you'd like to feel a bit more like a gentleman after all the traumatic experiences you've been through lately. Your other clothes smelled a bit like the Caspian Sea, after all. And as I said," he added with a gleam in his eyes again, "I take care of my own."

Jonas pulled his goggles off and looked Twist over quickly before putting them back on. "Ah, the new-guy special," he toned, turning to Quay. "How come I never got a top hat?"

"You're not a gentleman," Quay said simply, to which Jonas gave a reluctant nod. "Now, are we all ready to leave Hong Kong?" he asked the others, looking excited himself.

"You know I am," Cybele grumbled, already heading for the door. The others got up and followed after her, while Jonas and Twist drifted to the back of the group.

"Can I ask you something?" Twist asked Jonas as they all stepped out onto the cobblestone streets, under the shade of advertisements and signs that hung off the buildings around them. Jonas nodded. "Vane is immortal?" Twist asked, keeping his voice low.

"Foxes can live forever," Jonas said, "but they aren't invincible or anything. They can be killed as easily as anyone else. After a hundred years or so, they usually move on to the next stage of their existence and grow another tail. You can tell Vane is young because he only has one."

"I see," Twist said, filing the information away to work on understanding it later. "And Jiran," he said, keeping his voice low again, "is she a mute?"

A laugh escaped Jonas for a moment, before he caught it. "No, she's just quiet," he said, smiling as he spoke. Ahead of them, Twist thought he saw Jiran glance over her shoulder for an instant. "It's a big deal if she decides to speak," Jonas said. "But she certainly can. And her hearing is way above normal as well."

In obvious response, Jiran turned back and gave Twist a wink as the group turned a corner. Twist felt a brush of heat in his cheeks and looked away. Ahead of the others, Twist spotted tall sailing ships and steamers at the end of the long street, while clouds of airships floated in the air above them.

"Got any more questions?" Jonas asked lightly.

"A few," Twist said. "Arabel told me that they left Quay's airship at the bottom of the Caspian Sea. So how did they get to Nepal, and then here?"

"They probably stole another ship," Jonas said with a shrug. "In fact, I'm sure that's why they brought us to Hong Kong. This is the biggest airship port in Asia. It's full of sky pirates and the last of the old-fashioned sea pirates as well. If you're in Asia and you need something illegal done well and quickly—like forged airship ownership papers—this is the place."

"So, we're surrounded by pirates right now?" Twist asked, his eyes searching faces in the crowds nearer the docks. Each one looked rather foreign, battle hardened, and suspicious to him.

"I'm sorry," Jonas said with a sigh. "I know you don't like pirates."

"Thank you," Twist muttered. "Last question," he said, pulling himself steady again.

"Are you sure it's the last one?" Jonas asked. When Twist glanced at him, he found a smile playing at the edge of his mouth.

"For the moment, yes," Twist muttered. "What about the *Vimana*?" The mirth faded from Jonas's face. "Quay said that something happened to the ship, but what about the crew?"

"I know Ara is all right," he said softly.

"Do you remember more than I do?" Twist asked.

"Probably not. I just remember trying to hold onto you while my mind exploded into that white light. But, I know that Ara is going to live for a while yet. I saw her future once. She was old, with white hair and years of sunlight and life on her face."

"Ah, then you can control your visions sometimes," Twist said. "I thought you always saw someone's death when you looked into their eyes."

Jonas didn't respond, though his face showed not even a glimmer of light in it.

"Well, that's good though," Twist said, changing the

subject quickly. "If she's alive, then you and I have a chance to be found."

"True," Jonas said, nodding. "There's no telling what happened to the *Vimana*, or any of the others, but if Ara's alive then she'll probably try to find us. She's tenacious, that one."

In London, the airship docks had reached high above the rooftops in the center of the city, on thin limbs of strong, reinforced ironwork. In Venice, the docks had looked much like docks on water, hanging as they did at the edges of the flying section of the city. Here in Hong Kong, the airship docks were different still. Tall towers, barely wide enough to house the stairways within them, stood at the edges of the water docks in progressive layers of thinning red walls and wide, black tile roofs that curved upward at each level. Ships floated around these towers for what looked like over a hundred feet up into the sky. Twist looked up into the heights with a frown.

"Is there no one else in the world afraid of heights?" Twist asked as he and the others walked under the shadow of the airships that clustered around a tower like gigantic hummingbirds.

"Sure there is," Jonas said, grinning at him as he walked through the arch at the base of a tower and began to climb after the others. "They just never go anywhere."

"I liked not going anywhere," Twist said as he followed him. "It was very pleasant. I never got attacked, or kidnapped, or enslaved, and I always knew what to expect from my day."

"How dreadfully boring," Jonas said with a wrinkle of his nose.

"You vastly underestimate boring," Twist said.

Jonas laughed and shook his head. As Twist focused on his steps and did all he could not to let himself look down, they passed landing after landing. The group soon reached a landing at which they stopped. They then walked out to a thin bridge that hung from the tower on thin ropes, stretching out to the deck of an airship.

This ship looked smaller than the *Vimana*, but it was still massive. The two enclosed decks of the wooden hull hung in a long curve beneath a set of three tall, round, white balloons that floated above two masts and their single-piece, huge, red sails. Thin black supporting bars lay over the surface of the sails in a ray shape that reminded Twist of the sun. A giant copper propeller hung under the keel on a long, articulated arm. The ship's top deck was also rimmed with cannons.

Enamored by the look of this new airship, Twist continued to step forward until his foot landed on the thin, long, bridge that hung over empty space. The sudden difference in the sound drew his gaze down to see that the bridge was made of thin metal bars, all linked together like a basket, through which he could easily see the enormous drop beneath him.

Twist leaped backward onto the tower, where he clung tightly to the edge of the archway, staring down into the abyss, while his heart pounded loudly in his chest as if it were trying to escape.

"What's the matter?" Cybele asked from the deck of the ship, looking back at Twist.

"It's all right," Jonas said, already walking back over the bridge to him. "I'll get him."

"That's insane," Twist said, pointing to the depths that Jonas walked over so easily. "I can't do that!"

"It's perfectly safe," Jonas said, stopping beside him. "We all walked right across."

"You're all insane!" Twist snapped, unable to take his eyes off the horror.

"Do you want me to pull you over?" Jonas offered, already taking a light hold of the edge of Twist's coat sleeve.

"Get off!" Twist said, waving his hand to free it. "Go have fun in Indonesia without me. I'm going to stay right here on the ground, like the good Lord intended."

"Indonesia has ground too, you know," Jonas pointed out.

"Yeah, but that's in the way."

"Look," Jonas said, his voice growing heavy with impatience, "I'll push you over that bridge if I have to," he said, stepping behind Twist.

"Get away from me, you maniac!" Twist yelped, leaping to the other side of the archway.

Jonas gave a sigh and pulled his goggles off. "I'm sorry Twist, but you give me no choice," he said, stepping closer. Twist felt the heat in his neck take on its buzzing sensation again as he came well within reach.

"Now, just a minute!" Twist closed his eyes tightly and clung to the wall with one arm, swatting the other blindly through the air, in the general direction of Jonas.

Nevertheless, he felt a small motion at his waistcoat pocket and then sensed Jonas move quickly away. Realization struck him before he could even open his eyes to confirm his suspicion. He stared at Jonas in total shock and dismay as the other man stood halfway over the bridge. He was holding Twist's pocket watch out in front of him by its chain, with a sorrowful expression on his face.

"You bloody damned traitor," Twist hissed as darkly as his small voice would allow.

"Come on," Jonas said, reluctantly. "I wouldn't drop it, but I'll keep it if you don't come and take it from me."

"I hate you," Twist hissed, stepping to the edge of the bridge.

"I know, I'm sorry," Jonas said, stepping backward toward the air ship.

"I'm not going to forgive you for this," Twist snapped, glaring daggers at him.

It took him a moment to realize that Jonas's eyes were still uncovered as he stared into them. As he watched, Jonas's eye color shifted from their natural green to a softly glowing, azure blue. A flicker of confusion danced over Jonas's face as he stared back at Twist, not obviously affected by the visual contact.

"What the hell?" Jonas breathed in quiet disbelief, still staring into Twist's eyes.

"Why aren't you looking away?" Twist asked, his voice still hard.

"It's not...I don't have to," Jonas said softly. His eyes took on a soft lilac color. "Twist I can see you. Just you. Right now. What the hell is going on?" he asked, his words taking on the color of fear.

"What do you mea—" Twist began to ask until Jonas closed the gap between them in a rush and then reached out to take hold of Twist's arm. "No! What are you doing?" Twist yelped, trying to move away. Jonas was faster, and his hand gripped firmly over Twist wrist.

Twist braced for a vision, or for a strange and enormous white explosion, but none of it happened. The warmth at the back of his neck rose in a wave and crashed over his whole body while thin white fog billowed in his mind, before both fell away harmlessly to leave nothing but a light-headed glimmer at the edges of his vision and a faint, blurry sort of buzz in the air.

"What the hell?" Twist breathed, staring at Jonas wide eyed.

"What's the hold up?" Cybele's voice asked from the airship.

"Come on," Jonas said, turning and dragging Twist along behind him. Twist's breath caught in his throat while his feet hurried to keep up, scurrying over the thin metal and onto the solid wooden deck of the ship. The moment they were both on the deck, Jonas handed Twist back his watch. He didn't let go of his arm. Twist took the watch instantly, sparing Jonas another glare. Jonas watched with hesitance and disbelief still raging in his eyes, as they shifted from lilac to a deeper and darker purple.

Almost immediately after Twist and Jonas got on board, the ropes were all thrown off and the ship began to rise into the sky. They both went to the bow of the ship to get out of the foot traffic while the rest of the crew manned the rigging or went bellow. Quay took the ship's wheel, near the stern.

"Seriously, what's going on?" Jonas asked Twist, looking at him again.

"How long are you going to hold my wrist?" Twist asked him back.

"Does it hurt?" Jonas asked. "Are you getting anything off this touch? You hand is glowing a little…"

"No," Twist muttered, tugging at his grip and looking away from Jonas's now-piercing, azure-blue eyes. "It does feel really strange, though."

"Why? How?" Jonas asked, trying to catch Twist's eyes again. When he couldn't, he took hold of Twist's chin with his thumb and finger, pulling his gaze back. Twist shivered from head to toe at the feeling of Jonas's warm fingers on his skin. He stared back helplessly into the slowly changing colors of his eyes.

"I've never been touched, without a vision, for as long as I can remember," Twist said quickly when Jonas let go of his chin. "Not in reality, anyway. The princess could touch me, but that was a dream. And her skin was cold."

"Try," Jonas said, staring unblinkingly into him.

"What?"

"Pull at your Sight," Jonas said, taking his other hand

in his own. Jonas's skin felt so warm to Twist in the quickly chilling air that he could hardly focus on anything else in the world. His fingers felt solid, rough, and so much stronger than his own. "Try to get a vision."

"Are you completely mad?" Twist snapped back at him.

The color in Jonas's eyes darkened suddenly, taking on a rich, deep, almost-black purple for only a moment before he took in a sharp breath and snapped his eyes finally closed.

"What is it? Are you all right?" Twist asked.

"Yeah, I just..." Jonas said, blinking his eyes but not looking back yet. "I got something for a second." He glanced up again with a gentle, pale lavender in his eyes, and a light grin on his face. "Are you angry with me right now?" he asked curiously.

"You have simply brilliant deductive skills," Twist spat. "Let go of me," he said, pulling uselessly at Jonas's solid grip.

"Come on, try it," Jonas said, only letting go of Twist's wrist to take both of his hands instead. The new touch made Twist pause. "Please? Just for a second."

Twist glared at him, desperate to keep his mind focused on anything but Jonas's hands. His curiosity screamed at him in bitter frustration, desperate to open his Sight. Twist's thoughts turned to his Sight for only a moment, and his attention dove heedlessly into the soft warmth of Jonas's skin against his own. A vast whiteness, limitless as the sea and bright as the sun, crept into his mind to color every corner of it, but he didn't lose himself in it as he had before. Instead, he thought that he could begin to feel the blood pulsing through Jonas's skin, and he sensed the beating of the other man's heart: quick, excited, and fiercely hopeful.

Sudden and unexpected as a lightning strike from the

empty blue sky around them, a new thought came to him. After a lifetime of distance from every other living being, Twist was holding someone else's hands. Unlike holding Myra in those beautiful dreams, the man before him now was wholly alive. The shock of the concept was enough to bring his awareness back to himself, and to let him realize that those thoughts hadn't been his alone. He pulled sharply without warning and freed his hands to the cool air. The feelings of hope and excitement broke like the thin, colorful film of a soap bubble.

"Did you get anything?" Jonas asked, his blue eyes gleaming in the over-bright sunlight of the higher atmosphere.

"Emotions," Twist said, nodding. "Nothing else."

"So, what then?" Jonas asked, no longer even attempting to hide the excitement from his voice as he spoke very quickly. "We broke our Sights? I haven't tried to use mine since we woke up in Hong Kong. Have you? I wonder if we'll respond like this to everyone."

"No, my Sight still works like it always did," Twist said, jumping into the conversation when Jonas took a breath. "I touched my watch and didn't notice anything strange."

"But that's a thing. It's not alive," Jonas said thoughtfully. "One of us should try using our Sight on a person."

"Have fun," Twist said with a forced smile. "I'm not testing myself on any of them," he said, gesturing to the figures that still moved on the deck behind them.

Jonas took a breath in through his teeth, with a nervous expression. "Good point."

The ravenous, electric tension of their discovery began to fade once they had found the limits of their new personal borders. Even when Jonas wasn't actually touching him, though, Twist still felt a ghost of his touch on his skin like indelible fingerprints—as if Jonas had left a mark on him that no one else could see. The feeling was so new to him that Twist was left off balance in the deepest level of his spirit.

Glancing over the side of the deck, Twist found even more reason to feel lost in the sky. Puffy white clouds surrounded them as the airship sailed out of the dusty mist that sat low over Hong Kong harbor, and up into the endless blue sky. He saw nothing but open ocean below them, all the way out to the horizon; where the deep blue of the sea melted into the pale-blue haze at the edge of the sky. Twist felt the speed of the airship's flight in his bones. The sun beat down heavily on his back and stung at his eyes with all of its considerable might. He felt the enormous girth of the Earth far below him and the endless sky above. He felt his own fragile form surrounded and saturated by things so much larger than he was.

And it felt just like free fall.

Once the airship was sailing at a comfortable altitude, swaying gently on the gusts that rose off the sea, Quay left the wheel to guide Twist down into the cargo hold. There, in the dim, low-ceilinged belly of the ship, lay Myra's clockwork puppet in relatively the same condition it had been in when Twist last saw it. The limbs lay at its sides in gleaming perfection, while the body sat half open and still bearing the signs of damage and time on its skin. There was a simple cloth underneath it, making a sort of bed out of the rugged-looking wooden crates. Her dark-maroon wire hair hung like a waterfall off the side of the crate, still untangled and gleaming gently. Twist found his own tools in a disordered pile with the last free parts of the puppet that he hadn't yet replaced, but the crystal was absent.

Looking down at the still, cold, metal body, Twist saw only a shadow of the enchanting princess whom he'd seen in his dreams. Without her ghost looking on from the empty shadows in the cargo hold, without the palace crumbling into memory around it, the puppet looked much less like her.

When his fingers fell lightly on the metal above the puppet's exposed navel, his mind filled once again with damage and memories. Because she was a dancer, the delicate workings inside the body were vastly complex to give better flexibility to the thin, interlocking sheets of metal that made up the skin. The violent tumble that had broken the crystal had tangled and dislodged much of the fine inner workings.

"I assume you'll be all right?" Quay asked. "Is

everything there?"

Twist jerked at the sound of his voice and looked to him quickly, having forgotten totally about the man's presence. Jonas stood beside him as well, looking at the puppet quietly with uncovered eyes that seemed to glow much more brightly in the dim light.

"Yes," Twist said. "I have everything I need."

"Good," Quay said with a smile. "Come along, Jonas," he said, turning.

"I'll stay, thanks," Jonas said, not moving.

"No, you'll come with me," Quay said. Both Jonas and Twist looked to him curiously.

"No, you'll leave me the hell alone," Jonas said back quietly.

A flicker of something dark and silent moved through the pirate's eyes. "Your friend is doing his part," he said, gesturing to Twist. "It's your turn to do the same. I need you to come look at some things."

"We're already on a job, here," Jonas said, nodding at the clockwork puppet. "How many treasures do you plan to chase after at once?"

Quay looked to Twist. "Do you need his help to finish the repairs?"

"Not, exactly..." Twist toned slowly. Jonas seemed to ready a response, but Quay cut him off.

"Twist is not going anywhere," Quay said. "You can see him again in a little while. And obsession isn't attractive, you know."

"I'm not obsessed!" Jonas snapped instantly.

"Oh?" Quay asked back, his voice still soft. "Did I touch a raw nerve, there?"

"I'll touch your raw nerve," Jonas hissed.

"This is childish," Quay said with a sigh. "You're not nearly as stupid as you're acting. If you want to fight me, then just say so. I'd be more than happy to resume our sparring matches. As I recall, you were getting quite good with a sword. But just now, I need your help."

Twist watched silently as the pirate's words slowly broke down Jonas's defenses until he was left with nothing but a vaguely bitter curve to his mouth.

"Now, we should leave you to get to work," Quay said to Twist. "Come along, Jonas," he said, turning to the stairs.

While Twist watched, Jonas and Quay both disappeared up the stairs. At the last moment, Twist saw a note of frustration on Jonas's face. Now alone in the dim, quiet, cargo hold, Twist turned back to the puppet and resumed his work.

After a long day of diligent work in the cluttered and dim cargo hold of the pirate airship, Twist returned to the bow on the open deck as the sun began to finally slip into the western ocean. His fingers were sore from overwork, his neck was stiff no matter how he tried to stretch it loose, and his mind felt numb from so many hours of using his exhausted Sight. Without Aazzi or Arabel to pull him away for moments of rest, or the constant presence of Myra watching him from the shadows, the already intricate work had only grown even more tedious. Twist now realized that Jonas also hadn't returned to him, even once.

Twist crossed his arms and leaned heavily on the high railing at the bow of the airship, watching the gleaming, white capped, sapphire sea pass below the burnt-orange dying sky, and tried to work out just how far away from home he was.

"You finally got a break?" Jonas asked, walking up beside him. Lost in his thoughts, Twist hadn't noticed him approach, and jerked slightly at the sound of his voice, turning to look over his shoulder. Unexpectedly, a touch of bitterness wafted into Twist's thoughts, finally seeing him again.

"I'm almost done, so I'll leave it for tonight," he sighed, looking back to the sea when Jonas came to stand at his side.

"Almost done?" Jonas asked lightly. "So, might you be finished tomorrow, then?"

Twist gave a shrug. His thoughts shifted to the gnawing pang of bitterness that seemed to build slowly in the pit of his stomach. Maybe it wasn't bitterness after all, but some other uncomfortable sensation. A cold breeze wafted up over the deck, sending a soft chill down his neck and he shook his head to release the tension of it. Somehow, the feeling seemed strange to him as well.

"Well, they say we'll be over the islands by midday tomorrow," Jonas said, turning to look at Twist and lean his side against the rail. "I'm sure you can complete the puppet in time."

"It hardly seems to matter anymore," Twist said softly, "now that the princess isn't there to watch me. I got rather used to her, you know."

"You got used to a ghost?" Jonas asked with a smirk. "You're a morbid one, you know that?" Something in his voice sounded odd enough to catch Twist's drifting attention, like a tiny snag on silk. "Is that why you want to keep that puppet for yourself?" Jonas asked curiously. "Is it because you like having a dead girl around?"

Twist looked up at Jonas silently. Jonas didn't flinch even for the merest moment when their eyes met. The slightly taunting smile on his face faded as Twist watched.

"Well, whatever," Jonas said, turning away to look over the side of the railing. "But if you've got a plan to steal it away from these pirates when it's done, don't forget to include me." He looked back to Twist with a knowing light in his clear, green eyes and a slight curl on his lips. "We're friends, right?" he asked leadingly.

In a single flashing moment, Twist realized that the usual warmth of Jonas's presence was missing from the back of his neck. He reached up to rub at his neck, but his chilled fingers gave him a shiver.

"You all right?" Jonas asked.

"I'm cold," Twist breathed, pushing gently at the space where the warmth should have been. Just as in

Hong Kong, he found the buzzing sensation buried deep in the back of his mind. It felt as if Jonas was a fair distance away from him, and not standing just beside him.

Jonas gave a small, mirthless laugh. "Then go inside," he said unkindly. Twist's eyes snapped to his quickly but, search as he might, he could find no sign of a glow or shifting color within them.

"Vane?" Twist breathed hesitantly.

"What?" Jonas asked lightly, though a flicker rushed through his eyes for an instant.

Twist turned back to lean on the railing and scooted himself a foot away. "Go away."

"Ah, come on," the man who looked like Jonas said with a sigh. "Are you going into another mood on me?"

"Stop looking like Jonas, and leave me alone," Twist said, not looking at him.

"Huh," Jonas's voice remarked. "How'd you know?" Vane's voice asked as he stepped closer to Twist, now back in the first form Twist had seen him wear. "Did you see my tail?"

"No, and I'm not telling you how I knew," Twist said.

"Why not?" Vane asked, falling into a noisy whine.

"I'm not going to just give you something you could use against me," Twist snapped, shooting him a nasty look.

"You'd be surprised how many people do," Vane said with a wicked smile.

"Isn't there someone else you could go and bother?" Twist asked, dropping his forehead against his crossed arms on the railing. "I'm tired. Leave me alone."

"But I like bothering you," Vane whispered into his ear from only a breath away.

Anger burned through Twist so quickly—hot and electric like fire racing up his spine—that it stole a breath

from him. He spun a step away from Vane and pulled
back a fist before he realized what he was doing. His
shock managed to stop him, and he held still while
Vane's eyebrows shot up in surprise.

"You have teeth?" Vane asked brightly, grinning
now. "I had no idea."

"Leave him the hell alone!" Jonas's real voice
bellowed from farther up the deck. He rushed in to stand
between Vane and Twist. "What's wrong with you?" he
snarled, reaching out to shove Vane back a step—his
black goggles were firmly in place over his eyes, but his
aim was still perfect.

"We were only talking!" Vane spat back, re-taking
the step to come nose to nose with Jonas. "What's wrong
with *you*? Afraid I'd steal your boyfriend?"

Jonas's fist came back quickly, but Twist could
almost feel it move before he saw the motion, and he
reached out just as quickly to catch Jonas's arm. The
same warm wave crashed over Twist again when he
touched him, and once again fell away harmlessly. In its
wake, however, Twist realized that the rage he'd felt a
moment ago hadn't been his own at all.

"Stop," Twist said, smooth and solid, when Jonas
turned to him in the jerk against his sudden grip. "He's
just an idiot, and I'd much rather you weren't handcuffed
to anything again."

Jonas's jaw tightened, but he said nothing. He swung
his arm down sharply, freeing it before turning back to
Vane. "Bugger off," he snapped, nodding off of the side.

Vane gave an impressed whistle. "He's got you
wrapped right round his little finger, doesn't he?" Vane
purred slickly with a dark smile.

"One more word out of you and you'll wake up
tomorrow morning missing something furry," Jonas said
back with a dark smile of his own.

"There a problem, boys?" Cybele yelled to them from where she stood near a trap door to the lower deck, with a rather large rifle lying lazily across her wide shoulder.

"No," Vane said with a suddenly pleasant lilt. "Nothing at all."

"Has she got a gun?" Jonas asked very quietly.

"The big one," Vane responded just as quietly.

"We were just having a chat about this fine weather," Jonas called to her brightly.

"Play nicely together, or I'll have to separate you two," Cybele said flatly. "As a matter of fact, Vane, come help me with the supper," she added, heading down into the lower deck.

"Oh, do I have to?" Vane whined, though he moved immediately to follow her.

"And I thought that the *Vimana* crew was odd," Twist said, watching them both disappear under the deck.

"I really hate that guy," Jonas said. He then looked to Twist. "I'm sorry I didn't come back to visit you. Quay had me busy the whole day." To Twist's surprise, the tiny ghost of bitterness in his heart melted away at Jonas's words.

Twist gave him a light smile. "You shouldn't let Vane get to you," he said. "He's just doing things to get you all worked up."

"I know," Jonas said, turning to lean his back against the railing with a heavy sigh. "You know, I really didn't realize how much I don't like these people until I got away from them for a few days," he said thoughtfully. "Not that life on the *Vimana* was any better, mind."

"There's got to be somewhere you could be happy," Twist said, frowning to himself as he tried to think of one. As large as the world seemed to be, now that he'd seen so much of it, he couldn't believe that there wasn't somewhere in it for Jonas.

Jonas put on a smile and slipped his goggles down, letting them hang around his neck as he looked up to the sky through the rigging. "The only place I really like is up there," he said, waving a hand generally at the new stars in the darkest part of the sky.

"You want to live in outer space?" Twist asked, looking after his gesture.

"Not too bright, plenty of open space, and no one alive to deal with," Jonas said as if these things described absolute perfection.

"I thought you wanted to be closer to people," Twist said, watching the starts appear, one at a time in the deepest part of the blue. "I thought you hated being cut off by your Sight." Jonas's gaze fell to him with a warm weight and a subtle electric unrest that poured down his spine. Twist turned to find a new coldness in his now pale-green eyes.

"Says who?"

"Says you," Twist said back, watching him curiously. "You look into me now, every time our eyes meet. Did you think it was only one way?" Jonas looked down and shifted on the rail as if it were suddenly uncomfortable.

"Has anyone ever told you that you can be a little too direct from time to time?" Jonas asked, handling each word carefully.

"I don't usually talk to people," Twist said with a shrug as he returned to the rail himself, leaning on it to watch the horizon boil into red and gold as the sun began to sink below the waves. The sea had turned black with shadows, under the last gilded waves of sunset.

"So, you're never..." Jonas began to ask, but his words fell away. Twist guessed the rest of his question, but waited for him to finish it. Jonas turned to look over the side with him. "I mean, in London, didn't you have friends there?" he said instead.

"No," Twist answered easily. "I have customers that come back sometimes if they have more than one broken clock. Some days I might see people in the market who I've seen before. But I try not to go out if I can stay in. I usually try to stay away from people."

"And that minor contact is all you want?"

"Sure," Twist said, looking to him curiously. "No one ever believes me when I say this, but I'm really not lonely. I like the quiet."

Jonas made a thoughtful sound, his eyes shifting from pale to a mossy green as he looked back at Twist.

"See, you wouldn't be happy alone, after all," Twist said, smiling lightly. "You think I'm strange for saying that I was?"

"Oh you're strange," Jonas said quickly. "I already knew that." Twist shook his head and looked away. "The only time I've ever seen passion in you was when you were talking about a machine, after all."

"You've got your stars, and I've got my clocks," Twist said to the open air.

Jonas made no more remark after that point, but simply stood beside him, lost in his thoughts while Twist strolled listlessly through his own. As the last rays of daylight fell from the sky, with a flash of brilliantly golden light at the horizon, Twist found that his heart felt calmer in that moment than it had in ages. His fears fell from his tired mind as it rested on more pleasant ground. Though the air was turning cold in front of the night, the warmth at his neck was enough to keep him comfortable.

In his relaxed state, a strange thought came to him suddenly. For the briefest instant, he wondered what it might be like to move close enough to Jonas to feel the warmth of his skin again. The concept startled him enough to bring him back to his senses, but left him wondering where it had come from. As he struggled to make sense of it, he failed to notice Jonas move.

Jonas's hand rested on Twist's back as he stepped closer to Twist, bringing a pocket of warmer air with him. Twist held totally still under the touch, unsure how else to respond. The gesture seemed casual on Jonas, meaningless and empty, as if he hardly noticed that he was doing it at all.

"It's getting cold," Jonas said to him as he took in a calm breath. "Why don't we head down to the kitchen? Cybele should be finished cooking soon anyway."

"Sure," Twist managed to say without letting his voice betray him. Jonas's hand slipped off of him when they both turned to walk towards the trap door.

"Oh, but be careful," Jonas said suddenly, drifting closer as they walked, and laying an arm across Twist's shoulders that halted both of their steps. "Cybele is really touchy about her cooking. It's not bad, but she'd better think that you absolutely love it," he said gravely, looking at Twist with cool blue eyes that flashed gently to a dusty green.

"Oh?" was all that Twist could muster as he began to notice the subtle pulsing of Jonas's heart, so very near to him. Despite his best efforts, his voice came out a bit too high.

"I mean it," Jonas said, pulling away almost instantly and leading him on again. "Don't forget to mention that it's good, or she might take offense and throw a pot at you. Or a knife," he added, more gravely still.

"Got it," Twist nodded, his voice back under control now that Jonas wasn't wrapped around him any longer.

One deck below, near the back of the ship, Jonas and Twist found most of the others gathered together around a long wooden table that was covered with food. There was roast chicken with chestnuts, baked haddock in celery sauce, apple fritters, julienned-vegetable soup, mashed potatoes, braised turnips, and strawberries with whipped cream.

Each place at the table was set in a dignified manner: cutlery was placed to each side, there were both water and wine glasses, and a white cloth napkin was placed on each plate in a tin holder. A vase of colorful flowers sat at the center of the table, while a gold-and-crystal chandelier hung overhead, glowing brightly with gas-light.

"Ah, Mr. Twist," Quay said brightly, a jug of red wine in one hand and a glass in the other, "I was just about to send someone to fetch you. The meal is almost ready. Please, have a seat. We can't start without you, you know."

Twist stepped closer and found an empty seat beside Idris, who was busy spreading butter on a piece of bread. Twist couldn't help but stare. It seemed entirely strange for a magical djinn to eat bread and butter, though he couldn't exactly decide why.

"This is all British food," Jonas said, looking over the offerings as he sat at Twist's other side. "Where did you get it all?"

"You can get anything in Hong Kong," Quay said, coming around the table to fill Twist's and Jonas's glasses as well. "I thought Twist might like a little taste of home."

"This was all made because of me?" Twist asked,
wide eyed. The scents wafting up from the warm food
before him were all just as familiar to him as the wet,
sooty, aroma of London's cobblestone streets.

Quay smiled down at him through the black tattooed
lines on his face. "Of course. To celebrate our new found
friendship."

"I love new people," Vane said, smiling widely at the
roast chicken.

"I hate new people," Cybele grumbled, walking to the
table from another room with a large glass trifle bowl full
of layer upon layer of cake, cream, fruit, and nuts. "It's
always so much blasted work."

"But you do a fabulous job of it all," Quay said,
beaming at her.

"Oh, I simply love trifle," Idris said excitedly to
Twist, under his breath.

Twist did his best not to dwell on the absurdity of his
dinner companions, and instead tried to just enjoy the
familiar tastes. Everything was perfectly as he expected
it to be, and much of it was exceedingly delicious. Once
everyone had eaten their fill of the tasty meal—and
showered Cybele in compliments throughout—the plates
were all cleared away so that the trifle could be served,
along with cups of steaming hot, black coffee and cream.

As Twist sipped at his coffee—which was darker and
richer than any he'd had before, with light notes of
chocolate and cinnamon—he felt himself relax more
deeply than he had since he'd left London. He hadn't
thought of food very often on his journey, but the simple
pleasure of comfortable and understandable tasty treats
filled him up more completely than the food itself ever
could.

"Cybele, my dear, you are a master," Quay said,

finally tossing his napkin onto his now-empty trifle bowl.

"This cream needs more sugar," she muttered in response, poking at her own bowl with her spoon.

"It does not, I assure you," Idris said as he scraped up the very last bits of cream from his bowl with a finger. "Most people make trifle too sweet. But you, Cybele, understand the true nature of the animal."

"Yeah?" she asked back skeptically. Her eyes moved to Twist. "What do you think? You're a limey."

"It's very nice," Twist said instantly. "If I had a larger stomach, I'd ask for more."

"Heathen," Cybele muttered, but Twist saw the shadow of a grin on her lips.

"Well," Vane said with some finality, "I'm going for a walk under the moon. Care to join me?" he asked the forever-silent Jiran. She nodded vaguely and they both rose to leave.

"Who's cleaning up, then?" Cybele asked the room.

"I did it last time," Quay said.

"And I did it before that," Vane offered before walking away to the stairs with Jiran.

"Idris, I wish the dishes were clean," Cybele said the djinn.

Idris put on an unamused face.

"Come on, I made your trifle for ya," Cybele said, glaring at him.

"Fine, whatever," Idris said flatly. He waved one hand out over the table and then snapped his fingers. The dishes and cutlery all vanished into wafts of whispering purple smoke. Idris then pointed a finger at Cybele. "But only because of the trifle," he said before he stood and walked out of the room.

As the others each got up and left the table, Twist began to feel the full weight of the day pressing down on his slight shoulders. When Jonas got to his feet as well, giving himself a light stretch, Twist moved to follow him.

"Mr. Twist," Quay said, standing as well, "could I have a word before you go?"

"A word?" Twist echoed.

"I have something I'd like to show you, is all," Quay said, smiling gently.

"I'll find you later," Jonas said, giving Twist's shoulder a pat. Twist turned at his touch instantly to see nothing nervous or warning in Jonas's eyes.

"All right," he said, nodding.

"This way, please," Quay said pleasantly, leading Twist farther towards the stern through a heavy wooden door.

The room at the very back of the ship was just as large as the dining room, but much more lavishly decorated. There were oil paintings on the walls in gilded frames, Persian rugs strewn across the floor, golden gas lamps set about the room and burning brightly, a freestanding globe in a wrought-iron cage in one corner, and a cello made of gleaming red wood set in the other. A large wooden desk sat near the wide bank of windows that filled the far wall. A high-backed red velvet chair sat behind it, facing the door, and another, smaller, chair sat in front of it.

"I know you must be tired after all the work you did today," Quay said, walking towards the desk. "So I won't keep you for long." Quay sat on the edge of the desk as Twist came to stand near him.

"How can I help you?" Twist asked, his eyes flitting over the ornate flare of the room.

"It comes to my attention," Quay began, his voice smooth and curling lightly into his accent, "that you are not a man of this world." Twist looked to him sharply but said nothing. "You're from the ground. You don't like to travel. You've never been anywhere until now, and although you are splendidly resourceful, you don't seem to be a man of violence."

"I'm a clock maker," Twist said flatly.

"Quite," Quay said, grinning. "But we are now bound for a potentially dangerous place. And I fear that you are vastly underprepared."

"How dangerous?" Twist asked, holding back the uncertainty in his voice.

"Magical crystal caves in Indonesia have a nasty way of being full of creatures," Quay said lightly. "Although I have no intention of putting you in harm's way without reason, it might not be avoidable."

"Creatures?"

"You know," Quay said, glancing off to his memory. "Goblins, trolls, crazy civilization-hating weirdoes, basilisks, that sort of thing. We won't know exactly until we get there."

"Those creatures actually exist?" Twist asked slowly.

"Of course they exist," Quay said, smiling brightly. "You'll find that everything exists if you look into enough dark holes."

Despite his efforts, a flicker of doubt and apprehension flashed across Twist's face.

"So, I got you a gift before we left Hong Kong," Quay said, turning around to open a long, thin, black wooden box that sat on the desk.

Twist looked around Quay to see what he thought was a sword at first, lying inside the box on a bed of deep-blue velvet. It was a black walking stick with a shining silver hilt that was ringed near the top with a thin band of sapphire-colored glass under a slightly rounded silver cap. A band of black leather sat just below the silver hilt, with a small switch set into the bottom edge of it. There was also a thin silver coil around the tip of the long, slender, black cane. The whole piece shined in the

gas-light without so much as a single scratch or
fingerprint anywhere on it.

"This has never been touched by any human hand,
save the artist himself," Quay said, smiling down at it
proudly. "I made sure of it. You shouldn't get any visions
off of it. Go ahead," he said, gesturing for Twist to take
it from the case.

Twist hesitated for a moment, still awed by the
impressive perfection of it, but then reached out and
touched the smooth, cool, almost reflective black of the
walking stick's shaft. His Sight sent ripples of
information across his mind, but no emotional visions
met his senses. He closed his hand on it and lifted it out
of the case, finding it to be heavier than he'd first
expected. Holding it now, he instantly understood the
extra weight. It was filled with tiny workings that took
Twist a few moments to make sense of, even with the
help of his Sight.

"It's balanced like a sword," Quay said while Twist
let the rest of the information sink in. "And it's
reinforced with coiled steel along the whole length. Of
course, the coil has a double purpose," he added, meaning
to continue.

Twist finally made sense of what his Sight was
showing him and pressed a hidden switch at the base of
the hilt. Brilliant electric light shined to life inside the
hilt, beaming out in a rich swath of blue though the
sapphire glass.

"Ah, you found it," Quay said brightly. "It also has
another switch," he began.

Twist turned the light off and then flipped the cane
over to watch the tip as he hit the switch at the edge of
the leather grip, under the hilt. A tiny, white-hot spark of
lightning danced playfully around the shining metal wires
that had only seemed decorative before.

"Well, your Sight sure is handy, isn't it?" Quay said with a smile.

"There is a small weight inside the cane that charges up an electrical battery whenever it moves along the coil," Twist said, staring at the walking stick in wonder. "And the light itself is made by an electric current with no filament to burn out. It's completely self-contained and self-charging. I've never seen technology like this before."

"Well, I'm glad I got what I paid for," Quay said, sitting on the edge of the desk again and smiling at Twist as if fondly. "Do you like it?"

"You're giving this to me?" Twist asked.

"Yes, I am," Quay said.

"Why?"

"You're welcome," Quay said brightly.

"This must have been very expensive," Twist said, looking down at it while his Sight showed him exactly how magnificently it was built.

"That's not important," Quay said with a casual flick of his hand. "I like spending money on my friends. Besides, now you have a weapon with which to defend yourself should the need arise. Do you fence at all?"

"Not...exactly," Twist muttered, searching his memory or a moment when he'd even held a weapon in his hands before.

"Well, no matter," Quay said. "The steel makes it strong enough to use simply for hitting things with, and the shock at the tip would give anyone a nasty bite."

Twist put the tip of the cane down on the carpet between his feet and found that the cap at the top end of the hilt fit very comfortably in the palm of his hand; the height of it was just right to feel relaxing to his shoulders and wrists. The soft fabrics and perfect tailoring of his new clothes were still subtly comfortable, even after the length of the day. The tastes of dinner—the one that had been made especially for him—lingered on his tongue while the ship around him swayed gently on the night air.

"You are very good at this," Twist said softly.

"What was that?" Quay asked, leaning closer.

"Thank you," Twist said more loudly, looking up to him. "I like it very much."

"What's that?" Jonas asked, walking into the cabin that he and Twist shared.

Sitting against the headboard of one of the two beds in the small room, his legs crossed on the soft, thick bed covers, Twist rolled his new cane around in his fingers.

"A present from our dear captain," Twist said, not looking up. The silver on it gleamed brightly even in the amber dim of the one oil lamp on the small table between the two beds. Moonlight spilled cold and white through the two square windows in the outer wall onto the pale wood of the walls and floor.

"Ah, you got a present too," Jonas said with a knowing tone to his voice. "He gave me these when I joined the crew," he said, tapping the black lenses that sat snugly on his brow. "I was using a pair that I'd painted black, but the paint kept chipping. Very unreliable. These are much better."

Twist nodded thoughtfully. Jonas paused, watching him continue to roll the cane slowly across his knees. Twist felt the weight of his gaze run like warm water down his back.

"Let me guess," Jonas said with a heavy breath. "You feel like you're worth less, now that you've been bought."

Twist looked up at him quickly but said nothing. Jonas's eyes looked like pale opals, glowing softly in the low light.

"Don't feel bad," Jonas said, smiling gently. "Think of it like a job. You're just getting paid in nice clothes, good food, compliments and occasional presents, instead of actual money."

"I don't exactly intend to stay on this ship forever," Twist said.

"Neither do the rest of us," Jonas said with a shrug, walking over to sit on the other bed. "No one on this ship has signed up to stay for any particular amount of time. We're just here as long as it's good to be here. Even so, I know some of them have been with Quay for years now."

"But you said you hate them," Twist said, frowning. "Why would you want to stay?"

"The food's good," Jonas said, counting on his fingers as he spoke, "I've got a nice place to sleep. I get to see the world without having to see my family. Whenever we do a job I get a nice fat cut of the takings. I randomly get new things for just being around..."

"Yes, I get the idea," Twist said with a sigh. "The whole thing still makes me nervous."

"That goes away if you ignore it long enough," Jonas said with a hollow smile.

Twist and Jonas didn't talk very much more as they each got ready to sleep. The day had been long for each of them, and sleep beckoned. But while Jonas found it easy to drift away—his soft breathing running deep in the silence—Twist had trouble getting his thoughts to settle down. Eventually, he had no choice but to return to his pocket watch.

He took it from his waistcoat pocket and then curled up in the heavy, warm covers of his bed, holding the watch in his hand on the pillow before his tired, itchy eyes. When he opened the face, the quiet memory of his home rushed out to swallow up his sleepy senses. This time, however, the dim, quiet, attic room under the London gray, felt farther away than it ever had before. The sheer quiet and calm of it seemed so foreign to him now, that it chilled him even as he was under the warm blankets.

Twist closed his eyes and listened to his clocks ticking from the other side of the world, and felt himself begin to slip slowly into sleep. As he lost control of his own attention, he felt the warm, steady, gentle pulse at the back of his neck as well. Just before he fell totally from the conscious world, he recognized the familiar sensation as the steady beating of Jonas's heart, while he slept peacefully in the darkness.

The next morning, Twist awoke to find lush, dark-green forests and mountains gliding under the airship's shadow. When he asked, Jonas told him that the land below them was likely a place called Cambodia—which Twist had never heard of—and that they were now most of the way to their destination. After a quick but delightful breakfast and many more compliments to Cybele, he returned to the cargo hold to finally finish the repairs to the clockwork puppet. The only work that still needed to be done, however, was the most delicate and difficult of all; the disentangling of the tiny levers and sensors that transferred the vibrations of the central crystal to the rest of the body.

After three hours of diligent work, Twist was almost finished. Just when he stood back to stretch his stiff neck, he heard footsteps on the wood behind him. Turning, he found Idris's empty golden eyes watching him as he came closer.

"How's it coming?" Idris asked lightly.

"I'm getting there," Twist said. Idris looked over the puppet and nodded.

"Machines confuse me to no end," he said. "They're so complicated."

"Do you still have the crystal?" Twist asked, careful to keep his words light.

"Oh sure," Idris said, looking up to him. "Do you need it?"

"Can I just touch it for a moment?" Twist asked, trying desperately not to let his soft voice weaken.

Idris held out an open, empty hand. A purple mist

collected on his palm, growing into the shape of the crystal. With a strange little pop, the mist solidified into the crystal itself. He held it out to Twist easily. Twist moved one fingertip gently over the edge of the crystal before he took it off the djinn's palm, fearful that his Sight might shock him enough to drop it.

He felt the quiet, contented rest of Myra's sleeping spirit inside. The essence of her soul wafted slowly around the crystalline structure like living smoke, preserved and perfectly untouched inside the safety of the crystal. Her sheer peace was staggering. Twist let out a long, low breath, feeling her calm pour into his own heart.

"You look like a man with a wish," Idris said, smiling at him in gold.

"What?" Twist asked, blinking his eyes clear and wrenching his attention off the crystal to look at him.

"I haven't granted a good wish in a while," Idris said wistfully. "You look to me like you're brewing up a good one."

"But..." Twist toned, thinking quickly. "If you're a genie, aren't there rules about making wishes? What could I ask for?"

"Anything entertaining," Idris said with a shrug. "I can choose which wishes I grant, and I'm not granting any boring ones. That means no huge piles of money, no wishing yourself king of anything, and no simple transportation wishes. I've done those things to death."

Twist nodded as he hurriedly thought over any of the things he might actually want. Going home and being done with all pirates was chief among them. "So, if I wished to be sent home to London with this puppet, or even to the *Vimana*, would that entertain you at all?"

Idris's face washed over with a shade of disappointment. "Not in the least. How is that fun for me? If you're going to wish to be sent somewhere, at least think of some place interesting, like Mars, or Never Land, or something."

"Mars?" Twist gasped. "Heavens no. Isn't it crawling with strange alien things?"

"Care to find out?" Idris asked, grinning and rubbing his hands together eagerly.

"No," Twist said with clear certainty. Idris gave a sigh. "I don't mean to be rude, but I'm sure you must be the strangest person I'll ever have occasion to meet," Twist said, to which Idris's golden smile grew and deepened.

"You really need to get out more," he said smoothly. "I've met things in this world far stranger than I."

"With luck, I won't," Twist said. "I don't want to be made a liar."

Idris laughed and shook his pure white head. "I like you," he said once he'd caught a breath. "Learn to wish a little more elaborately and you and I could have a wonderful future."

"Well, for the present," Twist said, anxious to change the subject away from the possibility of that, "I suppose you'll want this back now?" he asked, looking down to Myra's heart in his hands.

"You can hold on to it, if you want to," Idris said lightly.

"Really?" Twist asked, looking up to him quickly. "I assumed you and Quay would want it out of my reach."

"Quay intimated as much," Idris said, nodding, "but at the moment I feel like making you happy instead." Something in his voice caught Twist's attention—an inference that he could only guess at.

"I wish I could keep this with me, without Quay knowing about it," Twist said.

"Ah, now that's a bit more interesting of a wish," Idris

said brightly. He reached out to the crystal and touched it with the tip of one white finger, and then raised his hand and snapped his fingers. Instantly, the crystal broke into silver smoke on Twist's palm, before recoalescing into a tiny version of itself that was set on a long, silver chain, as a pendant. "Done," Idris said as Twist stared at the item in his hands in total bewilderment.

"What...did you do?" Twist asked. His Sight showed the full, original form of the crystal still in his hands, while his eyes showed him the pendant and chain. The extreme paradox of it made his eyes water.

"It's just a bit of camouflage," Idris said easily. "To all the world, the crystal is now a great deal smaller. But, if you break that pendant off of its chain, then the crystal will return to its own form whether I'm involved or not. Wear it under your shirt, and no one will know."

"Thank you," Twist said, looking up to Idris in disbelief. "But, if Quay finds out that you gave me this, won't he think that you've betrayed him?"

"But I haven't," Idris said brightly. "He never actually asked me not to give it to you."

"But you said..." Twist said, pointing at him with his free hand.

"I said that he intimated," Idris said. "I'm a magical creature. We never play fair. It's simply no fun at all."

"I see," Twist said, more for the conversation's sake than for truth.

"We'll be near Indonesia soon now," Idris said. "You might want to finish this before we get there," he said, looking to the puppet.

"Yes, I do," Twist said, lifting the silver chain over his head to hang around his neck. His Sight could make no sense whatsoever out of this movement, though his fingers had no trouble with it. He tucked the tiny crystal pendant under his collar so that it was fully hidden, hanging near his own heart.

"Well, I'll leave you to it then," Idris said pleasantly
as he turned to leave. "Let me know if you think of any
more interesting wishes," he called over his shoulder
before climbing the stairs up to the next deck.

Twist looked down to the nearly finished puppet and
stretched his wrists as he thought through the last of the
work that needed to be done. As he reached back into the
inner workings of the puppet, his Sight filled his mind
with everything he needed to make the repairs, but it also
pulsed a steady stream of quiet, silent, peace straight into
his heart from the crystal pendant against his skin.

After what felt like a very long time, that had
inexplicably passed in an instant, Twist's hands finally
stopped working. He looked down at the puppet, now
gleaming, flawless, and perfect to the eye. Every piece of
it glowed in the sunlight that streamed in through the
small porthole windows. The copper skin and silver
notes gleamed with a polish so bright that it looked once
again untouched by time. Every joint and moving piece
was free and pliable, ready to move at the spirit's slightest
whim. When Twist reached out again to touch her, he
felt every single piece within, each in its rightful place,
polished and repaired as if they had never even been
used.

The clockwork machine was flawless and ready to
run, but nothing moved. The puppet was deathly still, as
if heedless of its own potential. Twist carefully replaced
the pink silks that had been left aside, covering the metal
body discreetly, and bound the wire hair into a tail as he
had seen Myra wear it in his vision. Looking down at her
now, Twist saw the echo of Myra's true beauty in every
detailed shape of the puppet. It was clear to him that the
man who had built it had loved her deeply. Twist had
seen his care and attention in every single part of the

terribly complex and artful creation.

"Twist!" Jonas's voice called as Twist heard footsteps on the boards above his head. He turned to the opening as Jonas came half way down the stairs with a smile. "We finally passed Malaysia, and Indonesia is in sight. Come up and see." He paused, looking around Twist at the puppet. "Is it finished?" he asked, coming the rest of the way down and walking closer.

"Only just," Twist said on a heavy breath. "I've never worked on anything nearly as complex as that. For a while I thought it might take the rest of my life."

"It looked bloody difficult," Jonas said, looking over the shining metal skin. "Nice work, though. It looks like she's just asleep. She could get up and go dancing any moment."

Twist nodded, smiling over his work.

"Well, it won't be long until she can, now," Jonas said, turning his smile to Twist. "Come on, let's go watch the approach," he said, reaching out to take hold of Twist's shoulders, turn him to the stairs, and give him a playful shove.

Twist let him do so, only slightly twitching at the effects of his touch now, and walked with him up to the top deck. The piercing sunlight of high atmosphere struck him the moment they stepped into it. Thankfully, Twist had his new dark-blue-lensed, silver goggles waiting, hanging round his neck by the leather strap. He pulled them on to dim the light and was surprised by how brilliantly they worked. The deep color of them cut the over-bright sunlight back enough to see easily, while bathing the world in a rich and vibrant blue that made the sky appear to glow in pure color.

Twist rushed to keep up with Jonas as he hurried to the bow of the ship. They both looked out over the edge at an island unlike any Twist had even seen. A huge expanse of heavily forested land lay before them, reaching out into the ocean with open arms, in the shape of a crescent moon. Other larger islands appeared in the vast distance behind it, off on the horizon.

As they watched, long, thin, pale beaches appeared out of the forests, at the edge of the azure-blue ocean. Palm trees hung over the surf, while tiny handmade villages appeared in among the trees. When the airship began to descend, Twist saw high, jagged, and lush green mountains reach up to them from the forests, giving the large island an even more dynamic face. The air warmed steadily as the ship drifted out of the sky, carrying the rich, moist, exotic scents of innumerable wild living things up to them.

"Welcome to the tropics, Twist," Jonas said brightly. "That sure doesn't look like London, does it?" he added with an elbow bump to Twist's side.

"It's like something out of a story," Twist marveled, unable to keep the grin of pure wonder off his face. "I'd thought people were exaggerating. But it's real, isn't it? Are those real palm trees down there?"

"And you didn't want to leave home," Jonas said, shaking his head.

The airship sailed low over the white-topped, cerulean waves to the left point of the island's arc. Twist saw tall towers made of bamboo standing at the edge of a long, pale beach as if to greet them. Where the land met the crystal-clear, blue water, it appeared in sweeping swaths of pale green and teal under the shifting reflections of pure-white sunlight. As they sailed nearer, the scent of saltwater and jungle rose warmer and warmer on humid air, carrying with it the sound of the gentle waves. For the first time in his life, Twist felt the sudden and decadent urge to run into that warm, colorful, clear water and splash about like a child.

The airship was tied to the bamboo towers, hanging only a few feet over the lightly lapping waves on the inside of the shallow bay, and the crew disembarked instantly. Vane was the first one to run down the creaking bamboo stairs—simply tied together by rough ropes—and down to the long, low pier that hung out over the clear water for a hundred feet from the white beach. Vane, however, didn't seem interested in the land at all. He ran instead to the edge of the pier where the water was still somewhat deep, and then dove in with an effortless arc and a brilliant splash. Following him to the edge of the pier, Jiran laughed to watch him, her usually silent voice surprisingly sweet. Vane's head came back out with a wide smile.

"Come in!" he called to Jiran. "It's so warm..." he purred, diving back down, only to come up just as easily, to smile at her again. The others, meanwhile, finally caught up to Jiran.

"I'm not dressed for swimming," Jiran said, her words striking Twist as quite British in color, as she smiled down at Vane in the water.

"Idris!" Vane called, swimming closer to where the djinn stood on the pier. "I really wish Jiran was wearing a tiny little swimming costume, like the ones some of these island girls wear."

"Don't you dare!" Jiran snapped instantly at Idris.

"But I'd like to see that, too," Idris said, grinning at her.

"I'll second that as well," Jonas said, raising a hand. Quay nodded silently, watching the exchange with great interest.

"Men are all alike," Cybele sighed, crossing her arms.

"If he grants that wish, I won't speak to you for a month," Jiran said coldly to Vane.

"You're not losing much," Jonas said to Vane.

"I'd take that deal," Quay offered. Jiran, meanwhile, was staring daggers down at Vane as he considered his options, hanging onto a loose piece of rope at the edge of the pier to keep himself afloat in the gentle bobbing of the light waves.

"All right, all right," Vane said, disappointment ringing in his heavy voice. "Never mind, Idris," he moaned, diving back down into the water and swimming under the shade of the pier.

"Damn it," Jonas muttered.

"All right, let's get to work," Quay said to everyone. "Once we finish with our chores, we'll all get to play. The weather is so nice, I'm thinking to stay here for a week or two."

Looking up to the sky, Twist saw only a handful of the puffiest, most delicious-looking white clouds he'd ever seen, sailing pleasantly through the perfect blue sky. Smiles broke to light on all of the faces around him, except for Cybele who wrinkled her noise.

"I guess it's not so humid right now," Cybele said, fanning herself with a hand. "It could be worse, I suppose."

None of the others seemed to hear her this time, each one breathing in the beauty around them with big, full, eager breaths.

Quay and his crew split up to ask for information at the various small huts that lined the beach at the jungle's edge. Many of them appeared to be small cafes and restaurants that served refreshments to travelers who arrived at the airship docks, or at the larger sea docks that filled the harbor further down the beach. Cybele told Twist to wait with her and let the others handle things. Apparently, neither of them would be very much help. Listening to her tone, Twist decided not to question her. They both sat at a small cafe table under a tall coconut palm that reached out over the white sand, and sipped at small cups of coffee. As Cybele seemed to be perfectly content to watch the gentle waves in silence, Twist obliged her and made no attempt to draw her into conversation.

Eventually, Vane came to join them, reporting that he hadn't found out anything useful in his search. Twist was surprised to see that he now looked perfectly dry, even after his impulsive swim in the bay.

"I'm magical," Vane said with a shrug in response to Twist's question.

One by one, the others arrived as well; each reporting little in the way of success. When Quay arrived, however, grinning broadly, he announced that he'd found a lead. Someone had told him of a puppet maker who ran a shop in a nearby city, selling magical puppets that seemed to move entirely on their own, as if they were alive. Once everyone had appeared at the cafe under the palms, they set out together to follow Quay's information.

To Twist's considerable surprise, the seemingly

endless and savage jungle that covered the island gave
way to a small but obviously thriving city of huts, with
palm-thatched roofs, that clustered together—in a rough
and very disorganized way—from the edge of the beach,
stretching deep into the jungle and up the nearest large,
jagged, green mountain. The trees, however, seemed to
be trying to retaliate against this intrusion. They grew
tall and wide, as if clawing at the edges of the city to drag
it back in. As the pirate crew walked through the largest,
relatively clear dirt street off the beach, Twist failed to
find a single face in the fairly dense crowd of people that
looked anything but foreign to him.

"Who owns this island?" Twist asked Jonas quietly,
while the natives—all dark skinned with Asian features,
and dressed in colorful clothes of shapes and designs
Twist had trouble identifying—all paused in their present
actions to watch as they passed.

"They do," Jonas said, nodding at the people around
them.

"Well, yes," Twist said quickly. "But this is South
Asia, isn't it? Is this island controlled by England?
Portugal? Or the Dutch, perhaps?"

"Oh," Jonas said, realization dawning. "Well,
technically, Indonesia is under Dutch rule right now, but
that's mostly over in Java. This little island is hardly
important to them."

"So, there isn't a real European presence on this
island?" Twist asked.

"You're off the map, mate," Jonas said with a grin
and a wink. "And I seriously doubt that anyone here
speaks English. You'd better stay with one of us."

Twist looked at him quickly. "You speak a language
other than English?"

Jonas gave a laugh. "You Brits are the weirdest ones
on the planet. Yes, I almost speak about four if you count

Spanish, though I'm much better at French. Then there's Mandarin and just a bit of Arabic. I can usually find someone to talk to."

"That's astounding," Twist said, wide eyed as he tried to imagine learning even one other language. "But what do you mean, 'you British are odd?' Aren't you one of us?"

"I might have been born in London," Jonas explained, "but I grew up in the rest of the world. That country means no more to me than any other. And your people are the only ones who have such an issue with speaking more than one language. In Lebanon everyone learns five as a national standard."

"Where's Lebanon?" Twist asked.

"See what I mean?" Jonas said instantly and then added under his breath, "Bloody imperialists..."

"Bleeding know-it-all sky pirates," Twist mimicked.

"Now just a—"Jonas began with an accusing finger at the ready.

"Gentlemen, if I could draw you away..." Quay called to them from the front of the group. When Twist looked to him, he saw that they had all stopped outside of one of the huts. The front appeared to be open to the street, displaying wares of some kind. Walking closer with him, Jonas stopped suddenly when he saw something on the ground just outside.

"That is a dead cat," he said, staring down with uncovered eyes at a metal cat that sat at the edge of the dirt street.

The cat looked back up at him with red jewel eyes, its thin, articulated metal tail waving lightly back and forth around its paws. Tiny white metal wires hung from its round, shining, copper face like whiskers, and its large ears flicked absently in the light breeze that played down the street. Overcome with curiosity, Twist stepped closer

and crouched down near the cat. He reached out a finger
to touch it, but the cat got to its feet in a smooth, perfectly
feline motion and stepped to the side. It watched him
carefully, while Twist admired the way the thin copper
and silver plates of its skin slid together and apart along
its slender body.

"It's not dead," Twist said, recognizing much of its
movements from Myra's puppet. "I think it's a cat ghost,
held in a metal body."

"That's damned disturbing," Jonas said, still staring at
it with a look of extreme unease.

"Can I chase it?" Vane asked excitedly.

"No," Quay said, peering into the depths of the
strange little shop.

Standing up to look as well, Twist finally saw the
items that the shop was selling. Every wall was layered
deep with bamboo racks of wood, paper, and metal
puppets of every imaginable size and design. The floor
was crowded with the largest puppets, while thin, light,
paper ones hung from the ceiling on strings like the
innumerable leaves of the jungle that hung over the huts.
While many of them appeared to be no more than
ordinary, lifeless puppets, each one was quite elegant and
fascinating on its own. A few of them, however, seemed
almost as complex and refined as the cat did.

As Twist admired one bird-shaped puppet—with
countless individual feathers of gleaming silver over its
round body, and emerald jewel eyes staring blankly into
space—it moved suddenly, opening its golden beak to
release a shrill cry to the air before blinking its eyes
quickly and turning to look in another direction. Twist
was so shocked to see it move among the lifeless forms
that he leaped back a step and collided into Jonas with a
solid thump.

"You see?" Jonas said, his hands falling onto Twist

absently. "This is all bloody creepy!" The moment of
contact from Jonas's hands flashed Twist's Sight with a
numb white fog that lingered at the edges of his mind.
He noticed instantly that his nervousness diminished.

"Wow, you jumped just like a frightened rabbit,"
Vane said, grinning at Twist.

"I didn't know that one was alive!" Twist said,
pointing at the bird puppet as he got himself back into a
dignified position, away from Jonas.

"Hey, can I chase Twist?" Vane asked Quay brightly.

"No!" Twist snapped instantly.

In all the excitement, he'd forgotten about the cat,
which decided at that moment to brush up against his leg
with its slinky metal body. Twist's Sight rushed over his
senses, displaying the complex inner workings of the cat's
clockwork body and the same driving crystal that he had
seen in Myra's puppet. This crystal, however, pulsed
with the vibrant life, memory, and feelings of a once-
living cat.

When the torrent of information ebbed away, Twist
returned to himself with a shallow breath. He looked
down at the cat for a moment—while Vane seemed to be
saying something clever—and then reached down to pick
it up under the front legs. The cat tried to scurry away,
but Twist managed to get a hold of it and lifted it into his
arms. The weight of it was about the same as a normal
living cat, and the metal was oddly warm to the touch.
Cradling it in one arm, Twist took its small metal paw to
look more closely at it. One of the little fingers wasn't set
properly, causing a catch in the movement of the paw.
The cat made a sound; Twist felt an array of tiny crystals
vibrate in its metal throat to create a sound that was only
slightly different than the voice of any other cat.

Twist snapped the loose piece of metal back into
place and released the cat's paw. It shook its paw and

then brought it up to its mouth to lick at it with a thin
copper tongue. The two pieces of metal made a sharp
sound as they rubbed together. The cat then seemed to
relax a little in Twist's arms, and a soft, pulsing, vibrating
sound began to pour out of its metal throat as it rubbed its
smooth copper cheek against Twist's chest.

"Hey, it likes you," Jonas said as he looked over
Twist's shoulder at the cat.

A new voice said something that made no sense at all
to Twist. He looked up to find a very old-looking man
now standing among the puppets in the dim little shop.
His dark, wrinkled skin hung loosely on his thin limbs
like the faded silks that wrapped his small, hunched form.
His eyes, however, were sharp and clear as he stared at
the cat, and at Twist, with a look of amazement. He
spoke again, pointing at them both.

"He says that the cat never likes anyone," Quay said
to Twist. "Apparently, he's never seen it let anyone pick
it up without scratching at them."

"Well, it was broken," Twist said, feeling somehow
awkward under the old man's steady gaze. "I think it's
just happy that I fixed it."

Quay turned to the man and spoke in words that Twist
couldn't follow. The man frowned, speaking again.

"He wants to know how you fixed it," Quay said,
grinning slightly. He spoke to the man again. This time,
the man's eyes widened in wonder. Jonas laughed quietly
to himself. "I told him that you're magical," Quay offered
to Twist.

Twist smiled lamely back at the old man, absently
stroking at the cat's metal neck. Quay continued to talk
with the man for a little while, as the others slowly lost
interest and began to wander off to look over some of the
other shops along the winding road. The cat continued to
purr softly, obviously content to remain in Twist's arms

throughout the conversation.

"That's still a dead cat," Jonas said, staring at it critically. "That's just not right at all."

"It's not dead," Twist said with a sigh. "It's just not...exactly alive."

"So, it's an undead, zombie cat? How's that better?"

"It's built exactly the same way that the princess's puppet was," Twist said, his voice low. "Its spirit is held in crystals, and they control the body. Whoever made this cat, must have some connection to the man who made her puppet as well. Do you know if he built it?" he asked, nodding to the old man.

"I guess so," Jonas said. He paused to listen to the conversation for a moment and then smiled. "Wow, you would love to hear all of this," Jonas said. "I'm only getting bits, but they're talking about crystals, clockwork, and ghosts." Before Twist could ask him for more than just that, Quay walked closer to them.

"He's protecting something," Quay said to Twist and Jonas. "I had to tell him everything about the puppet we've got on the ship before he'd even admit that he knew what I was talking about. Apparently, there are crystal caves nearby where he gets the crystals that he uses to make his clockwork animals. He said he'll take us there tomorrow morning."

"Why not today?" Twist asked instantly.

"He said he's not going anywhere near the caves in the dark," Quay said, glancing up to the sky. "The sun's going to set in a few hours, and he doesn't want to risk it."

"What's he so afraid of?" Jonas asked. "Did he say?"

"I didn't recognize the word he used," Quay said. "But it sounded like some kind of bat. Either way, there's no harm in playing it safe. Always listen to the natives."

After another lovely meal prepared by Cybele in the
pirate ship—this one consisting largely of grilled fish,
fresh albeit alien fruits, and fragrant rice—the crew split
up to pursue their own interests. Twist was left alone to
walk the length of an empty arm of the docking pier.
After all the madness that his life had become, it felt
unreasonably pleasant to simply sit in silence, his feet
hanging over the dark water and his back leaning against
the bamboo stilts of the tall, empty airship dock, with
nothing but the sound of the gentle waves to catch his
weary attention.

He pulled off his jacket and rolled up his sleeves, just
to feel the warm touch of the heavy night air on his skin.
As he leaned his head against the bamboo and looked up
at the silvery moon in the cloudless sky, Twist slowly
came to realize that the brilliant, countless stars above
him were entirely new to him. He'd had little chance to
see the stars in London. Here, away from any kind of
modern city lights, there were so many lights that he
couldn't find anything familiar at all.

As he searched through the endless foreign stars, he
began to feel them move, slipping below the horizon
while the Earth turned slowly. He felt nameless and
wayward as the moon, free of solid ground and lost in a
sea of stars he didn't know. To his astonishment, he felt a
sharp but tiny clap of excitement burn to life in his heart
at the thought. Somewhere deep within him, he liked the
feeling of the wind beneath his feet.

With his head full of strange notions, but his spirit
oddly calm, Twist eventually returned to the airship. On

his way, he noticed the clockwork cat that he had left at the shop, earlier in the day. It bounded up to him along the bamboo pier, its metal tail swirling happily behind it. Once Twist bent down to pet it with a cooing tone, the cat utterly refused to leave his side and ended up still beside him even as he climbed into bed.

"I don't think you're going to be rid of that thing any time soon," Jonas remarked, getting into his own bed as well, in the small cabin that they shared.

"I suppose not," Twist said, smiling and sitting up in bed to dangle the end of his watch chain in front of the cat. The cat swatted at it playfully with metal paws.

"Well, keep it over there," Jonas muttered, rolling to look away. "That thing is still highly disturbing," he added on the end of a yawn.

"Oh, don't listen to him," Twist said to the cat. "He's just a big meanie."

"A what?" Jonas snapped, turning quickly with a dubious expression.

"Go back to sleep," Twist said, waving a hand at him. "That was private."

"You're a bloody nutter, you know that?" Jonas asked, looking serious.

"If I'm insane, there's only your bloody sister to blame," Twist shot back instantly. "If she'd left me alone, I'd still be quite mentally stable. I certainly wouldn't be talking to clockwork cats."

"My dear Mr. Twist," Jonas said smoothly, with a piteous smile, "you've always been a strange one, and you know it."

"Leave me to my harmless illusion," Twist muttered, turning his attention back to the cat.

Jonas shook his head and turned back to his pillow. After a bit, Twist did the same and curled up under the warm covers. In the now almost-total silence of the dark room, he could only hear the soft sounds of Jonas's breathing, and the tick of the pocket watch that sat on his pillow before his eyes. The cat, however, began to add a soft, metallic purring sound to the mix as it finally settled down on the covers near Twist's feet, its jewel eyes closed and its tail tucked neatly around its nose.

Eventually, though, it wasn't a sound at all that swallowed up Twist's last conscious thoughts. It was the simple presence of Myra's crystal still lying against his own heart—silent, still, and sleeping peacefully—that filled his tired mind and pulled him down into a deep and dreamless sleep.

It only seemed like moments before Twist felt the weight of cold metal paws pressing down on his side. He blinked his sleepy eyes open to find two pure-red jewels staring down at him from inches away, wrapped in the rather loud sound of metallic purring. Realization dawned at the exact same moment as fright, leaving him staring back for a moment, frozen between desperate actions.

"Good morning, cat," he finally mumbled on sleepy lips.

Bright, luscious sunlight spilled over him from the uncovered window above his bed, and Twist snapped his eyes closed against it as he pushed himself up. The cat slid away, ending up on his leg while it continued to stare at him, unblinking. Twist's hand fell to it, petting absently, as he struggled to make sense of the world outside in all that light. The sun was definitely off the horizon, and already making its climb into the bright blue sky.

"Jonas, wake up," he called to the sleeping form in the next bed. "We've got a princess to save today."

A wordless groan was his only response.

"Come on, cat," Twist said, picking it up. "Go wake

up Jonas, now. There's a good cat," he said, slipping out of bed to approach Jonas.

"All right, all right," Jonas muttered. "I'm up. Keep the zombie cat away from me."

Twist laughed lightly to himself as he put the cat back down on the floor and stretched himself before moving to the wardrobe. It wasn't too much longer before both Twist and Jonas appeared on the open deck, now relatively ready for the day. The cat, naturally, followed at Twist's heels. Vane was talking with Quay, while Jiran stood silently with them.

"They are alive, after all!" Vane said upon seeing Twist and Jonas approach. "I was just about to go and wake you two up."

"Have I told you how much I love that wonderful cat of yours?" Jonas asked Twist quickly. "It's a marvel, a wonder, I tell you. Much better as an alarm clock than that blasted fox."

"Vane's not a good alarm clock?" Twist asked back, struggling to make sense of Jonas's statement. Vane grinned with all the innocence of a fox in an empty chicken coop.

"One of us would have ended up with a bucketful of water in the face, I'm sure of it," Jonas said seriously.

"I love this cat," Twist said earnestly. Jonas nodded quickly.

"Are we all ready to go yet?" Quay asked as Cybele and Idris both appeared from below decks.

"No, these two layabouts haven't eaten a thing," Cybele said, thrusting a plate of buttered toast at them. "You can't go marching through a rainforest on an empty stomach," she said sternly. Not wanting to argue, Twist and Jonas each took a piece of toast.

"Twist, have you got that gift I gave you?" Quay asked him.

"You think I'll need it in a jungle or a cave?" Twist asked with a frown.

"Our guide is worried about some kind of bat creatures," Quay said flatly. "I'd say we all definitely need our weapons. Oh, and here, I forgot to give you this part as well," he said, holding out what looked like a thin, black leather strap to Twist.

"What is it?" Twist asked, taking it.

"Slip it on over each shoulder and you can carry the cane on your back to keep it out of the way," Quay explained. "That jungle could get pretty dense, and you might need your hands to climb in the cave."

"Are you sure he should be going with us at all?" Jonas asked Quay. "I mean, he could just wait for us to get the crystal."

"No, we need him," Quay said, shaking his head. "He's the only one who can tell us, for certain, whether any particular crystal will work or not." Jonas nodded with a sigh.

Twist did as he was told and went back to his cabin to retrieve the black-and-silver walking stick. Sure enough, the leather strap that Quay had given him fit easily over his shoulders, and the walking stick slid smoothly through smaller loops against his spine, the silver hilt of it sitting in easy reach over his right shoulder. Thinking of the trial ahead, Twist took off his top hat and his long silver scarf, leaving them behind.

Now ready for battle with the unknown, Twist met the others on the pier below the airship, as the old puppet maker walked toward them from the beach. He spoke to Quay quickly, his face a mask of concern and sharp anxiety.

"What's going on?" Twist asked Jonas.

"He's talking really fast," Jonas said, shaking his head. "All I'm getting is that he's not happy about leading us to the cave. He keeps using different words for 'danger'."

"You know, I'm really not cut out for this sort of thing," Twist said nervously. "The last two times I was in any real danger I ended up unconscious for a few days."

A quiet laugh bubbled up in Jonas, but he made an obvious effort to keep it down. "Stay close to me," he said, forcing his voice calm. "I *am* good at this sort of thing."

Finally, Quay seemed to convince the old man that they were not going to leave without making an attempt to reach the cave. They all set out together, walking along the edge of the white sand beach under the outreaching palms. The clockwork cat still followed Twist, as they came to a narrow path through the dense trees, and stepped into the jungle itself.

The thin, winding trunks of the trees around them had long, clawing roots that stood out above the sandy ground, while wide, round leaves and long mossy vines filled the air around them. The whole jungle was bathed in shadows under the seemingly solid canopy high above. In places, the path was made only of large stones or small patches of sand that sat in what could have been an endless shallow river, that had flooded the whole jungle floor.

Occasionally, solid, albeit moist, ground appeared beneath their feet. It wasn't long before Twist stopped worrying about stepping over wet patches, and tried instead to just find anywhere solid to put his feet. The others, however, didn't seem to find this all that difficult. Out of desperation, Twist eventually followed Jonas's footsteps meticulously rather than trying to find his own path.

The clockwork cat bounded easily over dry roots and stones, sometimes climbing a tree to leap across the branches as it followed along. Twist couldn't help but feel somewhat jealous of it. His legs grew tired very quickly, but no one else seemed ready to stop even for a moment. The air in the dim, endless jungle was thick and heavy in the growing heat of the day, choking him tighter with every breath. When he thought he might not be able to go on at all, the group finally came to stop. It was only then that he noticed that the cat had disappeared into the jungle, wandering off to hunt in the damp shadows.

The trees opened up at the edge of a sharp cliff over a narrow, deep gorge. The jungle continued on the other side, while a small but violent river ran far below, rushing between the rock walls. The sound of tumbling water echoed down the gorge from farther to the left, around a wide bend. As the group began to move once again, Twist was horrified to find them walking along the thin, precarious ledge at the very edge of the cliff.

"Can't we go another way?" Twist gasped, reaching out to wrap his hands around the nearest tree.

"Do you want to hold my hand?" Jonas offered.

"No, I want to go home and live the rest of my life on the bloody ground!" Twist snapped back savagely.

"This is the ground," Jonas pointed out, gesturing to the precipice as the others began to move farther away from them.

"No, this is madness," Twist retorted. "One slip, and we'll fall to our deaths! Do I look like a circus performer to you?"

Jonas stared back at him for a moment, his jaw set determinedly. Then he stepped forward and peeled Twist's hand off the tree to hold it firmly in his own. He kept his eyes away while Twist's Sight washed over him in numb, warm, white light. Twist shook his head, clearing the fog to the edges of his mind. Jonas stood silently, as if waiting for this.

"Now," he said, still not looking at Twist, "reach out. What am I feeling right now?"

"I don't want to—" Twist began.

"Just look, Twist," Jonas said, cutting his complaints short. "How do I feel right now?"

Twist sighed. The pulsing, warm, white fog threatened to encroach again and bury him alive in numb, bright, calm. He focused on Jonas's hand, on the warm, rough skin pressed against his own. It took very little time at all before Twist began to feel the rhythm of the other man's blood running quickly through his skin, and he followed the flow right into his heart.

He found no fear whatsoever there, but was instead overcome with a light-headed and reckless excitement at the sight of the drop so nearby. The view was wondrous and the empty air tasted like freedom. He felt light, careless, curious and free. Jonas found nothing at all like fear in that drop, only a subtle joy at being alive enough to see it.

"Are you all right now?" Jonas asked after a silent pause.

"I suppose so," Twist said softly, suddenly unable to find his own fear as he looked at the precarious edge. Now that he had seen it clearly, he couldn't get the overriding sense of the other man's emotions out of his mind.

"Good. Let's go," Jonas said, pulling him back onto the ledge path.

To Twist's total astonishment, his own fear didn't return as he followed after Jonas, stepping lightly over the roots that clung to the rock wall. They caught up with the others at a quick pace. Vane looked back as they approached, and his eyes moved to their still tightly clasped hands.

"Is there something you'd like to admit, Jonas?" Vane

asked with a wicked light to his grin. Idris glanced back at well, his white eyebrows climbing slightly up his face.

"He's afraid of heights," Jonas snapped back at Vane. "I'm just helping him along."

"What, are you jealous?" Twist added with a sneer. He paused, wondering why the words felt odd on his tongue, as the rest of the group turned to look at him curiously.

"That was weird," Jonas said under his breath.

"Yes, it was," Twist agreed, nodding. "Let go of me. I can't find myself, in all of you."

"I really don't want to know anymore..." Vane said, moving to hurry onward.

"Come on, let's just get off this ledge," Jonas said with a sigh, pulling Twist on as well.

The old man led them expertly and quickly to the end of the ledge, where a tall waterfall crashed into the gorge from higher up the mountain. There was a small opening under the falls, into a dark, mist-filled cave. He leaped down easily, followed closely by Quay and Cybele. Twist and Jonas were the last to make the small jump over a wide, jagged crack in the rock. Once Twist had made the jump and landed easily on his feet in the dark cave, Jonas finally released his hand.

The roar of the falls behind them thundered against Twist's suddenly clear senses, and the chill of the mist that collected in the mouth of the black cave gave him a shudder. In a single instant, all of the fear that he hadn't been able to feel as he walked along the ridge, came screaming through his mind like a runaway train, crashing into rage with explosive force.

"What the hell is wrong with you?" he demanded of Jonas, taking fistfuls of Jonas's collar in his hands to glare directly into his eyes. Jonas let out a painful gasp, snapping his eyes shut while Twist continued to berate him. "That was completely mad! We could have been killed and you weren't concerned at all! Heavens above, you liked it!"

"What's going on?" Quay asked the group that now stood watching this display in silent shock.

"Lover's quarrel," Vane said softly to him from behind a shielding hand.

"We survived, didn't we?" Jonas spat back. "I had to do something. You were stuck back there!"

"Don't ever do that again," Twist hissed.

"Fine, whatever, I surrender," Jonas said, raising his hands submissively. Twist released him with a healthy shove and then turned away, his arms crossed and his steel-blue eyes blazing.

"Well, now that that's settled," Quay said, clasping his hands and looking to the old man. He spoke to him again, but this time the man shook his head sharply. When Quay spoke on, the man shook his head again and said only one word. Quay gave a sigh, staring at him with a frown. Twist looked to Jonas curiously.

"He's not going to take us any farther," Jonas said.

"Why not?" Twist asked back.

Jonas gave a shrug.

Quay tried once again to talk to the man, only to be cut off with a very determined-sounding sentence. The old man then held out his hand. Quay shook his head and pulled a small pouch from his pocket, handing it to him. The man weighed the pouch in his hand and then nodded, turning instantly to walk back out of the cave.

"We're on our own, then," Quay announced. "The little coward's too scared of these 'bat things' to go on. Still, we'd best be on guard," he added, drawing his pistol as he turned to the blackness in the depth of the cave.

Twist wasn't the only one in the cave who had an electrical light. He turned on the blue ring of light in the hilt of his cane, but left it on his back to shine out over his shoulder, illuminating the glistening moisture on the jagged, gray cave walls. A path led downward, deeper into the mountain. Quay walked ahead, holding out a small handheld electric lantern before him. The others fell into a line that snaked through the random formations inside the cave. The ceiling sometimes fell low over their heads, and sometimes flew away in the untold shadowy heights, while the walls seemed to do nothing but narrow in around them. Most of the path was slick from the mist, making the round, shifting stones even more untrustworthy.

After what felt like a very long time to Twist, the walls finally moved away into a sort of small cavern. As he and the others crowded inside, he saw not just one, but three more exits out into more narrow tunnels. The smallest of all was so narrow that Twist wasn't sure he would fit through it, let alone the others.

"He did tell you which path to take, didn't he?" Cybele asked Quay.

"He said that there were crystals all through these caves," Quay said, looking down each path thoughtfully. "Jonas?" he said suddenly. "Make yourself useful."

"What do you want me to do?" Jonas asked back.

"Have a look and tell me if you see us walking down any of these," Quay said, gesturing to the tunnel openings.

"That's not going to work," Jonas said back flatly.

"My Sight only works on people and things, remember? A hole in a rock is neither. Though I've met some people who make me wonder."

Quay gave him a displeased look. "Idris?" he asked instead.

"This is boring," Idris said with a sigh, glancing off to the side.

"All right," Quay said, already taking a seat on a large rock near the side of the cavern, "then we're going to have to send out scouts. There's no other way. Jiran, Vane, you're both small and agile. Take a tunnel each. Come back when you find something."

Vane made a show of being highly inconvenienced, while Jiran simply stood with her arms crossed and scowled at Quay. Twist shook his head, silently chiding himself for expecting anything else from a bunch of disorganized and mostly inhuman pirates. As he strolled listlessly around the small cavern's edge, he began to wonder again how he had ever ended up in such a ridiculous situation. If Arabel were with him now, she would be able to lead him directly to a crystal that would perfectly replace the one that now hung around his neck. But then, of course, every single thing that had happened to him since he'd left London was entirely her fault to begin with.

As he continued to wander, kicking idly at loose stones, Twist watched as the wide, flat, fan of blue light from his walking stick sent flickering shadows playing over the rocks before him. He didn't notice that the light didn't fall far below his line of sight, and didn't realize that the ground was less flat and level than he believed it to be.

He took one more step forward and the stone below him suddenly gave way, rolling down a long, previously invisible shaft, as quick as a cannon shot. Twist tried to catch himself on the jagged, slippery rocks around him, but his fingers found no purchase as he tumbled down the shaft with the loose stones. In his fright and confusion, he couldn't make a sound, but he heard Jonas's frantic call before it died away into the chaos as he fell.

Twist lost all control as he tumbled farther and farther into the black Earth, and the light of his cane went out somewhere along the way. After what felt like a terrifyingly long distance, his small frame battered against stones and rock walls all along the way, Twist finally came to a stop, lying in a heap on the cold wet stones, in total darkness. As his senses returned to him, all he heard was the quick beating of his own heart, and his own shuddering breath in an untold space.

Twist first tried to raise himself up to kneel on the uneven ground, but his battered limbs stung and shook from fatigue and shock. He caught enough of his breath to call out, but his small, shaking voice returned to him almost instantly, sounding caught and claustrophobic in the tight and total black. Sheer panic bubbled up his spine.

Something moved in the darkness behind him, and for a glorious instant Twist thought that it might be one of his companions. The sound, however, changed into a strange, half-human and half-animal growl. Frozen in fear, Twist could only listen blindly, desperate to gauge the distance of the sound. It seemed very close to him now, creeping quickly closer.

In a sudden flash of unseen movement, something launched itself at Twist from behind, forcing him to the ground again. He had no time to scream before two very sharp points dug deep into the soft skin at his exposed neck, and his thundering heart fell instantly to a painful stillness as he felt his blood run free. Twist's Sight burned to light, threatening to fill his mind with nothing but brutal killing and horrific death at the half-human hands of a monstrous creature he could never describe from inside its terrible mind.

Just as quickly, Twist was once again kneeling alone in the darkness. He threw his hands to his neck but found no blood or wound, no sign at all of the horrific attack. As he grappled with total confusion, he heard the same, inhuman growl from the darkness behind him. Cold fear gripped him so quickly that time seemed to slow down as he reached for the cane on his back. He drew it out, flipped it in his hand, and swung the solid silver hilt back at the source of the unseen movement behind him. The blow connected with a crack of bone and a screeching, animal wail.

Twist jumped to his feet and finally remembered that there was a light in his cane. He flicked it on to find the monstrous creature he'd seen in the vision now lying on the stones at his feet; thin, clawing hands clutched a large, ugly wound in its bulbous gray head. Its naked, leathery, only slightly human form was curled up on itself, but Twist could still see thin, black, bat-like wings hanging limply from its spindly arms.

The second one didn't make a sound before it jumped at him from the shadows. Twist looked up too slowly, but the creature froze suddenly in its flight and seemed to hang in space for an instant like a horrific puppet— clawing fingers mere inches from him, and two long, pointed teeth bared and aimed for his throat. Then, just as quickly, it disappeared entirely, only to jump once again from the shadows, exactly as before. This time, however, Twist was well warned. He jabbed the point of his walking stick out and hit the switch, sending a nasty jolt of electricity into the creature when it struck.

The creature screamed, falling away in a shower of bright sparks. Twist held up the light of his walking stick and saw many glistening black eyes in the shadows around him, all watching with an evil hunger. The rock around him now hung from the ceiling in long fingers while the ground reached up with its own. The eyes seemed to watch him from every black crevice. The shaft he'd come down was far too steep to climb, but Twist could see no other exit from this desolate place. He could still hear nothing but his own ragged breath as he stared around at all of the black, shining eyes.

Desperate for some salvation, Twist turned the silver cap on the end of the cane and pulled it off, revealing the bare electric arc inside. The light of it was impossibly intense, as if the sun itself were bound up in one point. Twist swung the wide beam of light around him, searching for anything that could lead him back to the surface. The creatures let out frightened-sounding shrieks and pulled back into the shadows when the light fell on them, providing at least some measure of comfort to Twist's terror.

The light suddenly returned to him, shining back brightly. For a moment, Twist thought that it was another electrical light like his own. But as he moved his aim, the returning light flashed off and then on again in exact response. Realizing it was a reflection, Twist moved closer. The creatures kept well out of the light, though they still watched silently as he crept nearer to a previously invisible opening into another cavern.

Twist crouched down and pulled himself through to find nothing but pure white crystals all around him: each one was hundreds of feet long and easily many feet wide. When Twist brought his light up, it bounced around the giant cavern, filling every crystal with light as well. It was so bright that he had to pull his dark-blue goggles on just to see. Knowing how little the creatures liked the light, he kept it burning at full force to be sure to keep them away.

As he walked slowly along a crystal that stretched out horizontally across the cavern, Twist was astonished by the sheer size of the crystal world he now stood within. Look as he might, however, he saw nothing but white crystals everywhere. Myra's had been red in color. Of course, he considered, the color might have nothing to do with it...

A sudden sound to his right struck Twist's senses like a thunderclap and he moved instantly this time, swinging the shining hilt of his walking stick at the source. To his surprise, the sound of metal clashing against metal met his ears before he could turn his eyes to see what he had struck.

Green jewels stared back at him from a silver, metal face. Twist stared back, perplexed by the form before him: a mechanical man standing on another crystal near him, his body shining brightly in silver. Unlike Myra's complex clockwork puppet, this one looked crude in comparison. Its limbs were simple, straight bars bound by visible gears and cogs, like a bare metal skeleton. Only the face was rounded by movable plates, though even they were not nearly as detailed or intricate as Myra's.

The metal man stared at Twist silently for a moment before glancing down to its own arm. Twist realized then that the metal man was cradling his arm in the other, and that one of the two bars of his upper arm appeared to be dislodged. The shoulder twitched suddenly with an ugly-sounding whir.

"Did I hurt you?" Twist asked breathlessly.

The metal man looked back up at him quickly, but remained silent.

"I'm sorry," Twist said, already moving closer. "I thought you were one of those things out there," he added, glancing at the tiny passage back to the dark cave outside. The metal man retreated from his advance, backing away a few steps before Twist finally stopped.

"Please, let me fix it," Twist said earnestly. "I know how. Just let me see it," he added, stepping slowly forward again.

This time, the metal man held his ground, watching Twist with intent, jewel eyes. Twist reached out and gently ran the tip of one finger over the shining silver at the top of the wounded arm. Instantly, he understood the reality of the mechanical life before him. It ran on the same exact principle that the cat and Myra's puppets both did, though this one was far simpler. Just as before, there was a ghostly force controlling it from within, from a central crystal much like Myra's broken heart.

Twist gently took hold of the shoulder in one hand, and expertly fit the support bar back into position before reaching inside the shoulder to fit the tiny, unseated gear back into place. The moment he was done, the metal man's form seemed to stiffen as if in shock. Twist backed away instantly, afraid he'd somehow hurt him again. The metal man looked down at its own limb, bending it slowly to test it, before looking back to him.

"Who are you?" the metal man asked, opening his solid metal lips like a marionette puppet, while fully formed words echoed out of his metal throat.

"Twist," he offered with a shrug, unsure how else to respond. "I fix clocks for a living, in London," he added, hoping it might help. Thin silver plates slid over the green jewels, giving the clear effect of narrowed eyes in the metal face.

"What?" the metal man asked. Twist took a moment to reconsider his position.

"I need a crystal," he said. "Like the one that runs your body," he added, pointing to the metal man's silver covered chest. "I'm trying to repair a..." He paused, unsure how to even refer to Myra in the face of her kinsman. "A puppet, like yours. The mechanism is complete, but the crystal was broken when I found it."

"There are none of us outside this cave," the metal man said.

"There are others?" Twist asked, wholly unable to keep the wonder from his voice.

"No," the metal man said instantly, straightening itself up slightly.

Twist shook his head, struggling to keep his battered mind on track. "The princess," he said, imploringly, "the one who lived in the mountains of Nepal. She was broken ages ago. I only just found her, and I'm almost finished fixing her. Please, will you help me? I've come from the other side of the world just to bring her back to life. She's been alone for so long." As he spoke, something slipped out of his mental grasp and he felt his eyes begin to burn while his voice wavered threateningly. He took in a deep breath, biting back his weary emotions.

The metal man's narrow eyes widened again slowly as he listened. He paused silently for a long moment before his chest rose and fell smoothly, as if taking a deep, resigned breath. Then, he took a step closer to Twist and gestured with one hand.

"Come with me," he said. "And turn that light out. It's far too bright."

Once Twist had replaced the cap on his walking stick and turned out its light completely, he saw the otherworldly white glow that seemed to live at the heart of every crystal in the cavern. However beautiful and strange, it was highly disorienting and he had to reach out to practically feel his way along as the metal man led him deeper and deeper into the crystal cavern. After what seemed like a very long walk on his now-aching limbs, the crystals around him gave way to a wide, open space unlike anything Twist could have ever imagined.

Tall crystals—now of pale blue, green, and gold— stood like the towers of a great city in the seemingly endless cavern around them, each one hollowed out into levels and rooms. More crystals stretched between them in ornately carved, glowing bridges of glass. Everywhere he looked, Twist saw clockwork people strolling through the crystals, talking together, running, laughing, playing, and living in a true city all their own. Each one was perfectly unique in design and complexity, though he saw many that reminded him of either Myra or his guide. Utterly bewildered by what he saw in the haunting natural glow of the crystals, Twist could only stop and stare at the impossibility that ran rampant around him.

"Wait here," the metal man said to Twist, watching him carefully. "I'll be right back."

When Twist made no reply, the man reached out a metal hand to lay on his arm. Twist's Sight flashed him a torrent of memories, far more numerous than anything he'd ever experienced. Because of the number, all he could grasp were flashes of a life lived in this crystal city, without so much as the sight of a single flesh-and-blood human being. Twist jerked away from the touch automatically, breaking the connection.

"I mean it," the metal man said. "Don't wander off."

"All right," Twist managed to respond.

Apparently satisfied now, the metal man turned and walked away into the crystal spires. Twist found it increasingly difficult to remain on his feet as he stood, watching clockwork forms tend to their own business in their inexplicable world. He leaned heavily on his walking stick and hung his head, trying very hard not to think about how much he hurt.

"You're not made of metal," said a very young, but still metallic-sounding voice.

Twist opened his eyes to see a small, clockwork boy staring at him from a few feet away. He looked to be no bigger than a five-year-old child, and his voice sounded about that age as well. He stared up at Twist from a chubby copper face, through diamond-clear eyes.

"I'm not," Twist conceded.

"But everyone here's made of metal," the boy pointed out.

"I'm sorry," Twist offered.

"But everyone who's not made of metal gets killed by the bat people," the boy said, tilting his metal head to one side absently. "How come they didn't kill you?"

"I can see the future," Twist said, allowing himself the luxury of saying it in a slightly spooky voice. "I hit them before they can hit me."

"Oh, that's very clever," the boy said, his bright, clear eyes appearing somehow very excited now, to match his voice. "How do you see the future?" he asked almost in a whisper.

"I'm magical," Twist answered flatly.

"I wanna be magical!" the boy said, hopping lightly

on his metal feet. "Can you teach me? Oh please, say you will!"

Twist could no longer keep the smile off his face, watching this. Luckily, he was saved from having to crush any tiny hopes.

"Run along, Willy," said another metallic voice. Twist and the boy turned to see what Twist recognized as clearly the most refined of all the clockwork people approach them.

"But—!" the boy began, pointing to Twist.

"What have I told you, Willy?" the new clockwork person said, raising a finger. "Never tempt a magical person, least of all a wizard. It's very bad for the health."

Little Willy gave a very large and aggravated sigh, pouting at Twist before finally turning to hurry away to a group of three other small clockwork children who had apparently been watching all the while. They scattered into the city at a dismissive wave from the new clockwork person.

Seeing her now from closer up, Twist was amazed by the craftsmanship in her golden face. The jewels of her eyes were a clear, brilliant purple, and the shape of her features reminded Twist instantly of Aazzi. Her form was wrapped modestly in fine, purple cotton that swirled into gray at her sandaled feet. Even so, Twist could only guess that her body had been built by an artist. It was nearly as lovely as Myra's, and obviously as flexible and intricate within as well.

"My name is Elizabeth," she said, bowing to him slightly. "I'm the governess of this city." She then held out a perfect, golden hand to him.

"Twist," he offered, taking her cool, metal hand ever so lightly.

It took all of his focus not to let the vision of her innumerable, vivid memories run away with him. As he had before, he found the still, constant, quiet warmth resting quietly at the base of his neck, even now that Jonas was so far away. He managed to wrap even that faint shield of warmth around his mind to retain his composure as he bent to lay a respectful kiss on the back of her golden hand.

"It's a pleasure to meet you, Governess," he offered, almost embarrassed by the inadequacy of his words.

"Please, call me Liz," she said, smiling gently as the metal sheets of her face moved silently to allow for the expression. Twist couldn't help but smile back into her amethyst eyes.

"I'm sorry, I can't," he said, bringing a light flash of confusion to her features. "A nickname is wholly inadequate. You deserve a much more unique and beautiful name."

Her smile deepened considerably. "Well, aren't you charming?" she toned smoothly, only now pulling her hand away from his. "Come with me," she said, gesturing towards one of the larger streets through the crystal city. "I hear that we have much to talk about."

As if in a dream, Twist walked beside the golden clockwork woman, through crystal streets filled with staring, jewel eyes. Each clockwork face that they passed seemed to focus on Twist, the clockwork people muttering quietly to one another just out of earshot. As they entered one of the largest carved out crystal rooms—decorated with long, hanging swaths of colorful cloth, shining crystal, and precious metal ornaments—he found little relief from the staring eyes, as the walls of this clear crystal palace were as thin as sheets of glass. Elizabeth asked him to sit on a low, purple velvet padded seat near the center of the room, while she sat across a small crystal table from him on another simple seat. Twist couldn't fathom why she didn't have a throne.

The moment his body came to rest, he realized just how far he had fallen down the dark shaft. Though he didn't think he'd broken anything, his whole body now ached. He let out a breath, fighting to keep his attention on other things.

"Are you all right?" Elizabeth asked him, looking concerned.

"Yes, I just..." Twist paused, smiling to her weakly. "I sort of fell down a hole out in the caves. I'm a bit sore now." Her amethyst eyes flashed with alarm. "Please, don't worry about me," Twist said quickly. "I'm getting used to this kind of thing."

"Well..." she toned, not looking totally convinced, "if you're sure that you're all right," she said slowly. Twist nodded instantly. "Well, my friend tells me that you're here for a purpose," she said. "He tells me that you found Princess Myra."

Surprise flashed across Twist's face. "You know her name?"

"She is the stuff of our legends as well," Elizabeth said, smiling to him. "Some say that she was the very first of us to be born into metal. But she has been lost for generations."

"Well, someone finally found her. She's been lying broken for a very long time. I've repaired the clockwork, and the other crystals are all undamaged, but the central one was cracked when I found it." It felt odd to say these things to her, and Twist wondered if she would understand or even be offended by his knowledge. Elizabeth, however, only listened and nodded thoughtfully.

"How did you know to come here for a replacement?" she asked him.

"Someone told me that her crystal came from these caves," Twist explained. "I had no idea that any...any of your people, were here."

"That's good," she said absently, nodding to her own thoughts. "Where did you find her?" she asked, watching him carefully now. "What was her condition?"

"She was in Nepal, in a crumbling old palace on the edge of a mountain peak," Twist said. "Her body had fallen at some point, leaving her soul trapped in the palace. I had to take every single piece of her apart just to repair all the damage."

"That must have taken you a while."

"Almost a week, I think," Twist said, nodding.

"Only a week?" she asked, smiling again. "Did you sleep?"

"Not much, if I'm honest," Twist said, smiling back lightly.

"And why would you go to all that trouble to fix her?" Elizabeth asked lightly, though the look in her crystal eyes was anything but light. Twist suddenly realized that these questions were not posed out of mild curiosity; she was testing him somehow.

"She was trapped, alone and forgotten in that crumbling old palace," he said, careful to keep his words as honest and clear as he could. "And her puppet is so lovely…almost as wonderful as she is, herself. It was a horror to see her broken like that. I couldn't have done anything else. I simply had to help her."

Elizabeth's eyes warmed as she listened to him. "Good answer," she said softly. "And if I help you to finish the repairs, what would you do with her then?"

"Whatever she wished," Twist said, his surprise at the question evident on his face. "It's not my decision to make."

"Isn't it?" she asked, her tone light. Twist searched her shining eyes, but any tension that might be in them was well concealed.

"No, it isn't," Twist said, letting his honesty speak for itself. "It's her life, and so it has to be her choice."

"I see," Elizabeth said, her expression warming. "Where is the broken crystal?"

"Ah," Twist toned, reaching for the chain that hung under his collar. He drew it out and over his head, before carefully taking hold of the tiny crystal pendant. Then, he pulled sharply at the chain, breaking it off. Instantly, the chain and pendant both dissolved into golden dust that swirled in on itself on his palm. Myra's broken crystal appeared out of the shimmering dust, back in its true form. "Here it is," Twist said, looking back to Elizabeth.

She stared at it in wonder, her eyes wide. "How ever did you do that?" she asked.

"Oh. I know a djinn."

"You do lead an interesting life, don't you Twist?" she asked, now looking at him with a glimmer of wonder in her purple eyes. "May I see it?" she asked, holding out a golden hand.

The moment that Twist handed her the crystal, the constant, peaceful presence of Myra's sleeping spirit vanished from his mind. He instantly regretted letting it slip from his fingers into any others hands.

"She's still inside?" Elizabeth asked, peering into the crystal.

"I asked her to return to it," Twist said. "There were others, at the time, who I thought might cause her harm. I asked her to return to the crystal so that I could keep her safe."

"There is no fear in her spirit," Elizabeth said, softly stroking the surface of the crystal with one golden finger. "She is perfectly at peace. No matter what you told her, you could only have left her in such a peaceful state if she actually trusted you." She looked up to him then. "From what you've told me, I can see that you honestly have no idea where you are. That's a very good thing," she added when Twist frowned. "But if I give you what you want, I want something from you in return."

"Anything I have to give," Twist said instantly as real hope burned to life in his heart.

She smiled again. "You got her to trust you, so I believe that I can too. But trust is only strong when it is even. You must trust me now."

"All right," Twist said, silently wondering what she could mean.

"I want a promise from you," she said, staring into him so pointedly that he thought she might be able to see through him. "I want you to give me your word, right now, that you will do exactly what I ask of you when I bring you back the replacement for this crystal."

"But, you won't tell me what you want of me, now?" Twist asked.

"Not yet," she said. "I want you to agree to it first. As I said, you must trust me."

A million possibilities flashed to Twist's mind in an instant. She could ask him to give Myra up and never return. She could tell him to return to this city with her and never see the living world again. Or, she could simply want him to stay with Myra and protect her for the rest of his life—which, by contrast, would be the easiest. There was no way of knowing what she would ask of him. It might not even be something he could do. He looked down to Myra's crystal, lying silently in her golden hands. He knew, undeniably, that this was the best chance he would ever have of bringing her back to the living world.

"All right," he said, surprised by the strength in his own voice. "I'll do whatever you ask. I only want to see her alive again."

Elizabeth watched him silently for a moment, before she gave a nod and rose to her feet. "Wait here," she said. "Believe it or not, this won't take very long."

With that, she left him alone in the glass-walled palace and took Myra's crystal away with her. Twist felt as if the weight of the world were crashing down on his weak and fragile form in the cold absence of Myra's spirit echoing in the back of his mind.

After what felt like a lifetime, the same silver man appeared and asked Twist to follow him back to the city entrance. When they reached it, Twist found Elizabeth waiting for them with a warm smile on her golden face.

"I assume I don't have to tell you to take good care of this," she said, holding a new, ruby-red crystal out to him.

Twist took it carefully, and instantly recognized Myra's sleeping spirit within the now-perfect crystal. He took the offered white cloth and wrapped it snugly inside.

"Now, for my payment," Elizabeth said.

"Yes, whatever you like," Twist said, steeling what little courage and determination he had left to offer.

"Never tell a living soul what you have seen here," she said, to Twist's instant shock. "Not ever, not anyone. Not even her," she added, gesturing to Myra's sleeping spirit. "If she should ever wish to come to us, then she will find us on her own and we will welcome her. But you are not to tell a soul about us or our city. We prize our isolation. We are down here because of it."

"But this place is a marvel! A miracle!" Twist said, unable to stop himself. "If anyone knew about it—" he began.

"You have already given me your word, Twist," Elizabeth said gently. "You must keep it now."

Twist stared back at her, as a sudden realization stung him. He would never see this place again, either. He would never again speak with Elizabeth, or even be able to speak of her to anyone else. She and her people would become a secret that would die with him. It seemed somehow unreasonably unjust.

"I will keep my promise to you," he said, forcing the words out of his reluctant soul.

"I knew I could trust you," she said, smiling to him one last time.

Twist etched the memory of her face into his mind before he turned to leave the city. The silver man who had first found him, now led him along a different path that climbed steadily up into the slick, gray rock, out of the gently glowing crystal caverns. They didn't meet any of the gruesome creatures on their way, even in the blackness of the tight rock tunnels. It felt like miles before the metal man finally stopped and told Twist that the way was now clear of confusing turns or hidden creatures. All Twist had to do was walk the rest of the way out.

Twist was grateful once again for his walking stick as he continued to climb through the darkness alone, along an inclined tunnel. The blue, electric light soon began to glisten off the rocks as they appeared moist again, nearer the surface, and the cane itself was a help as his limbs continued to complain against the effort. In the silence, he found himself reaching out for the warmth of Jonas's existence at the base of his neck. It wasn't long before the warmth grew into a nervous, electric tension.

"Twist!" he heard a voice call out, echoing off the stones.

Twist hurried his pace despite his fatigue, now feeling Jonas moving steadily closer to him. In a sudden burst of white, electric light, Twist turned one last corner to find himself faced with his companions once again. Before he even had time to speak, Jonas launched himself at him, wrapping Twist in his arms and showering his mind in numb, warm, white, calm.

"Shit, I thought you were dead!" Jonas gasped, pushing him back far enough to glare at. "Don't ever do that to me again!"

"I fell through a hole!" Twist snapped back in his own defense. "It was hardly on purpose, you know."

Jonas's hands gripped his arms firmly, while Twist recognized an odd mix of fear, pain, and relief on the other man's face. "I mean it. No more holes for you, got it?" Jonas said, his voice forced and not nearly as clear as it should have been.

"Fine," Twist said, unable to keep the light smile from his face. "I'll do my best not to almost die again, just for you. All right?"

"Good," Jonas said, taking a breath and wrapping one arm around Twist's neck as he turned back to the others. "Can we leave now?" he asked them.

"He's fine," Quay said, gesturing to Twist. "And we haven't found a single crystal yet."

"Twist and I are leaving right now," Jonas snapped savagely.

"Jonas—" Quay began, anger glimmering at the edge of his composure.

"Wait, wait, it's all right," Twist said, throwing up his hands to draw some attention to himself. "I have it. Look," he said, pulling the tied cloth off of his hip to hold up the wrapped crystal. He then quickly opened the cloth to reveal it to stunned expressions from everyone.

"How on Earth did you do that?" Idris asked, staring at the perfectly formed, round crystal. "Did you carve it with your fingernails?"

"It doesn't matter how I got it," Twist said, holding it up for Jonas to see. "Look at it, tell them the princess's spirit is inside it."

"It is," Jonas breathed, staring at it in astonishment. "But how—?"

"I've had a very trying day," Twist said, cutting off the question. "I've walked through a whole bloody jungle,

I fell down a dark hole, I was attacked by monsters—"
Twist felt a ripple of fear shoot through Jonas. "I'm all
right, though," he added quickly. "But I'm now in
desperate need of a cup of tea and a lie down. Can we
leave this wretched cave, please?"

The others found no other response than to begin the
journey back. It felt like a very long time before they
finally returned to the falls at the mouth of the cave.
Outside, Twist was too tired to even worry about the cliff
anymore, so he let Jonas lead him back along it once
again. The sunlight that broke through the ravine felt like
the most wondrous thing in the world as it fell onto his
bruised and battered skin. They took a few small breaks
on the way back through the jungle. Each time Twist
stumbled, it took longer to get back to his feet. Each step
felt more and more difficult to him, despite the small
rests.

It was edging into the afternoon by the time the group
of pirates emerged from the jungle, onto the white sand
beach, and began the walk back to the docks. Twist no
longer had any choice but to lean heavily on Jonas for
support by the time the docks came into view around a
bend in the palm-strewn beach. Distracted as he was
with simply continuing to move, he was the last to notice
the now-crowded airship docks, or the sea of men who
stood on the beach. The pirates ducked into the trees,
looking out at the crowds with great alarm.

"Jonas?" Quay said to him, looking over the figures
and the ships that hung in the air, so numerous that they
covered the beach in cool shadows. Jonas looked over
the crowd with uncovered eyes.

"That's the British Royal Air Force," he said, as if he
didn't believe his own words.

"This isn't a British colony," Vane protested. "What
are they doing here?"

"I specifically told the port authority in Hong Kong that we were headed to Russia," Quay said in total disbelief. "And no one was following us. No one knew we were here!"

"Is that the *Vimana*?" Twist asked, staring up at a familiar shape in the dense cloud of otherwise military-looking airships.

"And that's my sister, jumping up and down and waving at us in the middle of that crowd of soldiers," Jonas said, pointing again.

When Twist followed his indication, he saw a single form jumping happily on the sand, leading a wave of armed men in their exact direction. It was only moments before the British forces—dressed in red and white, and each man carrying a rifle—were well within sight.

"Captain Adair Quay!" called a voice through a megaphone, the owner of which Twist found easily at the front of the crowd. "You are under arrest for piracy, theft, and assault against Great Britain and many of the Queen's loyal colonies. Surrender now or you will be fired upon." Perfectly in time, the armed men on the beach took aim at the trees.

"Jon! Twist!" Arabel called happily into the jungle, almost looking at them directly through the dense cover of the trees. "I found you!"

"I hate your bloody sister," Quay growled at Jonas. "Vane, change into a fox and sneak around behind them. Jiran, Cybele, take up positions in those trees. Idris, could you lend us a hand?" he said, quickly.

"In addition," the officer with the megaphone called out, "our warrant states that we are to arrest Captain Quay and anyone on his crew. If any of you should decide to defect now, then we are honor bound to let you leave peacefully."

"What?" Quay spat. "That's the most ridiculous thing

I've ever heard."

"Are you telling me," Vane called back to the men loudly, "that if we all decide to leave Adair, we'll all be free to go?"

"Yes, exactly," the man with the megaphone said. "This is a special warrant for the captain alone. Come out peacefully and you will not be arrested."

"You can't trust them!" Quay bellowed to the pirates around him. "It's got to be a trick."

"Sorry, mate," Vane said with a meek smile. "No hard feelings." With that, he got to his feet and walked out to the beach with his hands up. "I surrender, good British gentleman!" he said as he walked. "That bad pirate made me join him! I'm a good boy, I promise."

"Me too!" Cybele said, following after him with her gun hanging harmlessly in one hand. "I'm American, by the way, well outside your jurisdiction, you know." Jiran gave Quay a sorrowful shrug before getting up to follow after them with her hands raised as well. As each of them reached the British forces, they were met with reluctant but polite nods.

"You're bloody damned traitors, the lot of you!" Quay bellowed after them. "Idris, please," he said imploringly to the djinn. "Haven't I always come up with the most entertaining wishes for you?"

"I'm already serving one debt to society by being here in your world at all," Idris said with a sigh. "I'm sorry, but I have no intention of being arrested here on Earth, as well." He too got to his feet and then vanished into a cloud of purple smoke, leaving only Twist and Jonas still beside Quay.

Quay only stared at Jonas and Twist silently, with a bitter desperation in his eyes.

"Thanks for getting me away from my family for a while," Jonas said, placing a hearty pat on the pirate's shoulder. "But this is where we part ways." With that, he helped Twist to his feet and led him out to the beach, where Arabel met them both with a wide smile.

"Oh, can you touch people now?" Arabel asked brightly. Twist was still leaning on Jonas, with an arm over the stronger man's shoulders.

"No, just me," Jonas answered quickly. "It's a long story."

"Damn," Arabel spat. "Oh well," she said with a sigh, reaching out to take Jonas's neck in one hand as she planted a kiss on his cheek, mere inches away from Twist. "I'm so glad to see you again!" she said, positively beaming at her brother. "And you," she said, smiling widely at Twist. "Oh, I would kiss you too, if I could."

"Thank you," Twist managed to respond while his face suddenly became very warm.

Once everything was explained to him, Twist was finally able to understand what had happened on the beach. After the attack by Quay in Nepal, the *Vimana* had been left crippled for a number of days. Once Zayle and the others had managed to get it sky worthy once again, Captain Davis had set a course for the nearest British port and hatched a plan to capture Quay, using the only tactic that the British Air Force had never tried before. Even though he had been a wanted man for many years, no one had ever been able to catch Quay because of the powerful crew members that he always had at his disposal. Only by offering them a pardon, at his expense, were they finally able to capture him. It was also the air force's opinion that culling the leader would do wonders to calm his crew.

His ship and possessions were supposed to be confiscated as damages against the crown, but Cybele insisted that she had stolen the ship all on her own, in the Baku harbor.

"Who did you steal the ship from?" the British official asked at the final meeting on the beach, below the dense cloud of airships, as Quay was led away, fuming and cursing, in handcuffs.

"A silk trader from Turkey, on his way to Russia," Cybele said.

"Well, Turkey isn't a British territory..." the official conceded.

"Now, just a minute," Vane interjected. "We all helped to steal that ship!"

"Do you want a ride back to Hong Kong, or not?" Cybele snapped at him.

"Oh, *that* ship?" Vane asked, pointing. "I thought you meant another ship. Yes, she stole it fair and square from the Turkish fellow," he said earnestly to the British official.

"Fine, you can have the ship," the official said with a sigh, checking over his paperwork. "I'll count it as yours, miss, but we will still require the captain's personal possessions."

"That's fine," Cybele said dismissively. "It's all damn gaudy stuff anyway."

The clockwork puppet, of course, had already been reported as stolen, and was instantly returned to Captain Davis once the British forces boarded the pirate airship.

It was laid out on the bamboo pier at Twist's request. He then set to work immediately, fitting the new crystal into her chest. He carefully made sure that every single part was perfectly in place before he closed the chest panel and re-covered her form modestly with the pink silk. Then, at long last, he bent down to her metal ear.

"Myra?" he said softly. "Wake up, my dear."

The puppet's metal eyelids fluttered open soundlessly, revealing the pure-blue jewels inside, and the metal lips parted with an expression of mild surprise. In a fluid, graceful motion, the puppet sat up quickly, holding her head in her perfect, clockwork hands. Then, looking at her hands, she bent them slowly, testing the motion, before turning to look at the world around her. As she did, her blue jewel eyes landed on Twist and stuck, her face blooming into a shining copper smile. Twist watched, transfixed, to see that her movements were just as life-like and beautiful as Elizabeth's had been.

"Twist!" Myra's metal mouth said on a voice that was only slightly metallic and otherwise sounded just like it had in his dreams. "You did it!" she said, her voice breaking into a happy, sprightly giggle as she threw her metal arms around his neck, pulling him close.

Twist's Sight blurred over at her now familiar touch, showing him nothing more coherent than the faint glow of her bright, ecstatic emotions. He held her gently in his arms as well, stunned by the sheer joy of such a simple pleasure. She pulled back just enough to smile at him, his hands still resting lightly at her slender metal waist.

"You're simply wonderful, do you know that?" she said, her words brimming with excitement and glee.

"I'm nothing but a clock maker," he muttered, almost unable to control his own thoughts in this blissful haze. "You're the miracle."

Myra laughed happily and pulled him close once again, fitting her nose into the curve of his neck, just below his ear. "I'll be your miracle if you'll be mine," she said, playful but soft.

Somewhere between all the fear, pain, and stress of the day he'd had, the sudden sense of successful completion, and the pure, unbridled bliss that he was now swallowed up in, Twist lost his grip on the world and fell finally, into a warm and gentle space of soothing darkness.

Twist woke to the sound of gentle waves and the rain-like ticking of palm leaves in the soft, warm breeze. Before he managed to open his eyes, he noticed that he was lying down and that his arms and throat were exposed to that moist, warm air. A cool, soft towel that pressed gently against his brow, drew his attention finally to his eyes. Blinking them open, he saw Myra's copper face peering down at him, her wire hair hanging over her shoulders like a shimmering maroon waterfall, in a halo of golden sunlight.

"Oh!" she said, happy surprise flashing onto her face as she took the cool towel away. "Welcome back," she said sweetly. "You gave me quite a start, you know," she added chidingly as she somehow managed to smile down at him crossly.

"I'm sorry," Twist said, finding his soft voice a little ragged at the edges. "What happened?" he asked, looking around to find himself lying on his back in the white sand while Myra sat at his side. One of her hands was resting in his.

"You fainted," Myra said, sounding concerned now. "Dr. Rodés said you'd be fine after a rest. Are you all right now?"

"Yes, I think so," Twist said, finding it more difficult than it should have been to lean himself up on an elbow. Myra moved instantly to help him and Twist was surprised to find a measure of strength in her slender arms. "Thank you," he said, smiling up at her as convincingly as he could. "I've just had a very long… well, actually I've had quite a number of long days, all in a row," he said, coming to the thought as he said it.

"Oh, you poor dear," Myra said, reaching out with a cool, shining copper finger to tuck a stray black curl behind his ear. Somehow, none of the trials that he'd gone through managed to stay in his thoughts as she touched him so casually. He could have spent the rest of time in that moment, and would have given anything in the world just to do so.

Myra then turned to the side and waved a shining hand in the air. "Arabel," she called, her sweet, childlike voice pouring from her throat effortlessly with a bell-like ring. "He's awake!"

Arabel hurried closer, stopping to kneel in the sand beside Twist. "Hey, look!" she said brightly to him. "You survived yet again! Do you know, you might just be cut out for this sort of thing after all?"

"I sincerely hope not," Twist said seriously to her.

"Wow, you weren't kidding about needing a lie down," Jonas said, walking closer as well. "Feel better?" he asked, grinning down at Twist.

"Somewhat," Twist said, silently checking himself over. The general state of aching pain seemed to have subsided from his bruised limbs, and the rest had restored some of his ability to focus properly. "I could really use a good cup of tea, though," he added with a sigh, wondering how many miles he was away from anything of the sort.

"Are you up for a walk?" Jonas asked. "There's a tea shop just down the way," he said, hooking a thumb at the beginning of the city behind him, nestled into the jungle at the edge of the beach. "They've got a nice Darjeeling. I just had a pot an hour ago."

Twist stared at him for a moment while he struggled to accept such a glorious idea. "I could walk the rest of the way around the world for a good pot of Darjeeling right now," he said in total seriousness.

"Great, let's get you up," Jonas said, laughing under his breath as he bent down to help Twist to his feet.

Arabel said something brightly to Myra that Twist couldn't quite follow, and whisked her away while Jonas led him on to the tea. They came to an open hut with a palm-thatched roof and bamboo walls, which sat on the white sand against the edge of the jungle. There were three small tables made of thin, tied bamboo poles, and thick, un-split logs set around them as seats.

Though Twist's hope for proper tea in such a place began to fade as he sat at one of the tables with Jonas, he had to admit that the view was lovely: the wide, white beach stretched out to one side, dotted with palm trees that swayed in the light breeze, the water—now a deep-azure blue in the failing light—lapped lazily at the sand, and the sun fell just behind the height of the jungle at the far end of the bay in an open sky of purple, pink, and gold.

Jonas said something to a girl at the back of the shop, and then turned to Twist. "You know," he said, "Quay has been arrested, Cybele is taking her new ship back to Hong Kong and Howell is taking the *Vimana* and his crew back to Bombay to collect his reward. That leaves you and I with a choice to make."

"Only you and I?" Twist asked, unsure where everyone Jonas hadn't mentioned was planning to go from here.

"Let's face it, Twist," Jonas said, looking at him squarely with pale-blue eyes, "Myra and I are the only people in the world you can bear to touch. You and Myra are the only two people in the world I can bear to look at. We would be much happier together than apart."

"Wait," Twist said, nervous of losing details with all his tired senses. "You can look at her as well?"

"I tried it," Jonas said, nodding. "All I saw were useless, random flashes of present and future. None of it bothered me in the least. I have nothing to fear when I look at her. I mean, its not like she can die again," he offered easily.

"And so, you think the three of us should stay together," Twist said.

"Don't you?" Jonas asked.

While Twist searched his mind for even a single good reason against what Jonas was saying, the shop girl appeared at their table with a ceramic teapot and a pair of what Twist found to be quite ordinary-looking teacups. She poured a cup for each of them before disappearing into the back of the shop again. Twist took a sip and was instantly overcome with both familiar comfort and a terrible and sudden homesickness. He let out a long breath, staring into his delicious tea.

"Am I ever going back to London?"

"Sure, we could stop by," Jonas said. "Why not?"

"I mean, actually going home," Twist said, looking up at him with a heavy feeling of defeat already pressing down on him. "I'm never going home again, am I?"

"Well, think about this," Jonas said. "Do you think Myra would be happy living in your little clock shop and never getting out except to walk around in gray old London?"

"It's a very modern and busy city, you know," Twist pointed out in his home's defense.

"While you were out, she kept asking us all about where we are," Jonas said, smiling lightly. "You should have seen it. She got more and more excited as Ara and I listed off the places we each had to cross to get here. I mean, she's been trapped in that cold, empty palace for who knows how long! The girl wants to see the world. And just look at her," Jonas said, waving a hand down the beach.

Twist turned around in his seat to look after his gesture and found Myra and Arabel talking to a fruit vendor in the distance. Myra turned and swayed, lifting her arms and moving her feet to an unheard rhythm, dancing happily in the sand while the vendor and Arabel clapped and smiled to watch her.

"She's glorious. We don't have to sell her to make a load of money," Jonas said, drawing an alarmed and pointed look from Twist. "She knows that she's lovely, and she likes to show off. If we set up venues and charge a fee for people to see her, then she'd be perfectly happy to dance for them, they'd be delighted to see her, and you and I wouldn't have any trouble to support her or ourselves for a very long time. Not to mention, she'd get to see a lot of the world if we bought ourselves an airship."

"You mean to turn that wondrous creature into a circus attraction?" Twist snapped, disgusted with the words even as he spoke them.

"Great opera singers travel around to perform," Jonas shot back instantly. "She's a dancer, and an impossible beauty of technology and magic. What's the difference?"

"What if people treat her like a side show freak?" Twist asked back, already feeling himself begin to give in to Jonas's ever-shifting logic.

"Is that guy treating her like a freak?" Jonas asked, pointing down the beach with his teaspoon. Twist turned to see the fruit vendor smiling widely at Myra as he handed her a small sack and bowed deeply to her.

Twist looked back at Jonas darkly. "Why do you have to make so much sense?"

"How about this?" Jonas asked, smiling now. "We split the proceeds, but you get the final word on any decision directly about Myra," he said, offering a handshake over the table. "If you don't like the way she's treated, or don't think she's completely happy, then things change."

Twist took his time, even if it was just to make Jonas wait, before he finally took the handshake. The instant he did, he felt the world turn around him, as if his whole life had just gone through an enormous change, never to be the same again.

"Hi boys," Arabel said, walking under the roof of the tea shop hut with Myra. "How's the tea treating you?" she asked Twist.

"Better than your bloody brother," Twist muttered, sipping at his tea.

"Oh, what are you doing now?" Arabel snapped quickly at Jonas, swiping at his arm with the back of her hand. "You brute!"

"Steady on!" Jonas gasped, a look of great injustice on his face.

"Here, I'll cheer you up," Myra said, stepping closer to Twist.

Without a moment of hesitation or warning, she turned and sat herself down comfortably on Twist's knee, dropping the small sack she'd gotten from the fruit vendor on the table in front of her. Twist's hand moved to her hip before he could stop it, and try as he might, it simply wouldn't move away. A lifetime of culture and propriety screamed at him for this radically undignified display. Myra, however, swinging her feet under the table, didn't seem to even notice.

"Here," she said, plucking one of the small, bumpy, red fruits out of the bag. "These are my favorite," she said, flashing him a smile. "Well, they were when I still had a stomach," she added easily as her fine, metal fingers began to carefully peel the red skin off of the little fruit. Once she'd bared the translucent white flesh inside it, she held it up in front of Twist's mouth by the stem. "Try one," she said brightly, waiting for him to comply.

At a total loss of any other options, Twist opened his mouth and let her feed him. The fruit itself had one of the most foreign flavors he'd ever experienced—gently sweet, cool on the tongue, and oddly akin to celery, all at the same time—while the texture was at once soft and crunchy. Once he got over the strangeness of it, he found that he quite liked this new taste.

"Well?" Myra asked, peering at him curiously from inches away. "Do you like it?"

"You know, I rather do," he said, smiling back at her in light surprise.

"Would you like another?" Myra asked excitedly.

"Yes please," Twist said, finally far too drenched in happiness to bother with propriety for another instant. He managed to move his hand off her hip and put it on her slender waist instead, to steady her on his knee. He found that, somewhere along the way, all of the tension and fatigue in his tired body had vanished without a trace.

"Oh I'm so glad you like them too," Myra said, reaching for another one from the bag. Twist felt the pressure of Jonas's eyes and glanced off of Myra to find a wide, knowing grin on the other man's face.

"What?"

"I told you you'd like lychee," Jonas said smoothly, gesturing to the image before him.

"Wait, your vision!" Twist said quickly as the memory returned. "You saw this? Back on the *Vimana* before we even got to Nepal, when you looked at me that day."

Jonas nodded, smiling.

"Then you knew, all along, that she'd be alive and perfect," he said, looking back to Myra's curious expression. "Sitting on my lap and being lovely—this

whole time, you knew?" Twist asked, looking back at
Jonas in astonishment. "You knew that we'd all survive
and end up right here, right now, just like this."

"I believe I told you as much, didn't I?"

"No wonder you're always such a know-it-all,"
Arabel muttered, staring at Jonas darkly.

Twist turned back to Myra and leaned in closer. "And
he doesn't like to use his Sight," he said softly to her,
before shaking his head.

Myra laughed lightly, sending a shiver of pure delight
up his spine. In that instant, Twist realized that it really
didn't matter at all where he was in the world, or what
sort of life he was living, so long as he was present to
witness her every joy.

~ oOo ~

Congratulations!

You have just finished the very first book in the Clockwork Twist series, you intrepid darling, you. Thank you for joining Twist and I on his first foray into the wide world! It's been simply marvelous to have you along. Just remember, though, this is only the beginning.

Read on to get a glimpse of the next volume in this series, *Clockwork Twist, Book Two : Trick*...

~ Bonus Content ~

Myra danced in the middle of the busy bazaar, surrounded by sprightly small children, in the clustered back streets of Bombay. The copper plates of her skin glinted in the sunlight and thickly scented air. The bright purple and gold sari that Twist had bought her twirled around her dancing form like sweet smoke. As Twist watched her, the sight of her blissful copper smile stole all his other cares away, and her bright childlike laughs tingled on his skin. He took another sip of his warm, creamy chai and savored the multitude of delights before him.

"Twist?" Jonas asked with an insistent tone, as if he had been repeating himself.

"Yes?" Twist asked, looking to him. Jonas stood beside him at the side of the bazaar with his own small cup of chai. Against the dark amber and chocolate tones of the crowded human landscape around them, Jonas's pale skin, short golden hair, and sharp sea green eyes stood out nearly as much as Myra's clockwork form. The cut of his sturdy but worn, European attire—brown trousers and jacket, white cotton shirt, and leather boots —didn't help.

"You didn't hear a word I just said, did you?" Jonas asked with an accusing glare. His eyes shifted from green to a chilly gray as Twist watched.

"No, no, I was listening," Twist lied.

"What did I say, then?"

"I think you're absolutely right," Twist said, nodding earnestly. "Whatever you said."

"Uh huh." Jonas glanced at Myra. Two children were holding her copper hands now, spinning around her in time to their own song. "So, I can get you to agree to anything while you're gazing blissfully at your clockwork girlfriend. Good to know."

"She's hardly my girlfriend," Twist snapped.

"Right."

"Now see here," Twist said, pointing a finger at Jonas's smug certainty.

"Can you focus for a moment?" Jonas asked, finally in possession of Twist's full attention. "Howell said he's taking the *Vimana* off to Perth from here. But I just know we should head to America with Myra. California still has lots of gold just lying around, and a population that's in love with novelty. There's no money in Australia these days. It's too new."

"So, what do you want to do?" Twist asked reluctantly. He glanced back at Myra, wishing he could neglect the rest of his life—the simple fact that he was half way around the world from his home, without even the slightest idea where he might find himself tomorrow —just for a few moments more. She tilted her shining body into an elegant arc and swung through the children's melody as carelessly graceful as a willow in a summer breeze.

"Like I said," Jonas went on, "we can probably catch a trading ship as far as Japan. From there, I know people in Osaka who could get us to California."

"Fine." Twist took another sip of his tea. In the back of his mind he tried to remember if California was still full of ruffians and bandits, or if the place had been civilized yet.

"But," Jonas continued, "if Arabel or Howell find out that we're leaving the ship, they'll try to stop us and that will be difficult and annoying. So, we need to pretend that we're staying on board, gather our things, and disappear quietly. Night would be best."

"You want to run away?"

"Of course. I hate my family. You know that."

"Well yes, but..." Twist faltered. He'd always heard that families stayed together, no matter how much they hated each other. They always did in novels, anyway.

"Life is too short to suffer fools," Jonas said, shaking his head.

Twist gave a shrug. "Your family, your choice, I suppose."

Looking to Myra again, Twist gave a subtle sigh. She loved the idea of traveling around the world with Jonas and Twist, dancing for audiences while collecting a steady income from ticket sales. Twist couldn't bear to disappoint her. Of course, he knew that he would be entirely out of his depth without Jonas's help. Though the idea of relying on anyone but himself was foreign and uncomfortable to Twist, he found that he now had no choice but to accept that he was at the mercy of Jonas's whim. He could only hope that he'd be able to see London again, someday.

"Then we should head back now," Jonas said before he finished the last of his chai. "We can catch dinner and then turn in early, say we're tired or something. Then we can sneak out just after midnight."

"All right," Twist said with another sigh.

He finished his chai as well and then walked closer to Myra in the pool of colorful, whirling, children. Looking now, he saw that a large number of shoppers had gathered to watch her as well, standing to the side of the open

center of the bazaar. Their faces showed shifting shades
of curiosity, wonder and enchantment as they watched
Myra's magical movements. Twist couldn't help but feel
a tiny jolt of pride as he called out to her.

"Myra, we should go," he said as loudly as his small
voice would allow over the children's song and laughter.
He caught her eye and beckoned with a hand.

Myra paused in mid-turn to look at him, her purple
sari and long, maroon, wire hair finishing the swirl
exquisitely, while her blue jewel eyes glinted brightly in
her copper smile. Twist's breath caught in the face of
such a beautiful and careless display. When she rushed to
him and took both of his hands in hers, he was too
stunned to realize that she was pulling him into her
dance. At her touch, his Sight flashed to life, filling his
mind to the brim with all of her innocent and heady joy.

"Dance with me," she said, her voice ringing as bright
as a bell.

She held tightly to his hands and swung him around
in the midst of the children. His feet complied, as if on
their own, while his mind whirled even faster with the
sudden and startlingly powerful high of her emotions.
Shivers ran down his spine as she pulled closer, wrapping
her slender arms around his neck as the twirl came to a
stop. Twist's arms curled around her back, while he stood
helpless in her joy, watching her smile from so very near.
There was sound, scent, and color everywhere around
them, but for a moment Twist saw only her.

Then, she turned and spoke to the children around
them. At first, Twist thought that there was something
wrong with his hearing because he couldn't make sense of
a single word. Then, he realized that she wasn't speaking
English. Some of the children made unhappy, pouting
faces, but others only waved and turned away. Myra
waved back to them, and then threaded her arm around

Twist's and led him out of the crowd.

"I like India," she said, as if the words tasted sweet on her silver tongue. "Where are we going next, my dear?" she asked, smiling excitedly. It took a moment for Twist to form an answer.

"Japan," he said finally. "Jonas wants to go to Japan."

"Oh!" Myra gasped, looking to Jonas. Twist was somewhat surprised to find him suddenly standing before them, and that Twist and Myra seemed to have arrived at the edge of the bazaar. "I'd like to see Japan," she said. "I've heard very nice stories about it. They say the Sun lives there."

"It's a fun place," Jonas said with a nod. He looked to Twist with a knowing smile. "Are you all right?"

Twist frowned at him, confused. He couldn't find a single reason for anything in the world to be wrong. Myra glanced to him, then back to Jonas with apparently the same thought.

"Myra, could you just let go of him for a second?" Jonas asked her pleasantly.

"Oh..." Myra muttered, removing her hands from Twist.

Twist watched curiously as she did this, at a total loss of why she ever would. The instant the contact was broken, however, the sun-bright joy and heady content vanished from his mind as a wave of fear, confusion, and cold unease washed over him. The last few moments re-played in his mind, in a wholly new light: Myra had swept him into the middle of a crowd. He'd been a breath away from touching the children; and suffering stabbing, burning visions of pain and fear from each one of them.

A shuddering gasp escaped him as his body trembled for an instant in an effort to process the violent change in his emotions. All of the new fright poured through his blood as his heartbeat jumped into very high speed.

"Yeah..." Jonas muttered apologetically.

"Twist?" Myra asked, her expression suddenly concerned. "Darling, are you all right?" She reached out a hand to his shoulder.

"Yes, yes, I just..." Twist said, slipping ever so slightly away from her touch. He took a breath to calm himself as he tried to finish his sentence coherently.

"He's fine," Jonas said gently to Myra. "Just give him a moment."

As he spoke, Jonas placed a hand lightly on Twist's arm. The contact numbed Twist's fears instantly in a thick cloud of chilly, impossibly white fog. It ebbed away quickly to hang on the horizon of his thoughts, but it washed his fright away with it. Twist let out a long breath as his heart began to calm down again. Jonas's hand fell away, and the white chill fell away with it, but this time Twist's own emotions returned to him more gradually.

"Myra, do you remember that he can't bear to touch anyone but you or me?" Jonas asked her. She nodded, though it was obvious she wasn't following him. "Children count as people," Jonas offered.

Myra's face snapped into understanding and she turned to Twist. "I'm sorry!" she said in sudden fear. "I keep forgetting to be careful with you..."

"It's fine," Twist said instantly, offering the best smile he could while his pride struggled to absorb the implications of her statement. He reached out to take her clockwork hand. The moment he did, a wave of worry washed over him through his Sight. But as he smiled reassuringly at her, it ebbed away into calm. "Shall we go?"

Sunlight glinted brightly in the heavily scented air, rising high over Twist's shoulder, prompting him to adjust his black silk top hat so it cast a shadow over his pale, fine featured face. The well-tailored, black and blue accented coat that a pirate had given him in Hong Kong, was of a light enough fabric to be comfortable even in the warmth of India. His electrically powered silver and black walking stick made a pleasant click as it struck the ground in time with his steps and made it much easier for him to feel like a gentleman, no matter where he was.

Walking with Myra and Jonas through the semi-European styled, wide, and straight streets of Bombay, Twist finally got his mind into some kind of order. Although the buildings were of a familiar design to Twist's eyes, with three stories each and a generally square appearance, the shop on the ground floor of each one spilled onto the street under cloth awnings in a seemingly disorganized and highly foreign way. The innumerable people walking by looked no different from those in the bazaar, and were a constant reminder that he was far from home.

As they walked through the crowded streets, Jonas kept his gaze solidly on the ground, rather than accidentally catch anyone's eyes. Myra's metal fingers still curled through Twist's, as if forgotten, as they walked and talked together under the occasional shade of palm trees planted along the streets. Through constant force of will, Twist managed to hold his own thoughts and emotions in the forefront of his mind despite the effects of her touch on his Sight. Twist was certain that he could learn to stop losing himself in her every time they touched—if he practiced diligently.

The three soon came to the imposing gothic facade of the Victoria Terminus railway station in the center of the city. The enormous building, so recently finished in honor of Queen Victoria—the Empress of India, as she liked to be called—reminded Twist of drawings that he had seen of French palaces. There were two huge three-story wings that opened out around a plaza before the central face of the building. A single gray stone dome rose above the entrance, simply covered with statuary, stained glass, and gargoyles. The proud figure of an ancient god stood in white stone on its zenith. Above and behind the station hung the massive cloud of docked airships, all moored along the edges of the top floor ramparts.

Seeing such a sight in the center of a bustling city half way around the world from London, Twist allowed himself a moment of quiet patriotic pride. Jonas glanced up at the building before he pinned his eyes on the ground again.

"You know," he said as he took the lead, heading for the airship docks, "all this cocky colonizing is going to turn around and bite England in the rear one day."

"How?" Twist asked as they walked into the cooler air inside the stone building and began to climb the stairs. "We have the widest sweeping empire the world has ever seen. The sun never sets on it, after all."

"Oh really?" Myra asked with great interest. "It's that big?"

"You know what they say about big things falling harder," Jonas replied. In the distance, a train whistle echoed off the stone, steel, and glass of the train platforms below them.

"What have you got against your homeland,

anyway?" Twist asked sharply.

"My homeland is the sky," Jonas answered with a smile as they reached the third floor and walked along the crowded open ramparts toward the docked *Vimana*, near the end. "All I ever got from England is my accent and a handful of ancestors."

The *Vimana* hung in the air beside the docks like a storm cloud. The large, three-level hull seemed to absorb all the color around it into its gray wood, while the enormous gray balloon above shaded it from the sun. The gangplank lay against the stone ramparts, inviting them back aboard, beside a number of large crates that hadn't yet been loaded.

"Someday," Twist said to Myra softly, as they came under the shadow of the *Vimana's* balloon and flanking wing-like sails, "he's going to realize that he's just as much an Englishman as I am. I'm sure it'll give him quite a fright." Myra giggled behind a hand, drawing Jonas's suspicious attention as he reached the gangplank.

"Get back!" a voice hissed to them as a hand covered in black cloth snatched at Jonas's arm. Aazzi Rodés pulled him behind a tower of large wooden crates to the side of the gangplank, and hurriedly gestured for Twist and Myra to hide as well.

"Ow, ow!" Jonas winced and pulled at the vampire's talon-like grip. "What's goin—"

Aazzi spun him around in an alarmingly fast movement and held him tightly from behind with one hand over his mouth and another pinning his arm to his stomach. His eyes opened wide in shock as she turned her mouth close to his ear. He let out a muffled sound and struggled to free himself, pulling at her immobile grip with his free hand.

"I'm not going to bite you," Aazzi spat impatiently on a hushed voice. "Now be quiet." She looked to Myra with silver eyes, from the darkness of her shaded face, under the red shawl of silk over her head. "You're in trouble, little one."

"What? How?" Twist asked quickly.

"There are Rooks on board, talking to Howell," Aazzi said. Jonas reached up with a finger to tap on the hand over his mouth. "Are you going to behave?" Aazzi hissed, turning her voice to his ear. Jonas's body shuddered visibly and his eyes flinched closed, but he nodded. The instant Aazzi released him, he moved well out of her reach to stand on the other side of Twist.

"God you're terrifying!" Jonas whispered harshly through clenched teeth. He rubbed at his neck, where her breath had been. Aazzi smiled at him slightly. "So, why are we frightened of magpies, then?" he asked her quietly.

"Rooks? Magpies?" Twist asked. "Why are we talking about birds?"

"Rooks, not magpies," Aazzi amended quickly to Twist.

"Oh, so it's just one kind of bird, then," Twist said, starting to feel his level of annoyance rise quickly.

"Shut up," Jonas said, holding a silencing finger before Twist's face as he spoke to Aazzi. "So, there are mags on the ship. What of it?"

"Howell registered a 'life-sized clockwork puppet' as belonging to him, when he brought the British navy to Indonesia to catch Quay," Aazzi explained quickly. "Apparently, the Rooks saw the report. Now, they're here for Myra."

"Shit," Jonas hissed darkly. "Would Howell sell her out from under Twist?"

"What?" Twist snapped. A jolt of Myra's fear crept through Twist's Sight as she wrapped both of her hands around his arm.

"Would he have a choice, is a better question," Aazzi said. She offered Twist a calming smile. "We all got paid well enough when we claimed the reward for Quay. Howell and the rest of us can see very clearly how important Myra is to you. We wouldn't take her from you." Twist nodded quietly, patting at Myra's nervous grip. "Howell might try to lie about her to the Rooks," Aazzi said, looking back to Myra, "but if they see her..."

"We have to get out of here," Jonas said to Twist, his tone now startlingly serious.

"We're not actually talking about birds, are we?" Twist asked slowly.

"Go to this cafe, and wait for me," Aazzi said, handing Jonas a small slip of paper. "If it's clear, we can come back together. If not, we can figure out our next move. Either way, wait for me to tell you what the situation is before you act," she added pointedly to Jonas.

"Sure," Jonas said, nodding.

"I mean it, Jonas."

"I get it," Jonas snapped. "We'll wait for you. Now go and figure out what's going on, will you?"

Aazzi seemed to accept his promise, and turned to glance around the crate before walking around it and onto the *Vimana*. The moment she was gone, Jonas nodded for Twist to follow him and turned to hurry farther down the ramparts behind the shelter of clustered piles of cargo. When they were a good distance away, he stopped, took a steadying breath, and then quickly looked over the people around them: aeronauts, merchants, passengers, dock workers, and disguised pirates wandered among their own business, all along the ramparts and docked ships. Jonas snapped his eyes closed and leaned back against the wall of the building to take a breath.

"Not a mag in sight," he said. "We're safe for now." Twist took a quick glance as well, not seeing a single feathered creature anywhere.

"What is going on, Jonas?" Twist asked. Beside him, Myra continued to hold to his hand tightly, sending a pulsing throb of worry wafting through his skin.

"It's a really long story," Jonas said, looking to him. "Basically, it's a huge secret society of people who steal strange or dangerous technology and remove it from the general populace. They say it's so it can't hurt anyone, but we all know their game. They always go for things that might cause more harm than good, like weapons or time machines."

"Time machines?"

Jonas waved his words away. "Like I said, it's complicated. They also try to police any magically inclined people, and generally cause strife and misery to anyone who they don't count as 'friendly.' They're a damned bloody nuisance and we do not want them interested in Myra." Myra gave a soft, nervous sound. Twist grimaced against her fear.

"What can we do about them?" Twist asked quickly.

"Not a lot, if they've got our scent," Jonas said darkly. "Mags—" He stopped suddenly. "Rooks, I mean, have a lot of money, a lot of power, and all of the dangerous items that they take away from people. They also have the best information network on the planet, and people stationed all over the world."

Twist nodded, listening, and willed himself not to panic. As he struggled to control his thoughts, a stray question slipped through his grasp. "Any reason for the obsession with birds?" he asked.

Jonas gave a sigh. "They call themselves 'Rooks.' It's probably because those birds are supposed to be mysterious, intelligent, and can predict death and whatnot, but the rest of the world calls these people 'magpies' behind their backs because they tend to steal and hoard all the best stuff. And it's usually bad luck to see them unannounced."

"They sound like something I should have heard about."

"They don't interact with the normal world," Jonas answered Twist. "You only see them when you get close to weirdness. But, once they appear, they have a tendency to take control. If they decide that Myra is high enough on the freaky scale—" Myra's face took on an affronted expression. "Not that you are, of course," Jonas amended. "We know that you're as harmless as a kitten. But if they decide to say that you're dangerous, that would justify taking you. And there'd be no way for us to stop them."

"Taking her where?" Twist's fingers tightened unconsciously on Myra's.

"There are rumors of stockpiles all over the world, but no one has ever found them. And believe me, plenty of pirates have tried. We only have two options here," he said, holding up a finger for each one. "One, we find some ridiculous way to prove to them that she's harmless enough to leave alone. Two, we run and hide and hope they never find us."

"Which one's better?" Twist asked.

"Neither," Jonas said with a sigh. "They could both fail and then we might never see her again." Myra gasped and Twist felt a fresh rush of fear burn off of her. "But if we try to run and they catch us, then we can always try to convince them as a backup plan."

Twist could already feel the future spinning wildly out of his limited control. He took a breath and tried again to calm his fears. "There has to be something else," he said. "I only just put her back together, for goodness sake!"

"I'm telling you right now, I had no idea they'd go this

far out of their way for her," Jonas said a little more gently. "Sure, they might be interested out of curiosity if we went and told them about her. But the fact that they came here without being called proves that they already think she's valuable."

"But she's not just some … thing," Twist said, finding the very idea offensive. "She's a person. They can't imprison her, can they?"

"Oh yeah, easily," Jonas answered with a nod. "Hence the problem."

"So, we're going to wait for Aazzi to return with good news, then, are we?" Twist asked on a heavy breath as he tried to accept this new reality.

"Does that sound like a good idea to you?"

"But you promised."

Jonas gave a mirthless snort of a laugh. "To hell with Aazzi. We were going to run away anyway. Now we've got even more reason to do so, immediately."

Twist felt as if the ground was turning and shifting under his feet. Things were changing so quickly it was making him dizzy. "But the plan was to advertise and let Myra dance for the masses. We can't exactly do that if we're trying to hide."

Jonas pushed himself off the wall and stepped closer to Twist, staring into his eyes while his own took on a stony, dark purple color. The deep, constant buzzing sensation at the back of Twist's neck grew more noticeable under the pressure of Jonas's Sight. "Would your world continue to turn if they stole Myra away from you?" he asked, his voice even but unkind.

"No," Twist answered instantly, glancing away to dim Jonas's ability to use his Sight against him. The buzzing at his neck itched and burned, making it hard to think of anything other than looking back into Jonas's eyes. Twist closed his eyes tightly and forced himself not to relent.

"I don't want to live with a hollow shell of you," Jonas said, crossing his arms. "And what about you?" he asked, as Twist felt his heavy gaze turn away. He glanced up to find Jonas now looking at Myra with the same deep purple eyes. "Do you want to be taken away from Twist?" he asked her.

"No, never," she responded just as quickly as Twist had.

"Then what choice have we got?" Jonas asked them both. "We can figure out the details along the way, but right now, all we can do is run."

"This is a damned bloody waste of time," Jonas grumbled for the fourth time since they had sat down at a table in the corner of the cafe that Aazzi had indicated. "They know we're not on the *Vimana*. They could already be searching the city for us."

"Are you trying to sound paranoid?" Twist asked as he stirred a little cream into his coffee and tried very hard not to look up at Jonas. Beside him, Myra leaned just a little farther behind the tall potted plant to the side of their shadowed table, and tugged her sari to hide her copper skin just a little more.

"Darling, what if he's right?" Myra asked Twist gently.

"I'm not going to fling you aimlessly across the world, running and hiding like a fugitive, unless I'm absolutely certain that I have to," Twist said, yet again. The words were starting to feel comfortable and well-practiced on his tongue.

"You keep saying that, and I might start to believe it," Jonas said darkly. Twist felt the heavy draw on his attention: the buzz at his neck sparking brightly as Jonas's eyes dug at him.

"What are you looking for, anyway?" Twist asked, reaching up to rub at his neck as he kept his eyes firmly on his coffee cup.

"Some kind of sense."

Twist shot him a glare. "Aazzi implied that there might not be any problem at all," he said with as much conviction as he could muster—well aware that Jonas could see it clearly in his eyes. "I understand your concern, but we might not need to hide at all. If we don't, we'll have a vastly better life from here on. I have to take that chance."

Myra made a mournful tone, her metal hands clasped tightly together on the table top. When Twist looked to her, he saw her face devoid of its usual brightness and joy.

"I'm so sorry," she breathed. "This is all my fault..."

"You've done nothing wrong," Twist said instantly, his voice considerably kinder when he turned it to her.

"If it wasn't for me, you wouldn't be in this mess," she said, looking to him sorrowfully. "You wouldn't be worried, or in danger, or angry with your friend," she added, glancing to Jonas.

"Oh no, we argue a lot anyway," Jonas said with a smile.

"I wouldn't remove myself from your side for all the trouble in the world," Twist added. "Please, don't blame yourself."

Myra smiled weakly back to them both in turn. "Oh, you're ever so sweet to me."

"Can't help it," Twist said, giving her hands a gentle pat. A flash of relief came through his Sight at the touch.

"Thank heavens," a voice said hurriedly, coming closer to the table. Jonas replaced the black-lensed goggles over his eyes again, apparently out of reflex. Aazzi took the open seat between Jonas and Twist, and set down a couple of bags at her feet. "I'm very proud of you," she said to Twist.

"What did I do?"

"You didn't let him push you into running," Aazzi said, nodding to Jonas.

"Hey!"

"You're as predictable as the sunrise," Aazzi snapped back at Jonas before turning back to Twist. Even a few feet away, Twist could feel true anger—and not just the frustration and annoyance he had personally caused—wafting off of Jonas like a toxic heat. It whispered at the vibration in his neck, calling his own heart to burn as well. "Now," Aazzi said to Twist, "did he explain anything about what's happening here?"

"Yes, he told me in great detail exactly why we can't let those men have Myra," Twist answered, fighting to keep his mind clear.

"Well, you're in luck," Aazzi said with a nod. "They didn't send Rook agents," she said to Jonas. "It's just a low grade, unarmed, collection team. They didn't expect a problem."

"They thought we'd just give her up?" Jonas asked, curiosity poking holes in his smoldering anger.

"They thought we'd sell her for the right price," Aazzi explained. "They don't seem to realize that we see her as a friend." Myra's face appeared surprised, but she said nothing. "Howell told them the truth—that you three were out exploring the city and that you should be back any time now."

"How is any of this lucky?" Twist asked, fighting very hard to ignore Jonas's anger.

"Because they still don't have any idea that we are going to run," Jonas answered.

"More than just that," Aazzi said, "we might be able to get them to back off completely."

"Wait, you want us to run too?" Twist asked.

"How could we get them off our backs?" Jonas asked tartly.

"I have a friend in Paris—Philippe's uncle, actually—who works in the field," Aazzi said. "He builds human-shaped machines that he calls robots. Apparently, it's a Bohemian technology that he's trying to perfect. They're nothing like Myra: just soulless shells that look something like people. But he's an expert on the subject and a consultant for the Rooks. If you can get to him directly, and get him to declare her just another robot, then they will have no cause to trouble us again," she finished with a proud smile. Twist looked to Jonas.

"Are you insane?" Jonas asked Aazzi sharply, seeming to glare squarely at her through the black lenses.

Aazzi frowned. "It's a perfect solution."

"We only have a handful of unarmed low-level thugs to deal with right now, but you want us to walk right into the middle of a hornet's nest, on purpose, and hope your weird uncle sees things our way. How the hell is that a good idea?"

"If we tell the thugs about her," Aazzi said with measured patience, "they'd still have to take her in to let their suppressor make the decision. If you go to them instead, it shows initiative and would help to show how much you care about her—that she isn't some *thing* that can be bought and sold."

"And what happens if this expert doesn't go along with it?" Jonas asked.

"He's family!" Aazzi said, exasperated.

Twist rubbed at his face while the others continued to argue. He could easily see the logic of both points of view, and the flaws in each plan as well. Neither one seemed like a perfect solution. His instincts had always helped him solve complicated problems before, but this time he couldn't use his Sight. He couldn't find the source of the problem in all the complexity of it.

He looked to Myra and found her watching the argument with a sheepish and forlorn expression. Twist reached out to touch her wrist, drawing her attention. Her emotions ran cold and fearful over his fingers. It dimmed his world to see her so unhappy. He leaned closer to her as Jonas and Aazzi's voice rose.

"My dear," he said softly to her copper ear, "if you could have anything in the world, regardless of all of this, what would you want?"

She smiled bravely to him. "I just want what you already gave me," she answered. "I don't want to be alone anymore. And I want to be with you," she said, reaching out to toy with the soft black curls behind his ear as her smile took on a deeper hue. Twist's skin prickled at her touch, sending a delicious chill down his spine.

"Could you be happy if you had to hide?" he asked. "What if you couldn't dance for anyone but me?"

"Well..." she said, her face taking on a hint of bitterness. "As long as I have you, I think I'll be all right," she said bravely. Twist felt the lie echo off her metal skin, no matter how she tried to bury it. Twist felt a solid shift in his own thoughts and emotions as he found the true source of his troubles.

"I understand," he said with a nod. He looked up to find Aazzi and Jonas still spitting shards of logic and spite at each other. He knocked on the table top with his knuckles until they paused to look at him. "I've decided. I'm taking Myra to your uncle in Paris," he said to Aazzi. Then he turned to Jonas. "Are you coming?"

"But—" Jonas began, while Aazzi smiled victoriously.

"There's a chance that she's right," Twist said, gesturing to Aazzi. "There's a chance that Myra won't have to hide and live in fear for the rest of her life. I'm taking it."

"And if they try to snatch her?" Jonas asked quickly.

"They'll have to kill me before they can take her from me." Twist felt a ripple of shock shoot through Myra at the resolute sound of his words. "I want exactly what you want," he said to her, squeezing her hand gently.

"You are one stubborn little bastard, do you know

that?" Jonas grumbled at Twist.

"I've been called worse. Are you coming or not?"

Jonas's face moved as if he were rolling his eyes behind the opaque goggles. "Yes, of course," he said on a heavy sigh. "Damn you."

"Wonderful," Aazzi said brightly, picking up the bags she had left at her feet and placing them on the table. "Here're your things, and here's the address." She handed Twist a slip of paper.

"You packed for us?" Jonas asked, pulling his goggles up just enough to frown at the bags on the table.

"I knew you were leaving the *Vimana* today the moment I saw the Rooks. The ship's too easy for the Rooks to follow. And no, Howell and Ara don't know yet. I'll explain things to them."

"Thank you," Twist said. Jonas said something under his breath. Myra smiled at Twist from under her purple sari, and he felt a flash of pride bleed through her touch.

~ oOo ~

Did you enjoy that little taste?

As you can imagine, this next adventure will set off from Bombay, and take Twist, Jonas, and Myra along a new journey of discovery, intrigue, and chaos. Pack your bags and don you hat, because *Book Two : Trick*, is available now!

Follow all things Twist at
clockworktwist.com

Join the Facebook page at
facebook.com/CWTwist

Made in the USA
Lexington, KY
15 November 2019

57101917R00177